Matrimony Redeemed

A Humorous, Inspirational Novel

By

Kathleen Cormack

Matrimony Redeemed is the second in a series following "Prayer for all Seasons"

Published by Kathleen Cormack

Copyright © by Kathleen Cormack 2012

ISBN 978-0-9852141-5-9

Authors Note

This is a work of fiction. Names, characters, places and incidents either are the product of the author's imagination or are used fictitiously, and any resemblance to actual persons, living or dead, events, or localities is entirely coincidental. Since the majority of the story takes place in Chicago, Il, certain well known places are used to add authenticity.

Dedication

In loving memory of my oldest brother, Wilbert Leon

Nichols

Thanks for all the wonderful memories, and a whole lot

of laughter!

You were simply the best.....RIP

Matrimony Redeemed

Acknowledgements:

Thank you first and foremost to my Heavenly Father for this wonderful gift! Without you, none of this would be possible!
To my copyeditor, Sonja Mack: Thank you once again for all of your hard work in ensuring all the "T"s were crossed and all of the "I"s were dotted. Thank you to my best friend and husband, John. You are truly amazing and I thank God daily for you. Thank you for your support!
And last but not least, to all of you who read my books: It is my hope that you have become inspired by my stories. I hope you will continue to enjoy the journey.
P.S. Love you mom; love you, dad. ☺

Kathleen@kathleencormack.com

www.kathleencormack.com

Proverbs 13:20

He that walketh with wise *men* shall be wise: but a companion of fools shall be destroyed.

<u>**Matrimony Redeemed**</u>
<u>**Copyright 2012**</u>

1

"You burnt the toast. I can't eat burnt toast." Conner playfully swiped his bride on her bottom. Five months ago they'd stood before 150 guests and exchanged wedding vows. He was a happy man. After 10 years of being married to a woman who turned out to be a bad choice, Conner was happy to have found someone like Pam.

"Sorry." Pam looked up from the morning newspaper. "I got distracted."

"It's okay." Conner winked as he sat beside his bride at the kitchen table. "I didn't marry you for your cooking."

Pam blushed, receiving her husband's comment as a compliment.

Pam's friends couldn't believe that she'd fallen in love with a man like Conner. Not that there was anything wrong with him. In fact, he had a lot of the things that many women believed a good man should have: a sense of humor, honesty, good looks, and he was quite the romantic.

"Well," Conner took a bite of his eggs, "you got my eggs just right." He placed his toast on the paper towel next to his plate.

Pam picked it up and bit into it. "Tastes just fine to me."

Conner's role as an assistant pastor had been part of the reason Pam's three closest friends were a little surprised at their union. Pam—a diva in her own right—had married a man of God. A church-going, on-fire-for-the-Lord Christian man who could recite passages from the Bible in "several different languages," which is what Pam had once said about her husband. Conner couldn't really recite the Bible in different languages, but he knew the Word so well that Pam liked to tease him that way.

When she and Conner had exchanged wedding vows, Pam noticed the raised eyebrows of some of their guests. Instead of keeping her eyes on her new husband, she'd peeked at them from the corner of her eye. Even two of her bridesmaids, Jackie and Tricee, and her maid of honor, Val, had been unsuccessful at keeping their eyebrows in their normal position.

"Who would have thought you'd marry a man of the cloth?"

"I had to pinch myself to make sure I wasn't dreaming."

"I'm still in shock. But it just goes to show you—God is still in the miracle working business."

The sentiments expressed by her three friends were all in fun. Pam knew they were truly happy for her. But the inside joke did surface from time to time. She would agree that she hadn't expected to fall for someone like Conner. He wasn't really her type. But she'd said the same thing about Jeff two years prior.

The Buckners' breakfast was interrupted by the ringing of their home phone.

"Good morning," Pam said into the receiver as she wiped her hands on a white dishtowel with a flowery print on it.

"Good morning, newly married lady!" Tricee chimed from the other end.

"Hey there, Mrs. Hatchett! I could say the same to you. How's married life?"

Conner looked up as if he was waiting to hear Tricee's response. Pam looked at her husband and mouthed, *Nosy.*

"Absolutely wonderful," Tricee said happily. "I think I'll keep him for a while."

A lot had happened in two years. Pam and Tricee were now wives, along with Val and Jackie. And as far as they all knew, each couple was enjoying marital bliss.

"Hunter's good for you. So, yeah, you should keep him a while longer."

Conner shook his head and smiled. He finished the rest of his breakfast and left the kitchen.

"How's Conner?"

"He's fine. But you know," Pam sighed, "since he's an assistant pastor, I feel as if I can't go off on him when he makes me upset." They both laughed.

"Girl, I'm serious."

Pam resumed her place at the kitchen table. A phone in the kitchen had seemed odd to Pam, initially. She'd asked her husband why they needed a phone in the kitchen. But she soon changed her tune upon realizing its convenience.

"I feel like the Lord will make me pay double if I go off on one of His own."

"You're one of His own, too. Remember that."

Tricee shook her head. She realized that Pam was teasing. But Pam had alluded to this before and Tricee sometimes wondered if her friend was serious. She had noticed a change in Pam since she'd married Conner. Pam seemed more subtle than she'd been in the past. This may not have been the case, but it seemed that way to Tricee.

Tricee liked Conner and felt he was a very good fit for her friend. But she was surprised that Pam found Conner physically attractive. She'd just never known Pam to date a biracial man before. Conner, who was born to a white father who was now deceased and a black mother, is light-skinned. Pam had said herself that she preferred brown to darker-skinned men and always had. Not to mention the fact that Conner's and Pam's personalities were like night and day. But that was easy to overlook since "opposites attract" proved to be a true statement for many couples.

Interestingly, when Pam first began to date Conner, she had shared with Val that he wasn't her type at all and that she was hoping that he wasn't looking to get serious. She hadn't revealed this to either Jackie or Tricee. But over time she really began to like Conner and recognized the special qualities he exhibited. It was also getting to the point for Pam where it was no fun being the only single one in the group. Pam started to view things from a different perspective.

"So what's going on with you on this beautiful Saturday morning?" Pam asked cheerily. In fact, she sang the question.

Tricee chuckled. *It must have been a good night,* she thought.

"What's so funny?" Pam took an emery board out of a kitchen drawer.

"Nothing." Tricee cleared her throat. "I was calling to invite you over for dinner next Saturday. That is, if you don't have any prior commitments."

"Okay. What's the occasion?" Pam began filing her nails.

"No occasion," Tricee said with a shrug. "I just haven't really hosted a dinner in a while and I thought it'd be nice to catch up with my girls."

"Yeah, especially since you have a bigger kitchen now," Pam teased.

"Well, yes. That, too." Tricee laughed.

Six months after Tricee and Hunter married they decided to purchase a bigger condo, a spacious unit with three bedrooms and two bathrooms and a beautiful view of the Chicago skyline. This condo, unlike the first unit Tricee had purchased, also had a partial view of the lakefront. She and Hunter decided to rent out her old condo and were elated to find the perfect tenant. It also helped that they'd only moved three blocks from the previous location.

"I'll understand, though, if you can't make it. You know, being a newlywed and all."

"Oh, please, I'm fine. Five months is long enough to have settled into a normal routine as a married woman."

Conner came back into the kitchen and poured himself a glass of water. He overheard his wife's comment and glanced over at her before drinking his water and leaving again.

"Not really," Tricee said slowly. "Hunter and I have been married a little over a year and I still miss him if we're apart for two hours."

Pam rolled her eyes. *She can be so mushy.*

"And stop rolling your eyes at me," Tricee blurted out.

"Dang, woman! Are you psychic?!" Pam asked. They both laughed. "You know we are all newlyweds. Except Val, of course."

"And Jackie." Tricee paused. "Well, it's only been—what, almost two years for her and Lem?"

"And as far as I know, they still qualify as newlyweds. But I guess it depends on the individual." Pam shrugged.

"Well, Hunter and I plan to be newlyweds well into our 80s."

"Why doesn't that surprise me?" Pam smiled as she shook her head.

Tricee's admiration for her husband was no secret. She felt so blessed. And seeing her three closest friends happily married was an even bigger blessing.

Tricee had shared with a few of her co-workers, all of whom bemoaned being single, how God had someone for them, too, as long as they stayed out of His way. It wasn't just the blessing of having a good husband, it was the contentment she'd felt when she was single. Each of the four women was blessed to have not only good husbands but satisfying careers, homes, and a relationship with the Father. Single or married, they'd all realized the importance of keeping Him first.

"It doesn't surprise you because you know I'm just a big old softie," Tricee replied.

A few moments later, Hunter walked into the bedroom. He bent over and kissed his wife gently on the neck. Tricee squirmed and let out a giggle.

"What's happening over there? I know that giggle when I hear it!" Pam asked as she stopped filing her nails.

"It's nothing." Tricee smiled as her husband left the bedroom. "I'll call you later this week. Tell Conner I said hi."

"I will. And you do the same."

"What? Tell Conner you said hello?"

Pam sucked her teeth at Tricee. "Bye!" She laughed as she hung up the phone.

Saturday was a whole week away but Pam was already looking forward to spending some time with her friends. It had been a while—too long it seemed—since they'd gotten together. She was looking forward to doing what they'd done many times in the past: eat, laugh, and just hang out and talk about anything that came to mind. Now that they were all married, there had been a shift in priorities, which meant that their time spent together was limited.

A year after Jackie married Lem, Tricee and Hunter eloped to St. Croix. Neither of them wanted the hassle of planning a wedding but they did host a reception two months afterward.

Pam tried not to take it personally when she realized just how much things had changed. After she became the only single one in the group, she saw the changes more clearly. Tricee had canceled two of their lunch dates in one month because something had come up with Hunter. Pam had been disappointed and even believed that Tricee was making excuses but she kept her thoughts to herself. Deep down she knew better but it still hurt.

"So," Conner began as he walked into the kitchen. "Five months is long enough, huh?" He removed a jar of peanut butter and some saltine crackers from the cabinet.

"Excuse me?" Pam began to polish her nails with one of the bottles of polish that was in the same drawer she'd taken the emery board from.

"I heard you tell your friend that five months was long enough to have settled into a routine." Conner spread some peanut butter on a cracker.

"Why are you eating peanut butter and crackers when we've just had breakfast?"

"Don't change the subject." Conner popped a cracker into his mouth. He kept his eyes on his wife as he waited for a response.

"I'm not changing the subject," Pam sighed. "It's no big deal." She finished polishing her last nail.

"Okay. So then you can tell me what you meant by your statement." Conner drank the rest of the water from the glass he'd poured and let out a loud burp. "Excuse me."

Pam sighed, got up from the table and attempted to leave the kitchen but Conner blocked the doorway with his slender, 6'2" frame.

"You can't leave the kitchen until you tell me."

"Please, Conner." Pam waved her hands to help her nails to dry. "I need to go and get dressed." She shoved her husband out of the way with an elbow. He followed her into their bedroom.

"Why do you keep things from me?" Conner asked, leaning against the dresser.

"Conner, I don't keep things from you." Pam blew on her nails and sat on the bed. Conner joined her and grabbed her by the waist. He laid his wife on her back.

"I love you but I haven't figured you out yet." He planted a kiss on her neck. Pam squirmed as she attempted to push her husband off of her. She loved the way he kissed her on the neck but now wasn't the time. She was meeting her cousin in an hour.

"Aww, Honey!" She whined. "You made me mess up two of my nails." Conner stopped being playful and rolled onto his side. Pam sat up and held up her hands. "See what you made me do! I was trying to keep you from having to give me money to get my nails done." She inspected the red polish. "Now I have to redo this hand."

"Your nails look just fine." Conner brushed her face with the back of his hand.

"Thank you." Pam kissed her husband on the cheek and rose from the bed.

Conner watched as she walked to the closet. She'd done it again. Each time they had a discussion in which he wanted to know something in particular, his wife would always change the subject. Sometimes Conner felt that she really was hiding something. He trusted his wife. He just wondered why she seemed so guarded sometimes.

"Why do you do that?" He remained lying on his side as he watched Pam pull a blouse and a pair of pants from the closet.

"Do what?" she asked, tossing her outfit on the bed.

"You have a way of not answering my questions. I'll ask you a question and if you don't think it's important, you don't answer it. It might not be important to you but if I ask, Honey, it is obviously something I need to know."

"Are you serious, Conner?"

"Yes. And don't look at me like that."

Pam sighed. "I think you're making a big deal over nothing. Besides, I don't ask you what you and your friends talk about." She headed back to the kitchen for her nail polish. "I allow you your privacy."

Conner bounced up off of the bed and was at her heels. "So if you heard me make a comment to one of my friends that left you curious and you asked me about it, you'd expect me to answer you, right?"

"What are you going to do?" Pam turned and faced her husband. "Follow me around the house?"

It was almost funny. He was so close to her she could almost feel the hair on his chin.

"Pam, it might seem like a small thing to you," he took a couple of steps back, "but it's not to me." He turned and walked out of the kitchen. Pam started to go after him but changed her mind.

"He'll get over it," she mumbled to herself before blowing on a newly polished nail.

Conner's career as a bus operator for the city of Chicago had its share of ups and downs. It paid well and came with great benefits, but he never knew what type of passenger he'd encounter on any given day. Being an assistant pastor helped a great deal. He once joked that had he not been a man of the cloth, there was no telling what he'd say to the unruly passengers he had sometimes. When he first began his career almost 15 years prior, he didn't hesitate to go word-for-word with his passengers. Since then he'd learned to ignore them and keep smiling. *That,* indeed, was the Holy Spirit at work.

His role as an assistant pastor was a different ball game. He'd been chosen to be the new assistant pastor of New Hope Non-Denominational church three years ago. He loved it and was known to go out of his way for the members of the congregation. Pam put a stop to that after they were married. Not completely, but she informed him that some things needed to change. Putting a stop to some of the single women who were calling seeking prayer was one of those things.

They'd only been married for two months when a woman who'd just separated from her husband began calling their home. Pam thought that was pretty odd since practically everyone in the church knew they'd just gotten married.

"Why is she calling you?" Pam had inquired.

"Honey, she's in need of prayer," had been Conner's reply.

Pam went on to inquire as to why the woman hadn't called the pastor instead. Conner explained that one of his roles as an assistant pastor was to assist the members of the church whenever Pastor Brooks wasn't available. That had been an acceptable answer, sort of. Pam learned that the woman was going through a rough time. It turned out that she'd started counseling sessions with the pastor, but the pastor had become unavailable tending to a family emergency. So she decided to reach out to Conner.

"But there are other deacons and one other assistant pastor at the church who I'm sure know how to pray." Conner allowed Pam to express her feelings without saying a word. He was all about keeping peace in his household. But he was also about handling His Father's business. Surely, he wasn't about to turn this woman away on account of his wife's overreaction.

Once when the woman had called, Pam sat in the living room along with her husband, pretending to be engrossed in a novel. The phone call lasted for at least 45 minutes—45 minutes too long. Pam could understand people needing prayer, but how long did it take to give a few scriptures and wrap up with the Lord's Prayer? She decided that if the woman called again, she'd explain to her husband that it wasn't her newlywed insecurity working it was her woman's intuition. But the woman resumed her sessions with Pastor Brooks so she and Conner never had that conversation.

A few weeks later, Conner began receiving phone calls from another female member of the congregation. The woman claimed that the enemy wanted her to go off on her boss so she could lose her job. Unlike the woman who had been recently separated, this woman was single. Pam knew of her though she didn't know her personally. The Sunday following, Pam noticed the woman standing too close to her husband. That had been the last straw. When they came home from church, Pam expressed her feelings.

"Something's fishy. Our home phone is not the prayer line. I suggest that these women get their prayer needs met elsewhere."

Conner pondered his wife's words. Even he found it odd how the woman had stood so close to him while they chatted after the service, among a couple of other things he'd picked up on. So when she called their home two days later asking Conner if she could meet with him for prayer over coffee, he laughed and tried to remain polite.

"Sister Vicky, I would suggest you pray over coffee with Jesus," he'd said. She must have gotten the hint because she hasn't called the Buckner home since. And Pam made sure she got the hint. She saw the woman at the grocery store not long after her last call. She gave Ms. Vicky her best "don't play with me" glance and Ms. Vicky hurried out of the produce section, dropping tomatoes and all. Ms. Vicky now sits in the very last row at church and is out the door as soon as service ends.

"She knew what she was up to all along," Pam had told her husband. They both had gotten a laugh out of the whole thing.

Pam adored her husband but there were times when he could really work on her patience. His asking questions that she felt were unnecessary irritated her. She concluded that she was still adjusting to married life. Even though she felt that Conner made things more complicated than they needed to be.

2

"You're not ready yet? I told you I'd be here by 1:30!" Pam walked into her cousin Sondra's bedroom which, up until a few months ago, had been her bedroom.

"I *am* ready!" Sondra grabbed her purse. "Let me go and tell hubby I'm leaving."

"You're wearing that?" Pam gave her cousin a once-over.

They were on their way downtown to have a late lunch and to window shop and Pam thought Sondra's attire was a little too causal. But before she could give her cousin an honest critique, five of her cousin's six children came running upstairs from the basement.

"Pam!" The oldest of the five ran up to Pam and grabbed her by the waist. "Cousin Pam, I have a new dress! You want to come to my room and see it?"

Before Pam could respond to her little cousin's excitement, the other four children gathered around her.

"I have a new dress, too! It's jello."

"Sweetie, it's yellow, not jello," her mother corrected her.

"Hi, Bam!" the youngest of the brood said excitedly. "You want to play with my toys?"

"Yes, I would love to play with you." Pam reached down and pinched her 3-year-old cousin on the cheeks and gave the other children a hug.

"I'm working on teaching her how to pronounce your name correctly." Sondra shook her head and smiled. If there was one relative who always got hugs and love from Sondra's children, it was Pam. "And this one," Sondra patted her 4-year-old daughter on the head, "is having a hard time with the letter 'y.' We're working on it."

Pam laughed. "It's pretty normal." She noticed that only five of the six siblings were present. "Where's your sister?" she asked no one in particular. It was the oldest who answered.

"She's with Grandma and Papa. Her birthday's today and they're taking her for ice cream. Papa said he's going to bring us some ice cream, too. And Grandma said that if we behave and eat all our vegetables, next Saturday we can come to her house and watch movies and bake brownies."

"And there you have it," Sondra laughed as her 10-year-old daughter gave Pam the full rundown, "straight from the news reporter on the Channel Five news team."

"Do we have a journalist in the making?" Pam teased.

"I like strawberry ice cream, Pam," the 5-year-old blurted out.

"That's my favorite ice cream, too," Pam said as she placed her arm around the girl. "Where did Parker go?" she inquired about her cousin's son who usually ran to greet her before his sisters. "I just saw him."

"He ran into the bedroom with his dad, I think." Sondra shrugged. "I can't keep up with those two," she smiled.

Pam and Sondra had been very close as youngsters. They used to take turns spending weekends at each other's homes. That started to change once they became teenagers but they still managed to keep their parents' phone lines tied up.

When Sondra, who is two years younger than Pam, got married and started having babies, Pam would sometimes tease her, "Once you started having babies, you didn't know how to stop!" Sondra had her first child at 25 and, 10 years later, found herself the devoted mother of six children ages 10, 8, 7, 5, 4, and 3. Spencer, her husband of 12 years, was just as devoted a parent as his wife. He joked often that he didn't know how he and his only son would survive in a house full of women.

Spencer loved it when his wife got together with Pam or one of her friends, which didn't happen often. It allowed him an opportunity to learn different ways to maintain his children's interest while mom was away for a few hours. Spencer took parenting very seriously. He looked forward to sharing with his wife what he and the kids had done or what they'd accomplished while she was away. It gave him a sense of pride to know that he could manage a household as good as any woman. Not to mention, Sondra being out allowed him an opportunity to spoil his children behind his wife's back. Although she did her share of that on her good days.

Sondra grabbed her purse and was just about to let her husband know she was leaving when he came walking into the living room. "Cousin-in-Law Pam!" he said and embraced her. "I thought I heard your voice. So how's married life treating you?"

Pam laughed. "That's the same question I asked my girl, Tricee, this morning."

"Yeah, I think it's an expected question when you're newly married."

"Well, married life is wonderful," she said and then tapped her cousin's long, tan coffee table. "Knock on wood."

"No worries, cousin. You don't need wood," Sondra commented. She looked at her husband and smiled. He winked and smiled back. "As long as Conner does everything you ask him to do, your marriage will remain wonderful."

Spencer shrugged his shoulders. "No argument here." They all laughed.

"Well, I'm leaving, Sweetie. I'll be back in a few hours." Sondra looked down at the children's book, with the penguin on the cover, in her husband's hand. "It must be story time."

"Parker needs to read it again," her husband replied. "I want him to explain it to me in his own words."

Pam's 7-year-old cousin came and stood next to his dad at the mention of his name. Other than giving Pam a hug when she arrived, he had remained silent, and ran back into his bedroom, while his sisters indulged her in conversation.

"That's my book for school," he said and reached for it.

Pam smiled at the adorable young boy who looked a lot like his father. "Do you like it when your teacher reads to you at school?" she asked him.

He nodded but was quickly reminded by his mother, "Answer the question with your words, Sweetie."

Parker looked lovingly at both parents and then turned back to Pam. "I like school and I like story time. But I don't like those girls."

Pam, Sondra and Spencer all got a kick out of his facial expression. The frown was hard to miss.

Pam rested her hand on her little cousin's shoulder. "Why don't you like your classmates?" she asked, trying not to laugh.

Still frowning he answered, "They smell like soap."

His parents laughed. This wasn't the first time they'd heard him complain about girls. There was one little girl in particular he'd mentioned before, so his parents weren't at all surprised when he provided Pam with more information.

"Tiffany likes to play with me and she tries to take my fire truck away. I don't like to play with Tiffany." Then he reiterated his point. "She smells like soap." Pam could no longer refrain from laughing.

"He just recently turned 7, so he's at that 'girls are yucky' stage," his father laughed. "But," Spencer continued, "give him a few more years. That will all change."

"I love it," Pam said with a light chuckle. "Yucky, but they smell like soap."

"You know, that has always tickled me pink." Sondra chimed in. "How you men," she looked at her husband, "despise the opposite sex when you are much younger, but then—*bam*! All of a sudden the opposite sex is the greatest thing to happen to you and for you." Sondra and Pam gave each other a high-five.

Before heading out, both ladies gave the children another hug. Spencer lightly grabbed his wife by the arm and planted a kiss on her cheek, right before he questioned her outfit.

"You're wearing that, Honey?"

Sondra gave her husband the side-eye. "Yes, I am. What's wrong with what I'm wearing?" She looked at Pam, then back at her husband. Pam looked away and began to chuckle softly. Sondra repeated her question. "What's wrong with what I have on?"

"You look pretty, Mommy," Parker piped in.

Sondra looked down at her son and smiled. "Thank you, Sweetie." Then she turned and looked at her husband and Pam. "I'm glad someone likes my outfit."

Spencer was about to speak until his 10-year-old daughter grabbed him by the hand.

"Dad, after Parker reads his book, we need to go to the grocery store so we can buy the food for dinner. We need to have dinner started in a couple of hours."

Pam and Sondra grinned and stole glances at each other. The way she expressed herself, it was sometimes hard to believe she was only 10. She was very good at helping out with her five younger siblings. And any time her mother was away, she pitched in to assist her father in every way possible.

"Okay, Sweetie." Spencer looked lovingly at his oldest child. "And you're going to help Daddy fix the tacos, right?"

"Yes, Daddy," she said and returned her father's warm smile.

Pam was touched. It was moments like this, watching her cousins interact with their children that made her feel like she was ready to start her own family.

"See you guys later," Sondra said, and then glanced at her husband. "And when I get home, we can discuss the issue you have with my outfit."

Sondra walked out first. As Pam followed, she turned around, looked at Spencer and shrugged. He laughed as he closed the door behind them.

Sondra and Pam climbed into Pam's 2009 black Mercedes and headed for the expressway. There was a couple of new eateries downtown that Pam hadn't tried yet and she'd asked her cousin last week to clear her Saturday schedule.

Sondra and Spencer began renting Pam's home after Pam and Conner got married. Pam loved her new home, a three-bedroom ranch—well, a four-bedroom one if you counted the room in the basement. It was actually a storage area but Conner decided to make it into a bedroom. This way, when they had family over, there'd be enough space for everyone, he'd said. Pam grunted when he explained his reasoning. She flashed her best smile at her husband and said, "Honey, there are a couple of hotels within 10 miles of the house." Hyde Park, the area she now called home, wasn't too far from the home Pam was renting to her cousin.

Whenever she visited Sondra, being in her previous residence always brought back memories for Pam. She marveled at how different the place looked. The basement had been transformed into what Pam referred to as "Spencer's place" because he spent most of his time there. There was a 52-inch flat screen mounted against the wall and a black recliner and sofa that didn't match. Pam couldn't even describe the sofa. She and Sondra had laughed and said it was a cross between green and some brownish color, something a woman would have never chosen for furniture. A square-shaped brown coffee table, if you could call it that, sat in the middle of the room. Along the wall were a few photos of some of the world's best athletes, some of whom Spencer had met.

During football and basketball season, Spencer would bring out extra folding chairs depending on how many buddies he was having over. He had only one rule: His buddies were limited as to how much beer they could consume in his home.

Spencer wasn't a big beer drinker and would usually have only one while watching a game. And his buddies were perfectly fine with his rule because the real perk about game day was Sondra's chicken nachos! Two of his buddies would phone a week before a game informing Spencer that they'd bought extra chicken strips. One day Spencer played what his buddies thought was a horrible joke. He told them that Sondra decided she was no longer going to fix her specialty dish. Spencer would never forget the look on their faces!

For now, renting Pam's home was the ideal situation. Spencer and Sondra had moved back to Chicago from Dayton. They sold their home a year ago, after Spencer's employers sold the company. He had been one of the few employees asked to remain with the new company. They had been renting a three-bedroom apartment on the city's north side that was certainly large enough, but when Pam offered to rent her home to them, they jumped at the chance. Though they expected to become homeowners again in the near future, they agreed that now was just not the right time. Not to mention, they had already started saving for their children's education.

Sondra shook her head as Pam parked her Mercedes in a downtown parking lot. "Pam, we could have gone somewhere else. It's expensive to park downtown."

Pam unfastened her seat belt. "No, we're here now. Besides, this is one of the least expensive lots. Stop worrying." She smiled at Sondra as they exited the vehicle.

"Okay." Sondra smiled back at her favorite cousin. She'd always felt that Pam was such a sweetheart but that her tough exterior sometimes made it difficult for that sweetness to show.

They walked toward Michigan Avenue, admiring the spring fashions on display. Sondra's best friend worked as a buyer for one of the downtown stores. She'd told Sondra that her buying decisions were generally pretty risky due to having to anticipate what people will buy. She'd also commented on the wide variety of fashions she got to see between the different shows in the various cities she visited.

"Look at that white pantsuit." Pam stopped in front of a store called Fashions Unlimited to admire the two-piece ensemble.

"I like it, but where would I wear it? Being a preschool assistant teacher doesn't allow me to dress up," Sondra laughed. "I can see it covered with every colored crayon in the box."

"You can wear it to church!" Pam said excitedly. "Come on! Let's go inside so you can try it on!"

"Not so fast, cousin. I said I liked it, I didn't say I wanted to buy it. Besides, they might not even have it in my size." Sondra was filled with excuses. She rarely bought herself any new clothes. Being the mother of six, she spent most of her time in clothing stores for children.

Pam exhaled. "Sondra, you know there's nothing wrong with treating yourself every now and then."

"I know, and being out with you on this Saturday afternoon is my treat."

Pam tilted her head. She looked at her cousin's long, brown skirt and flowery blouse. It was cute but it made Sondra look so plain. Pam rarely saw her in anything but long skirts.

"Sondra, I didn't want to say this, but you dress like you are much older than your 35 years. Your own husband questioned your outfit," Pam laughed.

Sondra let out a deep sigh and smiled. "I know why he asked me if I was wearing this." She pointed to her outfit. "He tells me all the time that I need to wear skirts that hit right at the knee to expose my calves more. I knew when he looked at my skirt that he was going to say something."

"But you asked him anyway?" Pam chuckled. "When you already knew what he was thinking?"

"He said my legs were the first thing he noticed when we met." Sondra smiled. "He told me once that he can understand why I wear long skirts to work, but that I should spruce it up a bit when I go out."

"And I agree, Sondra. Six kids doesn't mean you stop being sexy for your hubby."

"With six kids, I think I put the 's' in sexy!" She and Pam laughed.

"So are you in? I know Spencer would love that pantsuit on you, and you will love it on you. Let's look for a couple of knee-length skirts or dresses, too."

"Oh, I guess so," said Sondra, still very reluctant. "But they might not have a size 14, Pam."

"Stop." Pam tapped her cousin lightly. "I have seen women bigger than you who look jazzy in pantsuits. If you decide you don't want white, we can see if they have it in another color."

"Ok. But let's have our late lunch first. It'll give me a chance to think about it."

Pam giggled. "Okay. But if you want to eat first, before trying on clothes, you're going to be relegated to eating something light."

"That's cool." Sondra waved her hand. "I was just going to have a grilled chicken salad or something anyway."

They walked another two blocks before deciding on a restaurant. It wasn't either of the new places Pam had wanted to try but one she'd frequented before. She hadn't been there in a while so it was a good choice, especially because she loved their Monte Cristo sandwich.

Sondra felt her cell phone vibrate just as they reached the restaurant. "It's Spencer," she said. "I wouldn't answer it but when you have kids—"

"It's okay," Pam replied as she removed her Blackberry from her purse.

"Are you guys on the way to the store? Okay. Well, I don't need anything. Oh wait! Sweetie, can you please pick me up some female products? I just remembered. I'm all out."

Pam stopped scrolling through her Blackberry and stared at her cousin.

"Okay. Love you, too. Make sure Lamb Chops uses the bathroom before you go. She always says she doesn't have to go but is the first one to yell she has to use it as soon as she gets in the car." Sondra and Spencer referred to their 3-year-old as Lamb Chops on occasion, which always made the toddler giggle.

After her phone call they strolled into the restaurant. The server took their orders and, shortly after, brought over two glasses of iced tea. Pam sipped her tea.

"Spencer doesn't have a problem buying female products?" She wasn't shocked, just a little surprised.

That wasn't how it worked in her household with Conner. One would think that with one marriage under his belt, purchasing said item would have been as common as purchasing eggs. He was the father of 10-year-old twin daughters who would one day need them. What had he planned to do if his now ex-wife just hadn't been around when that day arrived? Pam had no idea.

"No, of course not," Sondra laughed. "He doesn't mind at all. Why?"

"I asked Conner to pick me up some one day and he almost had a stroke. Men can be so silly sometimes."

"You would think he'd had to buy them before at some point. Good night, the man is on marriage number two!" Sondra drank some of her tea.

"I know!" Pam shook her head. "I told him, 'Honey, I just asked you to buy a box of tampons. I didn't ask you to rob the store!'" They laughed as the server set their meals in front of them.

"Oh, that Monte Cristo looks good," Sondra eyed her cousin's sandwich.

"Would you like a piece?"

"Oh no, cuz. I'm good. I'm about to get into this grilled chicken and almond salad."

They bowed their heads, said grace, and dug in. They were having humorous conversation about relatives over their scrumptious meals when a gentleman with a smooth, brown complexion and deep voice approached their table.

"Pam? I thought that was you. How have you been?"

Pam stopped chewing. Her eyes grew big as she looked up. "Jeff?"

3

It had been two years since Jeff had seen Pam and, during that time, he'd thought of her often. Now, as he stood before the woman he'd once felt was more unique than anyone he'd ever known, he wondered if thoughts of him ever occupied her mind. The way things ended between them two years prior hadn't been very pleasant. When he attempted to call her several times after their last conversation, his calls went straight to voicemail never to be returned.

"Hi, Jeff." Pam managed to speak though her tone was softer than usual. Of all the people to run into, she had not expected to see Jeff. She tried her best to maintain a demeanor that said, *I haven't thought about you at all.* Though this sounded good in her mind, it wasn't entirely true.

"So." Jeff looked from Pam to her cousin Sondra. "I see you ladies are enjoying a late lunch."

He waited for Pam to make an introduction but she failed to do so. Then it suddenly dawned on him that she was probably feeling a little awkward. He couldn't understand why, since seeing her again had become the highlight of his afternoon.

Sondra put down her fork and looked from Pam to Jeff. She knew her first cousin well enough to know that this moment was, indeed, awkward for her. She wiped her hands with her napkin. "I'm Sondra, Pam's cousin."

Jeff shook Sondra's extended hand and smiled. "I'm Jeff. It's a pleasure to meet you, Sondra."

Sondra smiled. *He's a good looking man but something tells me he's full of himself.* "Likewise," she replied and went back to enjoying her meal.

From the expression on Pam's face, Sondra could sense that there was a little bit of tension between her and Jeff. She recalled Pam mentioning Jeff's name to her two years prior, when she and Spencer were still living in Dayton. Other than saying that she was seeing a "fine brother who made her laugh," she had shared little about her and Jeff's relationship. After this encounter, Sondra figured that Pam would likely have quite a few details to share. It would make for an interesting drive back to the south side.

Jeff tilted his head and looked at Pam, wanting for her to look him in the eyes. But she was looking away from him and rubbing the back of her neck.

"Pam, you're looking good." Jeff knew he had to say something. He had no intention of keeping Pam from enjoying her lunch with her cousin, but he had every intention of leaving her with a business card. "Are you still in sales?" Seeing that Pam hadn't even uttered a thank you after his compliment, he figured the next best thing to do was ask a question.

Pam sighed before answering. "No, I'm not." She looked him in the eye briefly and then turned to her cousin. "What time do you have?"

Sondra looked at Pam sideways. She knew her cousin was wearing a watch. Not to mention all Pam had to do was glance at her cell phone. But she put two and two together. "Uh," she began, then wiped her hands with her napkin and looked at her watch. "It's almost 3:30."

Jeff caught the hint and realized that Pam had no interest in chatting. But he was already making plans in his head to see to it that her feelings changed.

"I should let you ladies get back to your meal." He removed his wallet from his back pocket and pulled out a business card. "I don't want to seem pushy but here's my card." He gave Pam that smile she'd seen many times before. It had been this smile that kept her from being able to remain upset whenever he'd done something wrong. "I'll be back in town soon. I'd love to catch up."

Sondra looked at Pam and then at Jeff as she scooped up a forkful of her salad. She couldn't wait to hear more about this guy.

Pam reluctantly took the card. To say this whole scene had caught her by surprise was an understatement. She managed to say what she felt was most appropriate. "Take care, Jeff. It was nice seeing you." *Surely, you see this diamond on my left hand.* She was tempted to say this out loud.

Sondra was full of questions as soon as Jeff walked away. "Who was he? No, let me rephrase that question. Was that the Jeff you mentioned to me a couple of years ago? The fine brother who made your toes curl? Okay, wait. Let me not ask the obvious. That had to have been Jeff. What are you going to do, cuz? Are you going to call him? Why did you accept his business card? Did he not see the ring on your finger? He seemed sort of arrogant— assuming you would want to call him. Child, I couldn't be so bothered. I'm so glad I've been married to the same man for the past 12 years! No way could I ever do that dating thing again." Sondra grunted and shook her head. "That's for the birds. Girl, I tell Spencer all the time that if I ever," she shook her finger at Pam, "ended up single again, for whatever reason, I would not, under any circumstances, be with anybody else."

Pam began to laugh at her cousin's sudden declaration. "And you know what, Sondra? With six kids, you probably won't have too much of a problem staying single."

Upon hearing Pam's words, Sondra stopped eating and put down her fork. "Now see that's just wrong, Pam. That's just wrong."

A few seconds later the two women were laughing. But Pam felt the need to vent. She wanted to address Sondra's questions and she began by clarifying what she'd said about Jeff two years ago. But first she finished the rest of her iced tea.

"First of all, to answer your questions, I did not say he made my toes curl. I said he made me laugh."

"Same thing." Sondra shrugged before picking up her glass of tea.

"Whatever." Pam rolled her eyes. "He didn't start out arrogant although that was my first impression when we first met. As for assuming I would want to call him, he can think again. And as for seeing my ring, how could he miss it? But it doesn't matter anyway. It's all water under the table now." She wiped her hands and mouth with her napkin, then proceeded to open her bronze, Roxy Dusk, drawstring handbag.

"You mean water under the bridge." Sondra watched Pam pick the business card up from the table and look at it before tossing it into her purse.

"Yes. That ship has sailed. Besides, I'm a happily married woman now."

Their server approached the table before Sondra had a chance to comment. "Is there anything else I can get for you ladies?" He was a young black man who looked to be in his late 20s. His smile was as warm as it had been when they first sat down.

"No, we're good. Just the check please." Pam smiled trying to ignore Sondra's facial expression.

"Certainly," the server replied as he produced their bill. "You ladies come again."

Pam waited until he walked away. "You're nuts, you know that, right?"

"Yeah, I know. But if I wasn't an older married woman with six kids …"

"You'd just be another older woman with six kids." They chuckled as Pam paid the bill.

Once outside the restaurant, they walked in the direction of the clothing store where they'd seen the pantsuit.

"That was a nice tip you left," said Sondra.

"I believe in tipping well when I receive good service."

"I hear ya. But it does help when the server is fine, huh?"

Pam laughed. "Yes. It helps."

Sondra was still waiting to hear more about Jeff but decided to wait and see if Pam would bring him up again. She couldn't help but wonder, though, if Pam had forgotten all about seeing him just that quickly. It was obvious to her that Pam was, indeed, happily married. But there was something about the scene she'd just witnessed that had her curious.

They walked into the clothing store and were immediately approached by the sales clerk. She was an attractive Latina with dark hair that was pulled back into a ponytail. Her bright red lipstick matched her bright red nail polish. The huge orange ring on her right-hand index finger was hard to miss.

"May I help you ladies find anything?" She was carrying a bright green dress and a white top back to their rightful racks, but stopped to assist Pam and Sondra first.

"Yes," Pam spoke first. "We were interested in the pantsuit. The white one that's in the window."

"That's very pretty. Right this way." The sales clerk led Pam and Sondra to the pantsuit and Sondra immediately showed her disinterest.

"Why are you frowning, Sondra?" Pam asked, noticing the look on Sondra's face.

The sales clerk smiled and looked at Sondra. "Is it for you?" she asked.

"Yes, but I don't know about this color." She spotted the same pantsuit in dark blue. "Maybe this one would look better on me." She looked at the tag for the size. "That figures, a size eight."

Pam began to look through the pantsuits and found a size 14. "Now let's see if they have your size in white so you can try them both on."

The sales clerk put down the items in her hand and began to look for Sondra's size. "Here's a size 14." She smiled as she handed the white boucle pantsuit to Sondra. Sondra hesitated before taking it.

Pam let out a sigh, then looked at the sales clerk's name tag. "Thank you, Edith. She'll try them both on."

"I think it will look very pretty on you. The dressing room is right there. Let me know if you need anything else."

Sondra came out of the dressing room several minutes later wearing the white pantsuit. Pam's eyes grew wide. She looked absolutely gorgeous.

The sales clerk looked up from where she was standing at a nearby rack. She came and stood beside Pam. "That's lovely on you."

Pam agreed. "Sondra, you look great. I think we found a winner."

Sondra made a face. "I look like a big, white pillow." She did a couple of turns as she looked at herself in the mirror. Both Pam and the sales clerk laughed.

"You do not," Pam turned down the collar of the suit, "you look like a beautiful woman wearing a classic pantsuit."

"I like it on you. I have the perfect scarf to match," the sales clerk added. "You can wear a scarf or a nice necklace."

"I think a scarf will set it off." Pam turned to the sales clerk. "Let's see what you have."

The sales clerk walked toward the table where the scarves were on display while Pam continued to convince Sondra how nice she looked.

"Let me try the blue one." Sondra went back into the dressing room while Pam and the sales clerk began to look at three different scarves. When she came out again wearing the dark blue boucle pantsuit she was all smiles. "I like this one better."

Sondra made a couple of turns in the mirror and struck a pose, causing Pam to chuckle.

The sales clerk smiled and held up a blue and white silk scarf and a white one with small blue polka dots. "Either one of these would work," she said.

"I like this one." Sondra reached for the blue and white silk one but then hesitated. "But I like this one, too."

"Get them both. You can mix and match," was Pam's solution. Sondra was ready to protest but Pam cut her off. "You can wear them with other outfits."

They thanked the sales clerk for her help and proceeded to the register. Pam stopped as they were about to pass a rack filled with dresses. Not one to pass up a clearance sale, she began to look through the dresses for Sondra's size.

"Pam, I will pay for my dress if I find one that I like." Sondra smiled as she began looking through the rack.

It had taken a little convincing but Pam allowed Sondra to purchase the dress. They'd also found a pretty, olive one with ruching at the waist and a sheer white blouse. After about another hour or so of shopping, they walked the few blocks to the parking garage.

Fastening her seat belt, Pam commented, "This was a great way to spend the afternoon, cuz. We need to do this more often."

"I'm game," Sondra laughed. "But you might have to get through my six little ones first."

"I can handle them. I learned how to bribe children on my niece and nephew," Pam chuckled.

As they turned onto Michigan Avenue, heading south, Pam thought about the encounter with Jeff. *I'm not calling him. Hmph. He must not know who he's messing with. This woman has changed.* Her thoughts were interrupted when Sondra turned and looked out of the window.

"Doesn't that uppity cousin of ours live near here somewhere?" She grinned as she turned toward Pam.

"Yeah, she does." Pam tilted her head backward. "She lives a few blocks north of here. Her loft, I mean," she made a face, "her *luxury apartment* is near Huron."

Sondra chuckled. "She told me the last time we chatted that she was moving to Lincoln Park." Sondra didn't talk to their cousin often but, then again, neither did Pam. Although she and

Pam had been speaking more than usual lately. "Have you spoken to her recently?" Sondra asked.

Pam thought about the day two years ago when she visited her cousin. It had been the same day, later in the evening, that she told Jeff they were done. She had spoken to her cousin a few times since then. On one occasion, when her cousin mentioned Jeff, Pam immediately changed the subject.

"I talked to Maureen last week, actually. And she did mention something about buying a condo in Lincoln Park. I told her, 'Sweetie, you could get a big ol' home in the suburbs or on the south side and get more for your money.'" Pam laughed.

"Let me guess," Sondra chimed in. "She then went on about how she couldn't see living on anybody's south side or suburbs, right?"

"Bingo!" Pam blurted.

"She was telling me how she wants to meet a nice man. But she can't seem to meet any that seem normal." Sondra paused before continuing. "I was thinking of introducing her to one of Spencer's friends."

Pam gasped. "Uh, you'd better make sure it's one of Spencer's friends with a college degree. Otherwise, don't bother."

"I know, right?" Sondra sighed as she shook her head.

"I had to remind her that Spencer doesn't have a four-year degree and he does very well as an employee specialist for his company. He has quite a few friends with blue collar jobs who are doing quite well."

"She'll figure it out soon," Pam remarked. "I told her she's probably scaring men away and doesn't realize it."

The two women continued to chat until Sondra received a call from her 10-year-old. During Sondra's call, Pam thought about having seen Jeff again. She couldn't get the moment out of her mind even though she wanted badly to forget it. She broached the subject of past relationships as Sondra placed her cell phone back into her purse.

"Sondra, do you ever think about any of the guys you dated before Spencer?"

"No. I didn't date too many guys before Spencer. We got married young, remember?"

"Yeah, I know." Pam shrugged. "I was just wondering if you ever have any 'what if' thoughts."

Sondra knew where this conversation was headed. It had to have something to do with Pam seeing Jeff again. And since Pam had brought it up, Sondra felt it was well within her right to get nosy. Not to mention, she and her favorite cousin only had a little more time together. They weren't too far from the Kenwood area and Pam had already said that once she dropped Sondra off, she wasn't able to stay. She and Conner had dinner plans for the evening.

"Why are you asking? Does this have anything to do with that Jeff guy?" Sondra watched the expression on Pam's face and knew that the answer was yes.

"I just wondered, after Jeff and I stopped seeing each other, how my life would have been had we stayed together." Pam had just admitted something to her cousin that she hadn't admitted to her three best friends. "We were in the same field and had many of the same interests. I really thought things could have worked. Don't get me wrong," she continued while Sondra remained silent and let her bare her feelings, "I love Conner and wouldn't trade him for anything. But Jeff had an aura of excitement about him that I really liked."

"You know what? I take back what I said," Sondra suddenly blurted out. She decided to throw some humor into the conversation before sharing what she really felt.

"What's that?" Pam glanced over at Sondra for a brief moment.

"I do regret Denzel and me not getting married. I just can't get him away from that Pauletta."

Pam laughed. "You and about half the women in the world!"

"Only half?" Sondra asked. "I think it's more than that."

"I'm sure it is with the exception of me and a few other women I know. There are a lot of fine brothers out there. Denzel is not the only one."

"He is in *my* book! Goodness!" Sondra fanned her face with her hand. Pam laughed at her cousin's amusing behavior. "There are some fine men—period! Not just brothers," Sondra continued. "But anyway, back to the topic at hand. As for Jeff, cuz, that wasn't meant to be. But, surely, you know that already."

"Yeah, I know."

"And as for the excitement, I think it came from him keeping you guessing in a way. You know what I mean?" Sondra turned to look at Pam. "Jeff added excitement, if you want to call it that, because he wasn't ready for what you wanted. But he made sure to do all the things he knew would keep you interested. You know what I mean?" she asked again with a quizzical expression.

"I do know what you mean," Pam answered as she noticed Sondra's expression. "Stop making that face," they both chuckled.

Several minutes later, Pam pulled up in front of her cousin's home. They retrieved Sondra's shopping bags and were still standing by the Mercedes when Sondra reached over and gave Pam a hug.

"Thanks again, Pam. I love my pantsuit."

"You're welcome. You should have let me buy you the white one, too."

"You are too generous. Conner is blessed to have my cousin for a wife. You be sure to tell him I said so."

"Ok." Pam glanced at her watch. "I would come in but I need to get home. And if I do come in, your brood wouldn't let me leave."

"This is true. I'll tell them you said you'd be over again soon."

They embraced once more before Pam climbed back into her vehicle. Sondra was still standing by the passenger-side door. Sensing that Sondra had something to say, Pam pressed the button that controlled the window on the passenger side.

"What?" She leaned over to the passenger-side window as far as she could.

"Pam, you know how people say the grass is not always greener on the other side?" Pam nodded. "I really believe that. Many times I wonder if there is any grass at all." Pam remained silent. "You're a grown woman and I know you will do the right thing. But if I were you, I wouldn't call him."

"Okay. But I'm not sure I get the 'no grass at all' bit." Pam raised an eyebrow.

"Okay, look—don't try to figure out my philosophy." Sondra raised her voice in mock annoyance. "Just take heed to what I'm saying!"

"You should have been a comedian, you know that?" Pam smiled, gave her cousin a wave of the hand, rolled up the window and drove off.

As she headed for home and the husband she loved, she thought about what Sondra had said. She also thought more about seeing Jeff again. As soon as she arrived home, she walked into her bedroom and removed the business card from her purse. She looked at it for several seconds before ripping it in two and tossing it into the small trash can.

She turned to leave the bedroom and paused. She glanced down at the torn business card in the otherwise empty trash can and reached down to retrieve it. After removing a small envelope from her purse, Pam grabbed a pen off of her nightstand. She held the two pieces of the business card together and jotted down Jeff's cell phone number. Then she ripped the card into even smaller pieces and tossed it back into the trash can. *Don't want to leave any traces of evidence*, she thought.

4

"Hi, Hunter." Jackie gave Tricee's husband a hug. "It's good to see you." At 5'9" she was almost as tall as he was.

"How are Lem and the young ladies?" Hunter helped Jackie remove her sweater.

"They're all fine. Thanks for asking."

Jackie was mother to a 15-year-old daughter from her first marriage and stepmother to Lem's two daughters, age 18 and 19, who were both in college. She was telling Hunter how much her stepdaughters were enjoying college life when Tricee came walking out of the bedroom.

"Hello there, Mrs. Larson. So glad you could make it."

"So am I. But I thought husbands weren't allowed." Jackie smiled wide as she looked at Hunter. "I know you live here and all, but your wife said it was an all-wives affair."

Tricee playfully grabbed her husband by the hand. "I know," she said to Jackie, "but I had to use him to fry the chicken. We're not big on fried food but my honey can fry some chicken!"

Hunter laughed. "Yeah, she used me. What can I say?"

"Well, in that case, thanks for sticking around," Jackie laughed as the three of them walked into the living room.

Last weekend, after Tricee phoned Pam, she'd phoned Val and Jackie to invite them to dinner. She was elated when all three of her girlfriends said they could make it. Things had changed quite a bit in the past two years:

Val had given birth to a beautiful baby girl, Ashlyn Corie, who would turn 1 next month. She'd teased her girlfriends that her life had changed a lot more drastically than theirs. Sure, they were all married now but, unlike her, they hadn't experienced bringing another life into the world. Jackie could relate, although her "baby," Alesia, was now 15. But Pam and Tricee could only imagine it. Neither of them had experienced giving birth, at least not yet.

Ashlyn Corie was Val's and her husband Cory's pride and joy, and the whole childbirth experience had been beautiful. But Val had already told her friends that a second child was not in the making, even though Cory let it be known that he would like to have another one. Val would remind him of his 17 year old son Sean, from a previous relationship. It was her playful way of saying, "you have two children already."

On this warm spring evening in the Windy City, the women looked forward to catching up and having a good time, like they'd done so many times in the past. Tricee's phone rang just as Jackie and Tricee were about to take a seat on the sofa. "It's probably the doorman informing me that either Pam or Val is downstairs," Tricee said as Hunter answered the phone.

"You can send her on up. Thank you." Hunter smiled at his wife as he placed the phone back on its base. "That was your girl, Pam."

Tricee turned toward Jackie. "I guess Val will be here soon. I wanted her to bring the baby but she insisted that this was an evening for the women."

"Yeah, I don't think Ashlyn would have been willing to share her mom with us had Val brought her along." Jackie laughed. "Alesia still expects for me to tell her my every move. I have to remind her that I'm the captain of the ship and always will be. Therefore, I give the orders, not take them."

"I can't wait to—" Tricee immediately caught herself. She had news she wanted to share but not at that very minute.

"You can't wait to what? Have kids?" Jackie smiled as she waited for Tricee to respond, but their conversation was cut short when they heard Pam's voice.

"Hunter, good to see you again." Pam gave Hunter a hug and then handed him her jacket.

Tricee stood up. "No, forget it. We'll talk later."

Jackie raised an eyebrow as she watched a grinning Tricee bounce happily over to her front door. A few thoughts began swirling around in her head. She had a pretty good idea what Tricee's news might be.

Tricee had talked about having children now that she and Hunter had been married for a year and a half. She'd said before that she wanted to start a family within two years of being married. But regardless as to what she had to say, Jackie would learn before the evening ended that Tricee wasn't the only one with news to share.

"Hey, Lady," Tricee beamed. "As always, you're looking good." She and Pam embraced.

"So are you. I can see that Hunter is taking good care of you." Pam gave Tricee a once-over.

Hunter chuckled. "I do my best. It seems like married life has been good to you, too. How's Conner?"

"He's fine. At home preparing his notes. He's been invited to be a guest speaker at a relative's church. It's not until next month but he's preparing early."

"I'll keep him lifted up. I'm sure the Lord will move on his behalf."

"Thanks." Pam smiled. "He appreciates prayers from others."

"We could all use some intercession. Well, if you ladies will excuse me, I'll get out of your way." Hunter chuckled. "I'm sure there's a lot of girl talk waiting to take place." He turned and walked toward the bedroom.

Hunter had made plans to visit his mother but told Tricee he wanted to stop by the coffee shop on Broadway first to do some reading. It was the same coffee shop where he and Tricee had met two years prior. He joked with his wife that he wanted to relive that moment by standing in the exact spot he'd stood in when they met. Lately, some things had been weighing on his mind but they weren't anything he was ready to share with his wife yet. He believed there wasn't anything too hard for God to handle, and he trusted that God had already worked out a solution.

"Hello, Mrs. Buckner!" Jackie stood and gave Pam a hug, admiring her ruffled, paisley-print blouse. "I love the blouse!" She ran her hands along Pam's sleeves. "Look at you looking like a jazzy married woman." Jackie stepped back and tilted her head. "You're glowing."

"It's the tall glass of milk I drank before I got here," Pam said, laughing, "so don't get excited."

"Milk will do it," Tricee added. "That and the right moisturizer."

"Hmmm, then I'd better start downing some milk and change my beauty routine," Jackie remarked as she patted her cheeks.

The three women continued chatting and laughing. A few moments later, Hunter emerged from the bedroom at the same time the home phone rang.

"I'll get it, Babe," he shouted over his shoulder. "It's probably your other partner in crime." Moments later, Val walked into the Hatchett's condo.

"Hello, Val. Always a pleasure." Hunter and Val embraced. "How's the family?"

"They're fine. Cory's staying busy with studying but still manages to get a few hours of sleep each night since Ashlyn's sleep habits have changed a little."

"He's a busy man, indeed, with a new baby and his first year of law school. But I'm sure he can handle it."

"It's working so far. Let's keep our fingers crossed!" Val joked, crossing the first two fingers on her right hand. She turned around as Tricee appeared in the foyer.

The first thing Tricee noticed about Val was the short, dark wig on her head. It gave her girlfriend a totally different look.

"Babe, I'll see you later." Hunter kissed his wife on the cheek. "Enjoy your dinner and your friends. I'll be home before midnight. I promise not to stay out past my curfew," he laughed.

"Good," Tricee replied. "There's nothing better than an obedient husband."

"Amen," Val uttered as Hunter chuckled and left.

After Tricee took Val's shopping bag, which contained a huge container of her famous Cajun brown rice, they joined Pam and Jackie in the living room.

"Hi, Val. It's nearly 7:00. We almost started dinner without you," Pam teased. She and Jackie both stood up.

"It's good to see you, too, Pam." Val laughed as she and Pam embraced.

"Who are you?" Jackie asked, observing Val's wig. "I don't think we've met before."

"Very funny." Val reached over and gave Jackie a hug.

Tricee stared at Val's head once more. She couldn't believe just how much the wig changed her friend's appearance. It looked good, just different. It wasn't a look Tricee had seen before. She thought Val resembled a black Mary Tyler Moore, in an odd sort of way.

After assisting their host in the kitchen, everyone gathered in Tricee's dining room. In addition to the fried chicken Hunter had prepared, there was a green bean casserole, mashed potatoes and gravy, and a salad. And since Pam wasn't big on fried chicken, Tricee also made her famous baked chicken breasts. And Jackie made a lemon meringue pie so good you could slap somebody.

In the years she'd known her three girlfriends, Jackie had never mentioned how well she could prepare the delectable treat. It wasn't until sometime after she married Lem that her friends would get to try it. She made the best homemade lemon meringue pie they'd ever tasted.

"You know you need your tail whipped for holding out on us like this," Tricee had said after taking her first bite.

"Now we know why Lem married her, ladies," Val teased. "And we thought it was because of her personality."

Pam brought over a gallon of iced green tea and a container of white corn. She'd learned to cook a little bit but when she asked Tricee what she should bring, Tricee suggested iced tea, just to be safe. Then, after a bit of hesitation, she relented and allowed her friend to fix some corn.

"There's no way she can mess up corn," she'd confided to Hunter. "And please, Babe, don't tell her I said that." Hunter had laughed hysterically. Tricee shared a few of her girlfriends' traits with her husband, but only the things she felt were funny.

"Val, would you mind blessing the food, please?" Tricee asked once they had all washed their hands and were seated at her oval, cherry wood dining table.

"Sure," Val answered, and they all bowed their heads. "Heavenly Father, we thank you for this meal that has been placed before us and we ask you to bless those who are without. Bless the hands of those who prepared and provided this food, in Jesus' name. Amen."

"Amen," the other three women said in unison.

They proceeded to pass the serving platters around the table, each one helping themselves to the delicious meal they all had a hand in preparing. It was just like old times. They'd get together to eat and talk about anything and everything. Two years wasn't exactly a long time ago, it just seemed that way. Tricee wanted to ensure that they maintained their routine of hanging out whenever possible, and she was certain they'd agree to get together on a more regular basis. She would suggest, before the evening ended, that they attempt to meet at least once a month.

"Tricee, I love your new place. It's so spacious. And I love the view," said Val after swallowing a bite of the fried chicken. "You know, now you won't have to go downtown to see the fireworks. You can watch them from here. But then again, you were able to see them from your old place, too, right?"

"Yes, to both my dear. We can see them from here as well as from my old place. But Hunter and I still like going downtown to watch them. Maybe one of these summers we'll have you guys over for a Fourth of July celebration."

"I'm game. I love fireworks," said Jackie. "And my birthday is one day after the Fourth—just thought I'd throw that in there." She bit into Hunter's fried chicken. Once her mouth was free of food, she smacked her lips together. "Mmmm, this chicken is so good. What is your hubby's secret?"

"He won't even tell me," Tricee laughed. "But I do know he uses eggs."

"I tried that once," Val chimed in. "But somehow the eggs started frying around the chicken. After that, Cory insisted that I not try to use eggs again."

"That's funny. Maybe you hadn't used enough flour or something for the batter," Jackie suggested.

"Well, since I don't eat fried chicken, I wouldn't know," Pam added her two cents. "Conner thought I was playing when I told him I didn't eat chicken—well, fried chicken anyway. By the way, Tricee, your baked chicken is delicious as always. Thank you for preparing this chicken breast on my behalf."

"You are more than welcome." Tricee smiled. "We don't eat it fried often, but it's so hard not to because Hunter makes it so good."

"Pam, you don't know what you're missing. I like your breasts, too, Tricee, but—" Everyone laughed before Jackie could finish her statement. "You guys know what I mean!" She pointed her fork toward her friends and chuckled before continuing. "I like the way she bakes her chicken breasts, but I'm a stickler for some good fried chicken."

"Well, contrary to popular belief, not all black folks eat or like fried chicken. And if I have to explain that to one more white person," Pam jerked her head for emphasis, "it's on."

They all laughed.

"Isn't that the truth?" Val chimed in. "When will people stop with all the crazy stereotypes? I had a white woman ask me at work a few years ago if I cooked chicken several times a week. And I heard her ask a co-worker once if watermelon was her favorite fruit."

Tricee and Jackie both shook their heads.

"This woman sounds like an idiot," Jackie rolled her eyes. "As for watermelon, I don't eat it because I simply don't like it."

"Neither do I," Tricee commented. "I agree, though. She sounds like an idiot. Sometimes we need to educate folks on these sorts of things."

"Oh, she got educated alright," Val said after she sipped some of her iced tea. "I asked her if she made that old nasty potato salad that white folks make on a weekly basis. I didn't want to go there but I had to. Then I asked her why white folks cooked such weird foods to begin with. Now, granted—I don't believe *all* white folks are horrible cooks but she was asking for it." Val laughed as she continued. "And my co-worker really let her have it when she asked if watermelon was her favorite fruit. She read that white woman from 'a' through 'z.'"

"And after that, I bet you guys didn't have any more problems with her," Pam added.

"Not a one. In fact, I don't think she was liked much by too many of the folks on the job, black or white. I think it was just her. But she ended up leaving the company anyway."

"Speaking of which, when are you going back to full time, Val?" Tricee asked.

Val had taken maternity leave but after returning to work, she decided to go part time for a while. She was well liked by her employers. She was really good at what she did as a computer programmer for an IT company, and she was just two semesters away from receiving her master's degree in computer science.

Ashlyn was Val's priority right now. She and Cory decided that he should proceed with law school part time, as planned. This would allow him to continue working for the police department as a trainer at the academy.

They felt blessed to still be able to make all their ends meet after their income was cut due to Val's part-time work schedule. But with their savings and with Val returning to a full-time schedule soon, their circumstances were working out just fine. Val and Cory thanked God every day for allowing them to do what they knew many families weren't financially able to do.

"I'm actually going back full time this summer, the beginning of July. I wanted to wait until Ashlyn turned 1. My father will be visiting from Rockford around that time. He said he'd stay until mid-July or possibly longer because he has plenty of vacation time. I told him he didn't have to do that but he insists and says he wants to babysit his only granddaughter so they can bond. So between my dad, Cory's parents and our regular babysitter, we're in good shape."

"Cory must be thrilled that Ashlyn was born two days before his birthday," Tricee commented.

"Yes! He asked me why I didn't wait a couple more days and have her on June 10th," Val said with a hint of excitement. "I told him because she was ready to come out on June 8th and I was not about to argue!"

"I know that's right," Jackie said, laughing as she helped herself to more corn and Cajun brown rice.

They continued discussing a lot of what had transpired in each of their lives. While Val was close to earning her master's, Tricee was about a year and a half away from her Ph.D. in higher education. And Jackie had taken several more classes. In addition to remaining a high school principal, with a Ph.D. in educational leadership, she'd been offered a position teaching a freshman composition course this summer. Pam was using her master's degree in counseling but wasn't enjoying it as much as she'd enjoyed working in sales. When asked how things were going in her fairly new position, she didn't hesitate to say how she couldn't wait to either get asked back to her company after having been laid off, or find a sales position at another company.

There was silence at the table for several minutes after much discussion about husbands, careers and everything else the women felt obliged to discuss. Each of them was focused on their delicious meal and entertaining their own inner thoughts. For Tricee, it was Val's wig. *Val looks like a new person! I think I'm just going to come right out and ask what's up with the new hairdo.* Jackie was thinking about what Tricee had started to say earlier. *I bet Tricee's pregnant! I know that's what she wants to share. I'm so excited for her! I can hardly wait until Pam and Val find out.* Pam was thinking about her brief encounter with Jeff the prior Saturday. *I wonder how they're going to respond when I tell them I ran into Jeff. I know they're going to trip when I tell them I'm meeting him for lunch.* And Val had noticed the way Tricee had been staring at her all evening. *I know Tricee wants to ask me why I'm wearing a wig.* She had to keep from laughing out loud.

"Well, I think I'm there. This was great!" Jackie placed her napkin on her plate. "Tricee, you know what I'm ready for now?"

"Coffee," Tricee, Pam and Val all replied at once. Jackie's love for coffee was legendary.

Tricee stood up and went into the kitchen to turn on the coffee pot. "I'm all over it, girlfriend. I already have it set up. All I need to do is push the button."

Tricee removed Jackie's lemon meringue pie from the fridge as her friends began to join her in the kitchen to help her clean up. Once the dishes were washed and the table and counters were wiped clean, everyone headed into the living room.

Jackie and Pam sat on the sofa while Tricee and Val sat on the new loveseat. Other than the loveseat and the dining room table, Tricee and Hunter hadn't purchased anything new for their place.

Hunter was contemplating returning to school but since Tricee was already taking classes he decided to put his plans on hold. With a master's in education already, he was doing well as a consultant. Not to mention, he and Tricee had recently decided that they would adopt a child.

Hunter knew when he left his home earlier that evening that Tricee would share this news with her three closet friends. She'd already told Annette, her half-sister, who'd, responded with a burst of excitement. Hunter could hear her scream as Tricee laughed and moved the phone away from her ear.

"So, ladies! What's new and exciting in your world?" Val asked. "You ladies already know my daily routine. Other than keeping busy with a soon-to-be 1-year-old and keeping up with a 17-year-old stepson, my life is pretty boring," she laughed.

"Let's see," Jackie was the first to respond, "Alesia has decided to form a committee of some sort with a few of her friends. At 15 she has decided she wants to be a role model to young girls, other young ladies her age. She wants to teach the importance of having a healthy self-esteem. She calls Lem's two daughters, about once a week, to ask for tips. They love it."

"I do, too." Tricee got up from the loveseat. "I think it's great that she wants to embark on something of that magnitude. Wow, Jackie, you must be so proud of her."

"I am. She is too much, though," Jackie laughed. "She and her dad went into some store a few weeks ago after lunch. She came home and told me, 'Ma, Dad looked so uncomfortable when I was picking out a bra and panty set. What's his problem?' I had to explain to her that it was hard for her father to see her growing up, that's all. We were cracking up at him. He called me later on that evening and told me he hadn't expected that and that I should warn him the next time. I asked, 'Weren't there other men shopping with their daughters?' He said, 'Yeah, and they looked uncomfortable, too!'"

They all laughed. "That is too funny but also too cute," Tricee remarked before she disappeared into the kitchen.

"That is funny," Pam said as she stood up. "I can't wait to see how Conner is going to behave around his daughters when they reach their teens."

Pam joined Tricee in the kitchen. Tricee handed her the pie on a serving platter and four paper plates and plastic forks. She tossed a few tea bags onto the platter, too.

"I'm looking forward to bonding with Conner's daughters as they get older."

Tricee smiled at Pam's remark. She could see the warmth in her friend's eyes. "Aw, Pam. You really are changing," Tricee teased her friend. "That's so sweet." She removed four coffee cups from the cabinet. "Seriously, I know they will enjoy being around you. Why don't you start that bond now? Why wait?"

Pam frowned. "Because he has an evil ex-wife and I don't want to have to go Mike Tyson on her."

Tricee chuckled. "I was mistaken." They walked back into the living room. "You're still the same."

Moments later the women were indulging in the delicious pie and sipping hot coffee. Well, Jackie was the only one sipping coffee. Everyone else was having hot tea. Pam's small slice of pie hadn't gone unnoticed. When asked if she wanted more, she replied no. "Unlike you three," she said, "I have to watch the size of my hips." She'd lost eight pounds already and planned to keep them off.

"Oh, Tricee, I meant to ask you—" Val began, scooping up a forkful of pie, "Have you spoken to Karen recently?"

Pam made a face but then exhaled and forced herself to smile. It was no secret that she and Karen weren't exactly bosom buddies. But since Pam was now saved, she was trying very hard not to come off as negative.

"Hmm." Tricee set her plate on the coffee table. "I talked to Karen just last week. She's still doing quite a bit of traveling for work. She'll be traveling to Brazil for two weeks in June, I think. She still has her condo in the building I used to live in. I go check on my tenant from time to time and sometimes I see her."

Jackie and Val just nodded as Tricee spoke. None of them dared to mention what had happened two years ago when Tricee and Pam had seen Karen in Jeff's car while he was still seeing Pam. Jackie asked about the doorman instead who sounded like and sort of resembled the late Lou Rawls.

"What about that doorman that worked there? The one who sounded like my man Lou—"

Tricee cut Jackie off. "Tate? Yeah, he's still there." Her smile lit up her living room. "Sorry. Didn't mean to cut you off."

"Oh, that's all right." Jackie glanced at Val and Pam and then back to Tricee. "But what's up with the big smile?" she teased.

"Hmm, I caught that, too," Val added. "Tricee, were you seeing that man while you lived there?"

"No, I was not." Tricee poked her lips out in mock annoyance. "Tate's just a really nice man, that's all."

Pam poured herself another cup of hot tea. "Hmm, okay. Whatever you say. What about your white friend, Kenzie?"

Tricee sighed and dropped her shoulders. "Pam, why do you refer to Kenzie as my 'white friend?' You can't just say, 'How is your friend, Kenzie?'"

Both Jackie and Val were already laughing.

"Nope," Pam answered. "If she was Spanish, I'd say, 'How's your Spanish friend?' If she was Asian I'd say, 'How's your Asian friend?' And so on," she rolled her head around, "and so forth."

"You're crazy," Tricee pointed her finger at Pam. "Anyway—yes, I have spoken to my 'white friend' and she's doing fine. You have her contact information. Have you reached out to her?"

It was true. Pam had run into Kenzie two years ago, on the same evening Jeff had stood her up for the last time. It was during that encounter that Pam had to admit she found Kenzie to be a very nice person, indeed.

"Actually, we've exchanged a couple of emails. Has she been back to Chi-town in the past year or so?"

"Only once and we did meet for dinner." Tricee set her empty cup on the table. "Let's keep Kenzie and her husband in our prayers. I know they love each other but they're dealing with a few issues right now."

"Speaking of marriage …" Pam turned to face Jackie. "Jackie, you know what I've been thinking?" Pam placed the saucer to her cup on the table. "You did what was next to impossible."

"What's that?" Jackie asked as she poured herself another cup of coffee.

"You planned a wedding in less than a month. I mean, wow! You and Lem dated for only what—seven months before he proposed? You got right on it!"

"Well, yes, you can say that. But it helped that his family owns three catering companies. And his uncle is a pastor and was available *that* day, so that took care of the church."

"And it's not like she had to buy the traditional wedding gown," Val added. "She was able to find that gorgeous mid-length dress."

"Yep." Jackie took a sip of her coffee. "I immediately sent out the invitations and we only hosted around 50 people, so it all worked out." She blushed and turned to Tricee.

"It's something how you and I both got married after dating for just months. You and Hunter dated for eight months before he proposed."

"Correction." Tricee wiped her mouth with her napkin. "He *courted me* for eight months."

"I stand corrected." Jackie put up both her hands. "But seriously though, when you know you just know. It doesn't always take a long *courtship.*" She directed that last word to Tricee.

They had discussed this once before, how they both believed that if God was in the relationship, dating for years wasn't always necessary. Not to say that long courtships didn't have God in them. It was basically just a matter of what worked for the two people involved. The important thing was that God had a part in the relationship, no matter how long or short.

"Speaking of which," Jackie continued, "Lem and I had our first real argument the other night."

"After being married for close to two years? That's awesome!" Pam blurted.

"Not to get all in your business," Val snickered, "but since you brought it up you must need to vent. What was it about?"

"You're just being nosy." Pam punched Jackie in the arm playfully. "But she's right, you did bring it up. Why were you arguing?"

Tricee shook her head. In the years they'd all known each other, none of the women had ever shared anything they considered too personal. They all knew exactly where to draw the line. But now that they were all married, the discussions amongst them would change somewhat. There would be no discussion about who was dating or courting whom, or whether a particular man was a friend only. All of that was now in the past. At least it was for Tricee, Val and Jackie. But for Pam? That might be a different story.

"I don't mind sharing because it's no big deal." Jackie sat back on the sofa. "We were arguing over pork chops." She laughed. "Every time I cook pork chops, I notice he has something to say."

"Like what?" Tricee raised an eyebrow.

Jackie let out a sigh. "It's real silly if you ask me. But whenever I cook pork chops, he always mentions how good his sister's pork chops are. At first I didn't think anything of it, but he has said it every time!"

"What does he say exactly?" Val asked. She poured herself another cup of lemon tea and cut another slice of pie. "Does he not like the way you make pork chops?"

"He says I should ask his sister for her recipe." Jackie went into her imitation of her husband's voice. "You know, uh, my sister makes the best pork chops. I should, uh, get her recipe the next time I talk to her."

Her girlfriends roared with laughter. Jackie's "Lem voice" was spot on! None of them knew she could imitate him so well. Tricee was wiping tears from her eyes while Pam and Val were practically on the floor.

"Wow, Jackie!" said Val. "You sound just like him!"

"For real!" Pam added. "I wish I could imitate Conner that well!"

"That is funny!" Tricee stated. "But, really, it doesn't sound like he's being critical. He's only making a suggestion."

"No, you're just being nice. He obviously doesn't like my pork chops. I took offense this time and we got into it."

Jackie's tone was serious but her smile was hard to miss. She'd been upset when the incident happened but was apparently over it and was now able to joke about it.

"Had you cooked him pork chops while you guys were dating? I'm just curious if he said anything then." Tricee reached for the carafe of hot water.

"Yes, I did. A couple of times. And he never said anything."

Jackie thought back to two years ago when she and Lem were still dating. It had seemed so perfect. They never argued or had any major disagreements. They got along so well and it truly felt like their love was perfect. She knew and understood that arguments were normal within the institution of marriage, but still, Lem's criticism—at least that's what she called it—hurt.

"Well, …" Pam had stopped laughing but was still grinning from ear to ear. "It's obvious that he didn't want to say anything while you were dating for fear of hurting your feelings."

"Oh, Pam!" Tricee tapped Pam on the arm.

"Wait! Let me finish, Missy." Pam jerked her head toward Tricee. "Then you can give your commentary."

Jackie and Val laughed. Tricee couldn't wait to share her news but, for now, she was having too much fun listening to her friends and their issues. These moments made their friendship very special and, at this moment, Tricee couldn't imagine life without the three of them.

"He waited until he married you because now it's fair game. He probably thought that if he said something before, you would get offended—just like you did." Pam waved a finger toward Jackie. "So now you know and it shouldn't bother you. He's just being honest. Take it with a grain of salt—no pun intended—and get his sister's recipe." Pam stood up from the sofa. "And if that doesn't work, bake that brother a meatloaf!"

They all started laughing again.

"First of all, I don't even use salt," Jackie looked up at Pam and laughed, "so no pun taken. And second, I have been cooking my pork chops the same way for years, and I'm not about to ask his sister or anyone else for their recipe. Neither Alesia's dad nor Alesia have ever complained, so it's not me."

"Ok, now let me interject and don't get mad," Val added her two cents. "Sometimes, as women, we get so offended over nothing with our mates. Now, Jackie, you are no longer married to Alesia's dad so you can't really factor him into this situation."

Jackie crossed her arms and turned up the corners of her mouth as she allowed Val to finish. She wanted to laugh but, at the same time, she was now offended that Val was taking Lem's side.

"I agree with Pam. Now that's scary." Val moved to the side to avoid Pam reaching over to deliver another playful punch. "Lem is only making a suggestion, that's all. He means no harm."

"I agree," Tricee added. "I just think he'd like for you to try to fix them another way."

"Yeah! His sister's way!" Pam blurted out.

"Well, I told him that if he wanted his sister's pork chops then he should call her and ask her to cook some." Jackie chuckled. "Then I said something else I shouldn't have said."

"I hope you two have resolved this little spat." Tricee started gathering the empty cups and saucers from the coffee table to take into the kitchen.

"We have. That night I was upset and went to bed wearing my old gown. He knows not to touch me whenever I wear that old gown." Jackie laughed. "But, you know, an hour later, I woke up and sat straight up in the bed. Something my mother told me came to my mind. She told me once to not ever go to bed upset with your spouse because the next morning is not promised. So I reached over and kissed my honey on the neck. Of course, being a typical male, he thought it was about to be on."

"Of course," Tricee rolled her eyes toward the ceiling.

"I told him to go back to sleep. I just wanted to say I was sorry."

Tricee grabbed the serving platter, paper plates and plastic forks while Val took the coffee pot and hot water carafe. After taking everything into the kitchen, they rejoined Pam and Jackie who had moved into Tricee's dining room. Jackie held a framed photo of Hunter and Tricee in her hand.

"This is a nice pic of you two." She gave Tricee a warm smile. "I like Hunter. He's a sweetheart. But may I say one thing?"

Val and Pam looked at Jackie as she went and sat next to Tricee at the dining room table.

"What's that?" Tricee thought Jackie might comment on Hunter's dreds. He wore them pulled back and her friends were always mentioning how nice they looked and how well he wore them. But what Jackie said had nothing to do with her husband's hairstyle. She asked Tricee about Paul.

Paul had been Tricee's guy friend. He'd caught her off guard when he proposed two years ago. She politely declined explaining that she just didn't feel they were meant to be a married couple. She loved and cared for him as her friend but that was as far as her feelings went. Paul appreciated her honesty and they'd maintained a friendly relationship. They spoke maybe once or twice a month, if that often.

"I was certain that you and Paul were going to end up married. I guess I thought he was the one." Jackie leaned forward and put her elbows on the table.

Val sat down in the chair on the other side of Tricee. "Well, she told me she married Hunter because he had a big—"

"Val!" Tricee gasped and shouted her friend's name.

Val simply placed her hand on Tricee's arm and continued. "Because he had a big heart." Jackie and Pam had a hard time containing their laughter. "What on green earth did you think I was going to say, Tricee?"

"Ahh, never mind," Tricee answered in a baby like voice."

An hour later, after much talking and laughing, the women caught some of the 9:00 PM news. Pam had told Conner she'd be home by 9:30 PM. Val hadn't given Cory a time but she hadn't expected to be out past 10:00 PM. Lem was in Atlanta where one of his family's catering companies was located and Jackie had already spoken to him three times earlier in the day. But Alesia was expected to return home soon after being out with friends and Jackie wanted to be there when she arrived.

Tricee realized her friends would have to leave soon and she still hadn't shared her news. But first she had to satisfy her curiosity about Val and her wig. During a commercial, she turned toward Val. Jackie flipped through the current issue of *Ebony* magazine and Pam was busy texting Conner.

"So, Val. What's up with the wig?" Tricee blurted out. "You look so … different. Not a bad different, just different."

Jackie stopped turning pages and Pam stopped texting.

Val looked from Jackie to Pam and then to Tricee. She closed her eyes and giggled. "I knew you would get around to asking me." Then she opened her eyes and ran her hand through the short, dark tresses. "I'm just trying to keep my hubby entertained and keep the excitement in our marriage. Since I'm a new mom, I don't want things to get stale. And I'm actually not

Val. My name is Latessa Dominique La Croix." She rolled her neck with attitude.

"Alright now, *Latessa*!" Pam laughed. "I hear ya. Is it working for Cory?"

"Yes, it is," Val replied in her most proper voice.

"Well, that's all that counts!" Tricee laughed. "I was just curious, that's all."

Jackie looked over at Tricee. "Yeah, I was curious, too, but figured she was just going for different. I've been there before."

As soon as the sportscaster began to speak, Tricee picked up her remote, turned down the volume and stood up. "Well, ladies, I have some news to share."

"Oh, Tricee! I knew it! I knew it!" Jackie said excitedly, standing up to hug her friend. "I knew it was only a matter of time! I was wondering when you were going to tell us!"

"Ooooohhhhh, Tricee, you're pregnant!" Pam came over to where Tricee and Jackie were standing.

Val stood up and clapped her hands. "I'm going to be an aunt! This is great news! I knew you had invited us over for a reason!"

Tricee raised her hands and waved them back and forth. "Wait! No, no, no!" She grabbed Jackie's arms and removed them from around her shoulders. "I'm not pregnant! Hunter and I have decided to adopt!"

"Oh." Jackie took a couple steps backward. "I just assumed—"

"Yeah, I know. You know what they say about assuming, right?" Tricee laughed. "We hope to move forward with our plans in the next few months."

"Well, that's still awesome news!" Jackie hugged Tricee again. "It's so exciting!"

"That *is* exciting!" Val smiled. "So I'm still going to be an aunt! I mean an aunt to your child, seeing as I'm already an aunt."

"So when did you guys decide?" Pam was excited, too, but as always she was filled with questions. She and Conner had been discussing the possibility of adding a new addition to their family within another year or so but they wanted to make sure the timing was right, if that was even possible. When it came to having children, Pam wondered if there really was a "right time."

"We talked about it last year. We do want to have kids of our own eventually, we just believe there are so many kids out there who need a good home."

"This is true," Jackie added.

"Uh, Tricee, may I ask you a question?" Pam was forever thinking about how she didn't want to wait until she was 40 to have a child like her mom had done. She and Tricee were both 37 and she wondered exactly when Tricee planned to start a family.

"Sure." Tricee already knew what Pam was going to ask.

"When do you think you might try to get pregnant?"

"I figured you would ask that." Tricee smiled. "Maybe in a year or two. We'll see what God has in store."

A few minutes later, after all the sharing and hugs over Tricee's news, Tricee's friends gathered their purses, jackets and sweaters and prepared to leave. The containers that both Val and Jackie had brought to dinner were now empty and there wasn't enough rice or pie left over to take home. All of Pam's corn had been consumed, too, and she allowed Tricee to keep her Tupperware until the next time. They were all standing in Tricee's kitchen when Pam nonchalantly mentioned Jeff.

"I ran into Jeff last weekend. My cousin, Sondra, and I were having lunch downtown."

"Oh." Tricee had nothing else to say. They all knew that Jeff had relocated to Houston. Pam found that tidbit out from someone she and Jeff had known casually.

"He still lives in Houston, right?" Val asked, hoping the answer was yes.

"I don't know. I assume he does," Pam answered.

"Well, that's neither here nor there at this point. You did tell him you were married?" Jackie reached into her purse for her cell phone.

"He knows I'm married," Pam replied. But the look in her eyes suddenly caused her three friends to become concerned. She did know that Jeff still lived in Houston because he'd told her over the phone. He also told her how much he really needed to talk to her, practically begging her to meet him for lunch. But to divulge this information to her friends right now seemed irrelevant.

"Well, that's good," said Jackie. She had received a text from her daughter and was sending a reply.

"Yeah, I agree," said Val. "He knows you're married and have moved on."

"I bet he wanted to ask you out, didn't he?" Jackie chuckled. "He had his chance and he blew it." She turned to Tricee and gave her a hug, "Thanks, my dear! It was a blast."

"Yes, indeed," Val agreed. "And I like your idea about us meeting once a month for Bible talk."

"Me, too," Jackie chimed in then snapped her fingers. "That reminds me! If you ladies aren't busy this Thursday evening, I'd like to invite you to my church. We're having a guest minister and she is awesome! I've heard her before."

"I'll try to make it. Thanks for giving me a heads up," Val said as the four of them walked out into the hall.

"So will I. I don't have class on Thursday evening. I'll put it on my calendar and make sure I leave work on time," said Tricee.

The three of them looked at Pam.

"You think you can make it?" Jackie asked as they walked toward the elevator.

"Maybe." Pam shrugged. "I'm actually meeting Jeff for lunch on Thursday. If I don't get tied up at work I'll try to make it."

She can't be serious! Tricee thought, shocked at Pam's revelation. And she wasn't the only one.

5

"Pam, you can't be serious." Jackie gave Pam an incredulous look. "Tell me, what is it that you hope to gain from this lunch meeting?"

"I don't hope to gain anything, Jackie. For crying out loud, it's just lunch."

The elevator in Tricee's building had stopped on her floor several times, but now that it appeared that Pam was losing her mind, boarding the elevator would have to wait.

"I have to agree with Jackie on this one." Val was hesitant to respond at first but decided to voice her opinion. "Why even open that door again?" She glanced at her watch. She really needed to get going but talking some sense into Pam was important.

Tricee kept her thoughts to herself. She couldn't see any reason for Pam to have lunch with Jeff either but Pam was a grown woman. And no matter what they had to say, Pam's mind was already made up.

"Look, I know how you guys feel about Jeff." Pam looked from Val to Jackie to Tricee. "But I know what I'm doing. I see no harm in having lunch with him. It's been two years and I am so over him. Besides, I think it shows just how much I'm over him by agreeing to have lunch. I'll talk about how happily married I am and how my life is going just fine. It's my way of showing him what he missed out on."

Her three friends weren't buying it. If Pam was looking for their support, she wasn't going to get it.

The elevator doors opened again. Tricee smiled at the middle-aged white couple who lived a few floors above her. The couple realized that the four women weren't ready to board and smiled back as the elevator doors closed.

"I just don't see how any of it makes a difference," Val said, shaking her head in dismay. "But, hey! If you feel like this is what you need to do then whatever."

Jackie waited until Val was done speaking then picked up the big brown bag that held her pie container. She'd set it down when Pam told them her plans. It was as if Pam's news had suddenly caused the bag to become a heavy load.

"What if Jesus returns?" Jackie adjusted her purse strap on her shoulder and held the brown bag in her other hand. Her question got a perplexed look from each of her friends.

"What?" Pam looked at Jackie, baffled. "What are you talking about?"

Jackie exhaled. "I'm just saying. I wouldn't want to get caught doing anything I had no business doing when He returns. You know the Bible speaks on that."

Val and Tricee tried to contain their laughter but Jackie's choice of words made it difficult. They laughed but they knew where Jackie was coming from. Pam, on the other hand, did not and it was obvious that she didn't care to try to understand.

"It's–just–lunch," Pam repeated slowly, then rolled her eyes at Jackie and shook her head.

"I wouldn't care if you guys were meeting to discuss Dr. Seuss' green eggs and ham," Jackie wagged her finger at Pam as she spoke, "I–just–wouldn't–give–him–the–time–of–day."

Tricee and Val were enjoying the scene playing out before them as well as Jackie's strong stance on the matter. It wasn't meant to be funny but it was sure turning out that way. Jackie was just as determined to make her point as Pam was to make hers.

"First of all," Pam spoke directly to Jackie, "Jesus is not coming back during lunch. It's not like He needs to eat." She cut her eyes at Tricee and Val who were still giggling. "It says in the Bible that He's coming at night. But I guess you didn't quite understand that verse."

Tricee had a deadpan look on her face when she interjected, "That's a metaphor, Pam. No one knows exactly when He's coming back." She twisted her lips, which caused Val to laugh even harder. "I'm just saying."

"Look," Pam said, flustered, "thank you ladies for your opinions, but it is what it is." She glanced at her watch before turning to Tricee. "Actually, you haven't said how you feel about it. I'm sure you must have an opinion, too."

Pam was curious about how Tricee felt about the whole thing. Val and Jackie hadn't been shy at all about expressing their views, which had come as no real surprise.

"Noooo, I'm not in this one." Tricee shook her head from side to side. "This is a man who you almost allowed to ruin our friendship. I'll keep my thoughts to myself."

"Fine." Pam reached over and pushed the button for the elevator, hoping it would arrive soon. She didn't need to hear any more from Val or Jackie. Besides, it was close to 9:30 PM already.

"I don't blame you, Tricee," said Val. "I would have kept my thoughts to myself, too." She then glanced at Pam. "I am just a little surprised you agreed to see him again."

Pam remained silent. *Argh! Where is this elevator?*

"Well, I think it's a bad idea," Jackie reiterated. "But suit yourself."

"Please, Jackie. Don't get your panties in a bunch. You act like I'm committing some sort of sin," Pam responded not wanting Jackie to have the final word.

The elevator arrived but when Pam saw that Val and Jackie weren't boarding, she decided not to either. Interestingly, just 15 minutes prior, all three women were hoping to get home by a certain time. But now the mere mention of Jeff had changed all of that. She'd known that her friends would have an opinion but she didn't expect for it to come out so strongly. Surely, they had to know she wouldn't do anything to jeopardize her marriage. Maybe they still thought she was the Pam from two years ago. Hadn't they seen she had changed?

"Why not invite Conner to lunch with you so he can meet Jeff." Jackie looked from Val to Tricee in a last effort to get through to Pam but quickly changed her mind. "You know what?" she said, putting up a hand, "This is not really my business. You do what you have to do."

"Thanks," Pam responded with a hint of sarcasm. She almost regretted saying anything.

"Well, you ladies have a safe drive home." Tricee didn't know what else to say so she said what came naturally. She didn't really want to get into it with Pam about Jeff. A part of her believed that by the time Thursday arrived Pam would have rethought the whole thing and decided not to meet Jeff after all. "Val, kiss your little angel for me," said Tricee as her three friends boarded the elevator. "And I apologize about the parking—"

"Oh, please, girlfriend." Jackie cut her off. "We are so used to your being on this north side. We know what to expect when we come visit you." Jackie, Tricee and Val laughed. Pam did not.

A few minutes later they were stepping off the elevator into the lobby. The tall, heavyset doorman acknowledged them immediately. "You ladies enjoy the rest of your evening." His smile was warm but there was also toughness about him. He was pleasant but one could guess that he was a no-nonsense type of person. Tricee and Hunter had seen him go word for word with a couple of the tenants before—nicely, yet firmly. Hunter said he resembled a younger Harry Belafonte, only much heavier. Tricee, on the other hand, said she saw no resemblance between the two men at all.

"Thank you." Val spoke for the three of them. "You do the same."

"He's sort of cute," Jackie said as soon as they were outside.

"Handsome. Not cute," Pam added, once again with a hint of sarcasm.

Val and Jackie both looked at her as they continued walking to the end of the sidewalk.

"Okay. Handsome. So you're still speaking to me then?" Jackie asked.

"Jackie, you're allowed to voice your opinion. I *am* mature enough to handle hearing it. Besides, I knew when I mentioned his name how *you* would react."

They continued walking down Sheridan Road. Jackie had a hunch that Pam had mentioned seeing Jeff not only because she'd wanted to share some news but because she was curious as to how they'd respond. It was almost as if Pam was seeking their advice but indirectly. No matter the reason, Jackie felt strongly that Pam should have written him off. She saw nothing positive resulting from their getting together.

"Okay. As long as we're clear. I'm not trying to get all up in your business."

"Au contraire!" Val said, laughing.

"Oh, so you speak French now, too?" Jackie giggled and stopped walking. They had reached the intersection of Sheridan and Thorndale, where Jackie was parked.

"Yes. It goes along with the wig." Val tossed her hair like a model.

"Well, you better be careful before it falls off." Jackie gave Val a hug and then turned toward Pam. "You do understand where I'm coming from, right?"

"I do. I know it's a girlfriend thing—you know, not wanting to see your girl get hurt." Pam shrugged. "But you ought to know, Jackie, that I would never do anything that would cause problems in my marriage."

"Good." Jackie gave Pam a hug. "Because I happen to like Conner, and you have a happy life together."

"And you're still newlyweds," Val chimed in.

Pam looked at Val and then at her wig, which seemed to be a little crooked. "Okay, *Latessa*. I get the point."

The three of them laughed at Pam's comment as Jackie turned down Thorndale and walked toward her vehicle.

"I'm parked on Broadway," said Val as she and Pam continued down Sheridan.

"I'm going down Ardmore and then walking over." Val tilted her head in the direction of Broadway.

"That's fine," Pam replied. "I am actually parked on Ardmore. I got lucky. Someone was pulling out just as I was driving by."

They walked another block when they crossed paths with a middle-aged woman talking loudly to herself. The woman, who was dressed in a dirty, gray coat, glanced at Val and Pam.

"I'm not going back!" she yelled out. "You hear what I say! I'm not going back!"

Val and Pam picked up the pace.

"Keep walking." Val glanced over her shoulder at the woman. "Don't even look in her direction."

"No worries. I had no intention of looking at her. But you just did."

Moments later they reached Pam's vehicle.

"I will say this," Pam reached into her purse for her car keys. "There are some interesting characters on this side of town."

"Correction," said Val. "There are some interesting characters on *every* side of town."

"I guess." Pam pressed the button on her key fob and unlocked her car doors. "Let me give you a ride. Broadway is a few blocks away. No need for you to be walking around out here at night by yourself."

As they drove the few blocks toward Broadway, Pam thought about the incident that had taken place two years ago. It was near this very intersection that she and Tricee saw Karen and Jeff. It had taken a while to shake the pain she'd felt. And the way she'd treated Tricee afterward, she realized later, was very unfair. Pam thought she'd never see Jeff again, believing he would disappear forever.

But after running into him a week ago, new emotions had set in, though she didn't know exactly how to describe what she was feeling. When she finally got up enough nerve to call him, she'd almost hung up when he answered. They chatted for all of 20 minutes but by the time the conversation was over, they'd agreed to meet for lunch. "I really need to see you. Won't you please allow me to at least have lunch with you?" is what he'd said to her.

Jeff wasn't due back in Chicago again until the end of June, but he'd arranged to come back sooner just to have lunch with

Pam. He'd flown back to Houston the day after he'd seen her having lunch, but was already prepared to make travel arrangements back to the Windy City. He was all too happy when Pam relented, and agreed to his suggestion of meeting on a Thursday. He could not, nor did he wish to wait another month. He just hoped Pam wouldn't change her mind.

"Man, I am still full," Val patted her stomach. "I think I should have pushed myself away from the table before that third helping."

"It's easier said than done," Pam laughed. Val's statement had snapped her out of her reverie.

"I wonder what that woman was talking about when she said she wasn't going back?"

Pam shrugged. "Who knows? Probably just talking to hear herself talk." Then she quickly changed the subject to something Jackie had said earlier. "Hey, when Jackie said that she happens to like Conner, does that mean that if she didn't like him she'd be okay with me having lunch with Jeff or me seeing someone else?"

Val gave her a sideways glance. "You know what she meant."

Pam chuckled. "And you said that I should remember that I'm still a newlywed. Does that mean that if I wasn't a newlywed, *you'd be okay with it?*"

"No, it doesn't mean that. I was only reminding you that you *are* still a newlywed and that it's much too early for any nonsense."

"Oh, I see. So I need to wait until, what—at least a few years?"

Pam knew full well what the implications were from both her friends' statements. But to make light of it seemed like a good idea.

Val rolled her eyes and waved her hand. "You know what I meant, too."

Pam pulled up next to Val's minivan. "Get home safely. And call me when you make it."

"Okay. I'll let the phone ring one time and you'll know it was me." Val opened Pam's passenger door. "Okay?"

"That's so old school," Pam laughed. "But okay. I realize you have *two* babies at home just waiting for mommy to arrive."

Val laughed, reached over and gave Pam a peck on the cheek before she got out of the car. Pam waited until Val unlocked her door and stepped into her vehicle. She then motioned for Val to roll down her window. Pam then leaned her body across the passenger seat.

"I just wanted to tell you to fix your wig," she patted the side of her head. "It's not on straight."

Before Val could respond, Pam rolled up her window and sped off. Val could tell that Pam was laughing because of the way her head was moving. Val put her key into the ignition, let out a sigh, and proceeded to adjust her wig. She smiled as she pulled away from the curb.

"So how was dinner with your friends," Hunter asked as he removed his shirt and tossed it onto the bed.

"It was nice. I told them we've decided to adopt. Of course, at first, they thought I was about to tell them I was pregnant."

He laughed. "Well, tell them to exercise patience. It will happen at the right time."

"I know. I think Pam is ready to have kids soon." Tricee went to her closet to retrieve an outfit for church. "I just feel like she's really going to work on becoming pregnant soon."

"Good for her. I think she should if she's ready."

Hunter headed for the bathroom and Tricee followed. "Hey, you want me to iron anything for you to wear to church tomorrow?"

"That's okay, Babe. I don't think I'm going to church tomorrow."

"Oh, okay." Tricee shrugged and walked back into the bedroom.

Hunter hadn't been to church in three Sundays. Tricee felt that this called for a discussion—but at the right time. She was concerned but decided not to make a big deal of it. Hunter had joined Life Ministry Church, where she was a member, right before they were married. He'd talked about how much he enjoyed Pastor Downey's good-humored sermons. So she wasn't sure what the problem was.

What she *had* decided to discuss with Hunter, however, was Pam's situation with Jeff, just to see what he thought. Maybe she'd bring it up tonight or in the next couple of days. She'd chosen not to say anything earlier when Jackie and Val had both expressed how they'd felt, but Tricee agreed that Pam was making a huge mistake.

Later on, when she got on her knees to petition the Lord with her requests, she'd be sure to intercede not only for her husband who hadn't been to church in three Sundays in a row but for Pam as well. And, of course, keeping herself lifted up was a given. *Something's telling me the enemy is about to get real busy,* Tricee thought as she opened her top dresser drawer. She picked out a pair of off-black stockings to wear with the black dress she'd chosen for church in the morning. The scripture from 1 Corinthians 7:34 popped into her mind. It had taken her a while to learn the whole verse and now she repeated it softly as she walked back into the living room:

There is a difference also between a wife and a virgin. The unmarried woman careth for the things of the Lord, that she may be holy both in body and in spirit: but she that is married careth for the things of the world, how she may please her husband.

6

The sermon was powerful. There were a few women in the congregation wiping away tears. Pam looked around, wondering if men were ever moved to tears by a powerful message. Probably not, she reasoned. Lots of men were too cool to cry at funerals and weddings, surely they were too cool to cry for the Lord, even while in *His* house, no matter *how* much they'd been touched.

Her aunt, though not crying, was rocking her head back and forth. Pam smiled at the cute, soft-spoken yet feisty-when-she-wanted-to-be older lady who'd recently celebrated her 75th birthday. This was the same aunt who'd invited her to church a couple of years ago, and this was the church where she'd met Conner.

Pam had declined her aunt's invitation initially, claiming she had something to do that particular Sunday. But after giving it some thought and deciding that both the books of Ruth and Esther had left her hungry for more understanding of the Word, she phoned her aunt to tell her she'd be delighted to join her. Both books had been recommended. Tricee had recommended Pam read the book of Ruth, while Mrs. Rhodes, Pam's mother, had recommended the book of Esther.

"What changed your mind?" her aunt had inquired.

Pam laughed and replied, "I can't say there was any one thing that changed it, Aunt Polly. I just feel led, that's all."

"Well, good. When we're led, we know God is at work. Besides, you might just meet a nice, God-fearing fella who understands scripture, especially the ones that touch on the subject of how men are supposed to treat women."

Pam had tried to interject. The thought of meeting a "nice, God-fearing fella" had been the farthest thing from her mind, but her Aunt Polly was on a roll.

"You know, my love, I think women just make it too easy for these men nowadays. And then they wonder why the man won't ask their hand in marriage."

"Uh, well, Aunt Polly, sometimes—" Pam wanted to come to the defense of all the women who made it easy for men but Aunt Polly was quick with her words.

"Sometimes, my foot!" Aunt Polly screamed into the phone. "Don't you go making excuses! That's another thing that's wrong with relationships these days. Everybody got some old excuse."

Pam couldn't help but laugh. Aunt Polly was, indeed, one of a kind.

Now as she stood in church looking over at her aunt moving her head back and forth, obviously overcome with emotion from the pastor's sermon, Pam was glad she'd accepted her invitation two years prior. She credited Aunt Polly with her meeting Conner. He had seen her as soon as she'd walked into the building that Sunday but quickly looked away upon realizing that she'd seen him looking. Pam chuckled, thinking how women were not exempt from being given the once-over even in the Lord's house. *Men will always be men*, she thought silently as she sat down next to her aunt. She'd enjoyed the pastor's sermons ever since. Meeting Conner had just been a nice little bonus.

As Pastor Brooks brought his sermon to a close, Pam couldn't help but to notice the woman sitting in front of her. Her tight, green dress was hard to miss as were her long, bright green fingernails. Pam caught a glimpse of the woman's nails when she lifted her hands up to the heavens. Her eyes were closed and it seemed that she had also been moved by the message: Leaving the past in the past. Pam didn't want to pass judgment, but from the looks of that form-fitting dress and those fingernails, she could easily see why this message had hit home for this woman.

Just as the pastor concluded with the benediction "now go out and spread His love, and remember to pray for those who persecute you," Pam could tell that the woman's eyes were now on Conner. Even looking at the back of her head it was easy to see from the way it was tilted that the woman's eyes were toward the pulpit. She knew the woman wasn't looking at the pastor anymore because he had made his way down the short set of stairs, and the only one left standing in the pulpit now was Conner. Pam looked at her husband and, after catching his attention, gave him a wink. He smiled—actually, it was more like a blush—and the woman's face instantly broke out into a grin. Conner saw the woman, quickly looked away and turned to pick up his Bible. Pam decided to make her way to the front of the church to meet him, just in case Ms. Green Dress mistook Conner's smile for an invitation. She didn't want the woman to embarrass herself in the house of the Lord.

"Pastor, that was a wonderful sermon," Pam overheard one of the members say.

"Pastor, that message will be in my head all week. That was just what I needed," another member of the congregation remarked.

"You know, Pastor, that's something that I think a lot of us saints need a constant reminder to do. We need to let the past go. Oh, just let it go, let it go!"

Both Pam and Conner chuckled quietly at the way the middle-aged woman who was speaking to the pastor waved her hands and shook her head as she made her point, reiterating his message. The pastor laughed, pleased that he had, once again, spoken such a prophetic message.

As they exited the church Pam gently took her aunt by the arm. When they reached the parking lot, she walked her aunt to her vehicle.

"Aunt Polly, you be careful driving home now. I keep telling you we would be delighted to pick you up on Sundays and bring you to church."

Aunt Polly touched her niece's face lightly. "Sweetie, I'll be just fine," she said softly.

Pam had to laugh. It amazed her how soft-spoken her aunt could be when she wasn't in one of her feisty moods.

Aunt Polly then held Pam's chin with her thin fingers and looked her straight in the eyes. "Are you trying to say your aunt is getting too old to drive?"

"No," Pam said slowly. "I'm just offering to pick my aunt up for church on Sundays and make sure she gets back home safely." She bent down and gave the older woman a peck on the cheek.

"Well," Aunt Polly began, unlocking her vehicle and climbing in, "I appreciate the offer but I'll be just fine. "

Pam watched as Aunt Polly fastened her seat belt. Once she was settled, she rolled her window down.

"And I'm not deaf yet. Stop speaking to me in that slow way of yours."

Pam shook her head and chuckled as she watched her aunt drive away. Conner pulled up shortly and she climbed into their 2011 Buick. Conner looked handsome in his dark blue suit. He wore suits well but, because of his occupation as a bus operator, didn't wear them often.

Whenever they would go out, Pam was always pleased to see her husband wear some of his nice clothes. She thought he looked just as sexy in his work uniform, and she knew that quite a few of the females who rode the bus felt the same way. When she told her sisters what Conner did for a living, her sister Terri teased her. "Are you prepared for that? Because you know many of those bus drivers talk to everybody!" Her sister Lynn had come to Conner's defense. "That's not entirely true, Terri. I really believe that quite a few of those bus drivers aren't trying to be bothered like that."

"What a message! Pastor nailed it on the head today, didn't he, Babe?" Conner reached over and patted Pam on the knee.

"Yeah, he did the thing, didn't he?" They both laughed. "You know, I've been quite impressed with your sermons, too."

It was true. Conner had preached a few times before and Pam had been moved by her husband's passion. It was almost as if she felt an even deeper love for him on Sundays, like he was this different person. During the week he could really work her nerves.

After only five months of marriage, she sometimes wondered if that was normal.

"Thanks, Babe. I needed that." Conner pulled into the left lane. "Well, I'll be giving the message next month—"

"It's the last Sunday in June, right?" Pam asked, interrupting her husband.

"Yes, it is. And on the third Sunday I'll be preaching at my cousin's church. So maybe I'll give the same message." Conner laughed. "Do you think anyone will notice?"

"Sure. If the same folks are in attendance at both churches." Pam smiled at her husband. "Anyway, sorry to cut you off. What were you saying about giving the message next month?"

"Oh, nothing." Conner shrugged. "I guess I was thinking out loud and hoping folks would be moved like they were during this morning's sermon."

"Well, I have no doubt. I'm sure you're going to do just fine." Pam reached over and patted her husband on the leg.

Conner smiled and looked briefly at his wife's hand before redirecting his eyes to the road. "Now don't start something you're not willing to finish," he teased.

"Please." Pam rolled her eyes and let out a giggle. "Man, we just left the Lord's house and you talking fresh."

"I'm talking fresh to my wife. I think that might be okay with the angels, Babe."

As they pulled into the garage, Pam thought about the woman in the green dress. She'd been thinking about her since they left church. It was just something about her.

"I need to confess," Pam uttered as she unfastened her seat belt.

"About what?" Conner looked at his wife as he removed the key from the ignition. "You didn't go off on somebody at church, did you?"

"No, I didn't go off on anyone." They walked to their back door. Conner unlocked it and stepped aside, allowing Pam to enter first. "I was judgmental, toward someone at church, not that I was trying to be. The sad thing is I probably wouldn't even feel bad about it if this were a weekday. The fact that I was at church only makes it worse."

"Don't be too hard on yourself. Just ask God to forgive you and work on not being so quick to pass judgment, no matter what day of the week it is."

Conner removed his tie as they walked into their bedroom and Pam unbuttoned her white, ruffled blouse. She took it off and tossed it onto the back of a chair. She'd put the chair in the bedroom for times she wanted to sit and read but it came in handier as an object to toss clothes upon.

"That's becoming a bad habit," Conner nodded toward the chair that held his wife's blouse and now his tie, suit jacket and shirt. "I think hanging our clothes would make us seem less sloppy."

"I agree," Pam said as she took off her long, gray skirt. She walked over to the closet and removed a few hangers. "But I have this thing about putting my clothes back into the closet as soon as I take them off, remember?"

"Right. You said your clothes need to 'air out' first. Otherwise they leave a musty odor in the closet."

Pam smiled. "I never said anything about any odor. If I thought that, I'd wash them first."

Conner took off his trousers, replacing his Sunday best with a white T-shirt and some black sweatpants.

"So," he said to his wife as she buttoned the short-sleeved, light blue blouse she'd put on, "who were you judging in church?" Before Pam could answer, he spoke again, answering his own question. "I bet it was the woman with the braids and the tight, green dress."

Pam stopped dressing and looked at her husband. She was wearing only her top and underwear. Conner's comment caused her to pause before reaching for her pants.

"So you noticed her?"

"Of course." Conner sat down on the bed. "Who didn't notice her?"

"Uh, the pastor, maybe?" Pam stepped into a pair of black slacks. Her husband's comment had aroused her curiosity. Conner didn't usually remember details.

"No, the pastor noticed her, too. Why do you think he was smiling so much every time he heard 'Amen' being shouted out during his message?"

Conner laughed and Pam realized he was only joking. But she had to wonder how the pastor, or anyone else for that matter, could miss her. In Pam's opinion, the woman had stood out from the crowd.

"So you caught her when she smiled at you then, right?"

"No, Babe. I don't pay attention to that while I'm in church. I'm just messing with you."

"Yeah, right. You noticed her enough to recall what she was wearing." Pam hadn't even thought about the woman's hairstyle. "And her braids."

"You have to stop taking everything I say so serious." Conner grabbed his wife's hand and pulled her down onto the bed next to him. "Has anyone ever told you that you think too much?" Conner kissed her on the cheek and she had a sudden flashback to when Jeff told her the very same thing when they were dating.

They were to meet for lunch in just a few more days. The mere fact that she was even thinking about him, which she was trying hard not to do, was distressing. The way her husband made her feel, Pam had no intention of ruining what they had between them. Seeing Jeff again was, for her, an effort to get the closure she hadn't gotten the first time. But now she was having second thoughts. She had gone from feeling bad about having judged someone she'd never seen before to wondering if she would go through with meeting Jeff for lunch. Maybe she did overthink things.

"I'll work on not analyzing everything, as well as seeing only the good in others. Until they prove me wrong." Pam stood up. "But for the record, I noticed the way she looked at you. And she thought you were smiling at her."

"Were you judging her for the way she chose to dress for church?" Conner asked. He knew his wife better than she thought.

Pam nodded. "I thought today's message hit home for her because she looked to me like someone with quite a past, wearing that tight dress and all. I know it was wrong but I asked God to forgive me on the way home. I had a quick, private chat with the Lord while you were driving."

They both got up from the bed and headed into the kitchen.

"Good. Now just know you're forgiven and let it go." Conner removed a white container from the fridge. "I'm hungry. Can we eat now?"

"Yep. Let's hope the lasagna turned out good enough for us to eat."

Pam went into the fridge after Conner and took out some lettuce, tomatoes, mushrooms, and cucumbers. She prepared a salad while Conner heated the lasagna. Once they were seated they said a blessing.

"This is good, Babe. My mom gave you this recipe, didn't she?" Conner scooped a forkful of the lasagna into his mouth, pleased that it had, indeed, turned out quite well. It wasn't exactly like his mom's but it was close enough. Pam's cooking had improved, much to his delight.

"You already know the answer to that question," Pam laughed. "I admit your mom makes the best lasagna. I'm just glad she was willing to share. You know how some folks are so secretive about their recipes."

"Well, not my mom. Especially when it comes to me. She wants to make sure her son is eating only the best," Conner licked his fingers, "so she's all too willing to share her recipes with you."

"Please don't do that in public," Pam remarked as they both laughed.

They finished their meal and Pam cleared the table. Dinner was still a good six hours away and she planned on asking Conner if they could go out to eat. He might have been willing to do leftover lasagna but she wasn't.

Conner turned on the television in the living room and, before becoming engrossed in whatever was on, opened his Bible. This was his regular routine. He'd read the Bible some more after church and then watch a little television.

After placing the dishes in the dishwasher and being satisfied with the now clean kitchen, Pam retreated to the bedroom. She went through the purse she'd taken to church to remove anything she'd need to put in the purse she was taking to work tomorrow. She'd promised her parents she'd pay them a visit after church. She'd also promised herself that she would look over some notes she'd taken on two of the new women who'd entered the shelter this past week. But going over notes wasn't exactly what she wanted to do at the moment.

On a Sunday afternoon after church, all Pam wanted to do was relax. Conner had said early on, when they first got married, that because he had such a busy week, all he wanted was some peace and quiet when Sunday rolled around. Pam was fine with that but she laughed at him whenever football or basketball season was in full swing. Peace and quiet on a Sunday sometimes meant watching the games with Lem, Cory, and Hunter. Pam and her girlfriends were amazed at how men could yell and show such emotion when it came to sports. Jackie had joked once, "The next time Lem makes love to me, I'm holding a football over his head—you know, to add a little something extra to an already passionate situation." Her friends had laughed uncontrollably. "Touchdown!" she yelled out.

When Pam removed her cell phone from her purse, she noticed there was a message.

She dialed her voicemail and upon hearing Jeff's voice, she closed the bedroom door.

"Hi there, Pam I hope you have a good week. I am so looking forward to seeing you on Thursday."

Her first inclination was to phone Jeff and cancel but now obviously wasn't the time. She opened the bedroom door wondering silently why she'd even closed it in the first place. It was her subconscious making her realize she was hiding something from her husband. She deleted the message. *I'll call him tomorrow and cancel.*

She then thought back to the pastor's sermon. *We have to leave the past in the past. God can't move on your behalf unless you're willing to submit. Stop beating yourself up for your past mistakes. He knows what we're going to do before we even think it. Turn with me in your Bibles to Romans 12, verse 2.* The pastor's message could be taken any number of ways as most sermons could. That was the awesome thing about God's Word. It affected everyone differently. Right now, she could surely sense that there was something in that message meant for her, though she wasn't exactly sure what.

As Pam placed her cell phone into the purse she'd carry for the rest of the week, the doorbell rang. They weren't expecting anyone and no one usually stopped by without calling first.

"Babe, can you get that?" Conner yelled from the living room even though he was closest to the front door.

"Are you expecting someone?" Pam yelled back.

She looked out of the peephole and was surprised to see Conner's ex-wife. She exhaled before opening the door and prayed silently, *Lord, give me strength as I try not to conform to being unkind. I was not expecting evil to show up at my front door today.*

7

Conner jumped up from the sofa and rushed to the door when he heard his ex-wife's voice. "Are my daughters okay?"

His ex-wife let out an exasperated sigh. "The twins are fine. I—"

"Then what are you doing showing up unannounced?" Pam's tone was sharp. She ignored the inner voice reminding her that she'd come from church only an hour or so earlier.

Renita was Pam's least favorite person. But it wasn't because she was Conner's ex-wife. It was simply because of the sour puss attitude the woman seemed to carry around on her slender body. Too slender Pam thought. "Did she eat at all during your marriage?" she'd asked Conner the first time she'd seen Renita.

Conner stepped aside, allowing Renita to enter and Pam shot him a nasty glance. Renita was wearing a lavender skirt suit and a pair of bone Bella-Vita pumps. Pam assumed she'd just come from church.

"Can we talk, please? I promise it'll only take a few seconds." Her tone was sarcastic as she addressed Conner, and then gave Pam a brief once-over.

Pam couldn't see how Conner had ended up marrying someone like Renita. They didn't appear to have much in common. Their personalities were so different. Conner was laid back and really sweet. Renita was evil, pure and simple. Pam's friends tried to tell her that she felt this way because Renita had shared with Conner what she now shared with him—a bed. But Pam refused to accept that line of reasoning. She explained to her friends that if Renita had been friendlier, she would have felt differently about the mother of her husband's children. She wasn't asking that Renita bow down whenever they saw each other, she just wanted Renita to leave her nasty attitude at home. Or wherever it was she was coming from.

I'll hold my peace. But if she says one thing to me that I don't like ..., Pam thought, letting out a sigh as Conner led Renita into the living room. She read the expression on her husband's face and went into the kitchen, leaving him to talk to Renita in private.

She took a bottle of water from the fridge. Fuming, Pam sat at the kitchen table and wondered what Renita could possibly want. She'd said the twins were fine. This made Pam even more curious, especially since Renita hadn't stopped by unannounced before. As she and Conner had been married for only five months, Pam reached a likely conclusion. This would not be the last time Renita would make a surprise appearance. Pam was willing to allow it once more, and that was only if there was a problem with the twins. No exceptions, whatsoever.

The old Pam would have sat right there in the living room, listening to every word. The new Pam, having grown in her spiritual walk, allowed her husband and his ex-wife some privacy. She could tell by Conner's expression that he was asking for a moment alone. Well, that moment was almost up. If Conner and Renita weren't done discussing whatever it was that she had interrupted their Sunday afternoon for, she would walk right into the living room and shoot daggers from her eyes.

After what felt like a full hour, Pam finally heard Conner's voice. Until then he and Renita had kept their voices low, which made Pam even more furious.

"I'll keep the situation in prayer. Instead of worrying, which is useless, just turn it over to Him."

Pam heard Renita sigh, exasperated. "I *have* been praying." She closed her eyes briefly and shook her head. When she opened her eyes she saw Pam standing only a few feet away. Without acknowledging Pam's presence, Renita turned and walked toward the door. Conner followed.

"I'll talk to you soon. Don't forget you promised to take the twins on Tuesday, after you're done with work."

Conner nodded. "I won't forget. I'll come and pick them up sometime after 5:00. Give them a big hug for me."

He opened the front door and watched Renita climb into her black Dodge minivan. He then returned to the living room where Pam was now sitting on the brown leather sofa. He noticed that she'd turned off the television. He smiled, hesitantly, holding out his hand for the remote, which Pam was holding.

"Do you mind, dear?" Conner sat down on the matching recliner, still holding out his hand. He'd hoped Pam wouldn't start in on him with a ton of questions but he should have known better.

"So what did she want? It must have been important for her to just drop by unannounced."

Here we go, Conner thought and sighed. "Proverbs, chapter 27, verse 15: A continual dropping in a very rainy day and a contentious woman are alike." He winked at his wife and his smile broadened.

"What?!" Pam was none too pleased with her husband's attempt at humor. And using a Bible verse, especially the one he'd chosen, certainly wasn't helping.

"Conner, don't play with me!" Pam stood up, the remote still in her hand. She pointed it at her husband. "What did she need to discuss?! I didn't *have* to give you any privacy! I'll tell you what, the next time she pops up …"

"Hon', calm down. Please." He stood up and then walked toward his wife, reaching for the remote. "You're using that thing like some weapon. If you just calm down, I'll tell you." He turned his palm up and blew his wife a kiss.

"You know," Pam began, angrily placing the remote in his hand, "I'm sick of you trying to make a joke out of everything, Conner!" She turned to walk away but Conner grabbed her by the elbow.

"I'm just trying to keep you from getting all upset over nothing, Pam. I don't have a problem sharing with you what we talked about, but why do you feel the need to blow up over the smallest things?"

Conner's face changed into the frown that formed whenever he was fed up with his wife's over reactive behavior. He loved Pam more than anything, but she could be a real handful at times. Conner knew that underneath all the sass Pam threw around, her guard was up more than it needed to be. He understood that this was human nature, because some people were more suspicious than others, but he wanted so much for his wife to show a little more trust and faith in him and what they shared together.

"Conner, I have every reason to get upset! How would you like it if my ex came over without warning and then asked to speak to me in private? Wouldn't you have a problem with that?"

"No." Conner released his wife's arm and stepped in close, putting his face near to hers. "Because I *trust* you." Then he stepped away, sat down on the recliner and turned the television back on. "Besides, you don't have an ex." He didn't look in Pam's direction when he spoke. He just kept flipping through the channels, his eyes on the television. "If you did have an ex-husband with whom you had children, I would respect that."

"Well, I guess this is what I get for marrying a man with an ex-wife and kids." Her tone was full of sarcasm as she angrily left the room.

"Hey! I thought you wanted to know what we discussed," Conner called out.

"Leave me alone!" Pam slammed the bathroom door.

Conner just exhaled. He was too tired, mentally, to say or do anything more.

Pam emerged from the bathroom and grabbed her purse and car keys. Now would be a good time to go and visit her parents. She'd probably have to let herself in since her parents usually didn't get home from church on Sundays until around 3:00 PM. Although she'd planned on visiting later, she had to get out of the house now. It was either that or go at it some more with her husband.

Conner came into the kitchen just as she was about to leave. She had previously mentioned her plans to drive out to Matteson, a Chicago suburb where her parents resided.

"You going to see your parents?"

Pam nodded.

"Tell them I said hello, okay?"

Pam nodded again.

She couldn't help but to notice the way her husband stood before her, looking like a kid who'd done something wrong. His facial expressions were always a dead giveaway as to what he was feeling. Pam wanted to go over and plant a big kiss on him but that would likely lead to something else. Besides, he wasn't exactly off the hook. She was still upset.

She wasn't as upset with Conner as she was with the way Renita just seemed to come so easily into their home. That wasn't what she'd planned to have to deal with when she and Conner said "I do." She pictured a different kind of married life, one where she and her husband were free to devote all of their attention to each other. *Welcome to married life* is what she'd sometimes say silently to herself.

"I'll be home before 8:00," she said, glancing at her watch.

"Be careful. And when you get back, we can, you know, talk about what Renita wanted to discuss."

Pam shrugged. "Okay," she responded and then left.

She was still very curious but whatever it was that Conner and Renita had discussed could wait until later. It couldn't have been too major. The twins were fine and she knew Conner had no interest in going back to his ex. That wasn't a concern of hers. But she would tell Conner later that it was important that he let Renita know there were boundaries. She thought he'd done that already. But just in case Renita had somehow forgotten, Pam would make sure that he reminded her.

As she turned to get on the Dan Ryan Expressway, Pam's thoughts turned to the upcoming Thursday. Maybe seeing Jeff again was just what she needed. It would take her mind off some things. They could chat—about nothing too serious—just life and all that had happened with them over the past two years. They were two people meeting for lunch and conversation. Two people who used to date, yes, but she was married now so what was the harm? Besides, Conner had an ex-wife who would be in the picture forever, pretty much, since they had children together. So what was the problem with her meeting—just this once—a guy she dated before she even knew her husband?

Pam stopped for gas and picked up some diet soda for her father and some grapefruit juice for her mother in the gas station convenience store. She then reached into her purse to retrieve her cell phone, and the envelope that she'd written Jeff's number on, since she'd deleted his number from her cell phone. She dialed the number, sort of hoping to get his voicemail, but he answered on the fourth ring.

"Hello?" He answered sounding as if he had no idea who was on the other end.

"Hi, it's Pam."

"Hello there, lovely lady! To what do I owe this pleasant phone call?"

Pam could hear the excitement in his voice now.

"I was just calling to tell you I'm looking forward to lunch on Thursday." She bit down on her bottom lip, feeling her nerves dance throughout her body. Was she really looking forward to seeing him? A part of her was but there was another part that wasn't so sure. Feelings of guilt started to rise up within her, but when she thought about Renita's and Conner's "discussion," the guilty feelings went away. "I can't wait to hear what you feel we need to discuss." She felt boldness come over her. Now seemed a perfect time to try to make Jeff sweat after what he'd done two years ago. It was what he hadn't done actually. And that was not allowing their relationship to go beyond just dating.

"Oh, my! Well, I'm looking very forward to seeing you, too. But you know that already." Jeff laughed as he raised a glass of iced tea to his lips. "There's a lot we need to discuss. Wouldn't you agree?" He sat back in his black swivel chair. When his phone rang, he'd been busily preparing reports for later in the week and now wasn't the best time to chat. But since it was Pam on the other end of the line, the reports could wait.

Pam started her engine. "I guess we'll find out on Thursday." She pulled out of the gas station, ignoring the short guy who waved at her as he got into his vehicle. "Call me by 12:30. I take my lunch break right at 1:00 so I trust that you'll be on time." *You'd better be on time,* was more what she was thinking.

Pam had already planned to stay at work a little longer on Thursday, just in case lunch went over the hour she was allowed. She could take an hour and 15 minutes, but anything more would be pushing it. And she had no intention of giving Jeff the upper hand, no matter how well the conversation between them went. This time the ball was definitely in her court and she planned to keep it that way.

"I will call you by 12:30 and, yes, I'll be on time. I promise." Jeff drank the rest of his iced tea. He was hoping Pam would join him for dinner as well, but decided against asking her over the phone. *One step at a time,* he told himself, although he was certain she'd be amenable to seeing him again after their lunch date.

Pam turned to get back on the expressway. "I'll let you know then where we should meet." She'd already informed him that she worked on the north side. So he had an idea of what time he'd have to leave the hotel downtown.

"Sounds good to me," Jeff smiled and nodded his head slowly as he placed his cell phone on his desk. *This is going to go very well,* he thought. *I feel it.*

"I hope he doesn't have his hopes up too high," Pam mumbled as she tossed her cell phone onto the passenger seat. "But then again, who knows …" She smiled and pressed the volume button, turning up the music on her car stereo.

8

"So how are your parents?" Conner's inquiry came as soon as his wife walked through the door. She hadn't even had a chance to lock it. "Did your dad have any Jell-O Pudding Pops to share?"

"Very funny." Pam shook her head as she removed her jacket. "My dad looks nothing like Bill Cosby and you know it."

When Conner first met her parents, he told Pam he'd thought her father favored Bill Cosby. No one else had ever said that before so Pam thought he was just being funny. But every chance he got he'd joke about their "strong resemblance."

Seeing her parents had helped Pam take her mind off Jeff and her not-too-pleasant afternoon with her husband. "Where's Conner? I thought he was coming with you," had been her mother's first words, more like her mother's assumption, when Pam walked into their home. She'd let herself in even though her parents were both home. She said that Conner was fine and that he'd decided to stay home. That wasn't entirely true. She'd had no intention of asking her husband to join her. They'd needed some space, even if only for a couple of hours.

"Well, I think he looks just like Mr. Cosby. Did you enjoy your visit? I take it you did since you didn't get home before 8:00. You didn't tell them we had a little spat, did you?"

Pam rolled her eyes as she walked into their bedroom. Conner sure was full of questions.

"You know I don't involve my parents in my marital issues," Pam stated as she removed her blouse, "unlike you who tells your mom everything."

Conner shot his eyes toward the ceiling, an expression he made whenever he felt his wife had made an untrue statement. And what she'd just said was totally untrue. While he was very close to his mother, in no way was he *so* close that he shared his personal affairs. In fact, he'd been more likely to share things of that nature with his father, with whom he'd also been close. Pam never got the chance to meet her husband's father because he'd passed away a couple years before they met.

When Pam met Conner's mother for the first time, a striking woman with a smooth cocoa complexion, she could tell they shared a very close and warm relationship. So much so that she thought he was a mama's boy. He was an only child and no longer had a father, and in Pam's eyes, those two things alone made him a mama's boy—big time. But she didn't divulge her initial impression at first. She waited until they'd been dating a few months to tell him. And once, during an argument after they'd married (okay, it was more like a serious discussion), she'd blurted it out: "You ain't nothing but a mama's boy!" Conner had replied,

"Yeah, right. You know that's not true. And I can't believe an educated woman like you would use the word 'ain't' in a sentence." That comment had only upset Pam even more.

Conner pulled back the covers on their king-sized bed. He tossed the extra pillow to the foot of the bed. "Whatever, Dear. If you say so. I'm tired, I'm going to bed. I'm glad you enjoyed your visit."

Pam sighed and walked over to her dresser where she retrieved a white, oversized T-shirt from a drawer. H&P University was printed across its front. The shirt had been given to her by her sister, Cassie, who was entering her junior year this fall. Pam would normally wear the shirt when she was lounging around the house or when she was running errands. She'd wear it with a pair of jeans. But tonight she would sleep in it. There'd be no romance in the Buckner household tonight.

Conner noticed the T-shirt in his wife's hands as he picked up his alarm clock. He set it for 4:30 AM and lay on his back. He said nothing as he watched his wife head into the bathroom. A few minutes later, Pam's cell phone rang in her purse. *Probably one of her girlfriends calling to check on her,* Conner thought. *I'm sure she told one of them we had a spat.*

He shook his head and smiled. Unlike his wife, he wasn't one to stew long when they had a disagreement. And tonight he had no energy left to go another round with her. That's why, when

Pam made the comment about him telling his mom everything, he didn't try to battle. Besides, she hadn't said anything he hadn't heard her say before.

Conner didn't intentionally compare Pam to his ex-wife, but Renita had never accused him of being a mama's boy. And he and Renita hadn't argued and carried on after just five months of marriage, the way he and Pam did.

Life had thrown Conner a curve ball. He'd always thought he'd marry once and that he and the mother of his twins would have lasted until the "'til death do we part'." His way of dealing with the unexpected had been 1) prayer and 2) not staying upset for long. He found grudge-holding a waste of time. But this wife of his—well, she had her own ideas about how to handle things. Many times Conner found Pam's behavior to be pretty hilarious. Sometimes he wondered if she picked arguments just because.

After fifteen minutes, Pam emerged from the bathroom. The hot shower had felt good against her skin. She'd washed and conditioned her short mane, which felt soft and silky. And thanks to Val, it smelled of strawberries. Val had recommended the shampoo and Pam was hooked.

Conner was now lying on his side, propped up on one arm. He watched his wife as she proceeded to her dresser where she sprayed her neck with a squirt of body mist. When she reached for her black stocking cap, he winced.

"You're already coming to bed wearing that big T-shirt. Now you want to make it even worse by wearing that rag." He'd hoped to talk her into some play time. She couldn't be that upset.

"It helps my hair to stay moist, you know that." Pam picked up a tube of hand lotion.

She didn't always come to bed in the "rag," as Conner called it, but she'd done it tonight purposely.

"Oooh, Darcy, I don't know if I can. Let me see how much I get accomplished. I'll let you know by noon. Is that okay?"

"That's fine. I was thinking we could grab something and just eat it here. I need to vent, you know?" Darcy rubbed her temples.

Pam knew then that it was likely the same issue that had her colleague sounding She knew how Conner felt about her bed attire. A big T-shirt and a stocking cap meant one thing: sleep. No touching, no petting, just good night. All she wanted was a good night's rest to get ready for the start of another busy workweek, not to mention her important meeting on Thursday. She was looking forward to it, that much was true, but not in a I-still-desire-the-guy-I-used-to-date kind of way.

Pam climbed into bed and turned out the light on her nightstand. Conner didn't budge. He would usually turn the light off on his nightstand, but this time he just lay facing his wife.

"I know you're not going to allow an unexpected visit from the mother of my children cause you to go to bed angry. Pam, think about it. Don't you think it's kind of silly?"

Pam rolled onto her back and folded her arms. "I just don't want this to become a problem," she said, sighing. "I feel like you two have secrets that I don't know about."

She knew Conner was right—sort of. It was *kind of silly.* She just didn't know how to explain how she felt. It wasn't that she was insecure. She knew her husband loved her and that he had no intention of going back to his ex. She was even certain that Renita had no desire for Conner. But still.

Conner had said he would share what they'd discussed and Pam knew he would. She wondered if Renita knew of Conner's plans to tell her what they'd talked about. Pam figured Renita had to know there was only so much Conner would and could keep from his present wife.

"Take this rag off." It was both a plea and a command. Conner smiled and Pam caught a glint of mischief in his eye. Her husband definitely had a certain way about him. "Your phone rang while you were in the shower," he whispered. "You need to get into the habit of turning it off after 9:00 like I do." He chuckled.

"I forgot to turn it off. I was too busy being upset with you." She smiled. "I guess I can stop being upset for a minute."

Conner raised an eyebrow. "A minute? Uh, how about we not say a minute?" They both laughed.

Pam got out of the bed and walked over to her purse. She glanced at the missed call from Jeff on her cell phone. *Okay, I see I need to address this immediately;* she made a mental note to herself, then turned off her phone and rejoined her husband. Her thoughts tried to turn again to the week ahead but she pushed them from her mind. Right now she wanted to focus on her husband. Thursday would take care of itself. Pam felt she had total control of the situation. She didn't know she was in for a rude awakening.

9

"Mrs. Buckner, you have a call holding on line one." The receptionist looked up at Pam briefly as she spoke. The day had started like any other Thursday—busy and then some. Pam had stepped away from her desk and was returning from the ladies room. She was glad she hadn't stepped outside for some air or gone next door to the bakery for a bagel.

"Thank you, Deena," Pam smiled. Given all of the demands placed upon the 20- something-year-old receptionist, Pam decided not to inquire why she hadn't just allowed the call to go to her voicemail. She thought the young lady did more than her share of duties, some not even related to her job description. She overheard one of the social workers as she proceeded to her office.

"Deena, would you mind making copies of these two files, please?"

Pam looked over her shoulder just in time to catch the half-smile on Deena's face.

"Sure. Right after I make copies for Ms. Beacon."

That's right, Deena. Let it be known that your boss comes first. She picked up the phone while simultaneously glancing at her watch. Unsure of how long the person had been holding, she added some extra politeness to her voice. "Thank you so much for holding. This is Mrs. Buckner."

She spent close to 30 minutes on the call. The visit to the Uptown library branch that she'd scheduled for two of her clients had been cancelled. Something about the head librarian and an important meeting. Pam asked if there were any other staff members who could fill in.

"Unfortunately, it's library policy that only the head librarian conduct the sessions with clients. Sorry."

Pam could hear the sincerity in the woman's voice, even though she didn't like their policy. "Okay. Well, flexibility is important. I'll use this as a teachable moment when I let my clients know I had to reschedule."

She'd arranged for two of her clients to meet with the librarian to learn how to better utilize the library's database. Being able to search for books and other resources was an important tool, something Pam felt everyone needed to know how to do. This was only one of the many ways the women at the shelter learned to gain independence. It had been a successful venture with a couple of her other clients who were faring well since they'd left the shelter.

The session was supposed to have lasted an hour, with Pam accompanying the clients. Her boss was perfectly fine with her having to be out of the office for that amount of time. "Anything to help these women get back on their feet gets a vote from me," the middle aged woman had stated. She had 30 years of experience working with women who lived temporarily in shelters and Pam respected her genuine concern for others.

"I have next Tuesday available at 10:00. Will this time work for you?" At least the staff members at the library were helpful. Pam flipped through her planner. Tuesday looked good.

"That will work fine. Thank you." As soon as her phone call ended, there was a knock on her door. Seeing that it was partly open, Pam's co-worker entered without waiting to be invited in. She was a stylish social worker who dressed "to the nines" daily and Pam could tell she was not having a very good morning.

"Pam, do you have any Advil, Tylenol, Aleve—something that will make this headache disappear?"

Pam pulled open her top desk drawer. "I might have—"

"Oh, you are a life saver!" Her colleague cut her off as she reached down and grabbed the bottle of Aleve in Pam's drawer. Pam watched with a raised eyebrow as the 40-something-year-old woman with a caramel complexion tilted her head back and swallowed two tablets. She had never been able to comprehend how anyone could take any type of pill without a glass of water.

"Thank you. I'm about to blow up at somebody. I'm trying to be nice but—" She stopped short and exhaled, spreading her hands in a downward motion. "Breathe, Darcy, breathe."

Unable to contain her laughter, Pam shook her head. "You're having more than just a bad day. What gives?"

Pam and Darcy shared a closer bond than any of the other employees at the shelter, but neither woman would describe their relationship as very close. Darcy had been at the agency for a year prior to Pam's arrival. And since the two of them were the newest kids on the block, they sort of fell into a comfortable working relationship.

Both had come to the agency after being laid off from their previous jobs. Darcy had been a marketing manager and hadn't used her master's in social work for several years. During a conversation over lunch, shortly after Pam began working at the shelter, Darcy shared how she missed working in marketing. She'd ended up in that field sort of by accident and found that she really loved it. Unlike Darcy, Pam hadn't really used her degree in counseling with the exception of one temporary position. And after graduate school and after the temp position, she'd found a job in sales and loved it.

It had been that conversation that helped to form an understanding between them. They both agreed that on some days they loved their jobs. Helping women who were less fortunate was a great feeling. But then there were other days when they didn't feel like that at all. Today was one of those days for Darcy.

"I was supposed to be in court," Darcy began, glancing at her watch, "20 minutes ago. But our lovely boss informed me that my case had been assigned to one of the other social workers. It would have been nice to have known this sooner."

"Did she say why it was reassigned?"

Pam figured there had to be a good reason. Darcy was good at what she did—as were the other four social workers at the shelter—but Darcy was the only one who could handle the not-so-kind ways of some of the judges in family court. Pam had heard the other four social workers, on several occasions, complain about the decisions some of the judges would make. Their feelings were justified, she believed that, but Darcy had a way of finding the positive in a negative situation.

This morning, though, it was obvious that she was unable to do that. Which actually took Pam by surprise. Darcy got along fine with their boss, the director of the shelter, so there had to be something else. She decided to probe a little deeper.

"Something tells me there's more to your frustration than a reassigned case." Pam crossed her arms and sat back in her oversized maroon chair.

She hoped Darcy wouldn't think she was prying even though she was. It was obvious that she needed to vent and, if she could do it in less than 10 minutes, Pam was all ears. She watched as Darcy closed her office door, which Pam was just about to suggest that she do. No need to give the other folks at the shelter anything to wag their tongues about.

"I really should've left my personal matter at home." Darcy ran her hand through her medium-length auburn hair. She often received compliments on how nice that color looked on her. "You're right. It is more than just the case—though I'm not exactly crazy about it being handed to someone else."

Pam nodded and then glanced at the clock on her wall. Darcy smiled and caught the hint.

"I had an argument with my husband last night. He seems to think there's nothing wrong with an ex-girlfriend showing up at our door unannounced."

Whoa! Pam thought and shifted in her chair. Darcy's statement really got her attention. This sounded all too familiar. She wanted to hear more but couldn't help but to interrupt.

"When did this happen? And why is she showing up without being invited?"

Pam found herself catching an attitude and was ready to toss blame at Darcy's husband, without even knowing the details.

"Last week. And he doesn't seem to understand why I'm upset. He says she was only stopping by to say hi and to ask about his father. She'd heard his father was really sick and—"

Pam's phone rang and she held up her finger. Darcy glanced at her watch. There were seven more hours to the workday and she knew it would be better to have this chat some other time, but just as she was pointing toward the door, indicating that she was leaving and that they'd talk later, Pam ended her call.

"Has she stopped by before? How long were they dating?"

Darcy laughed at the expression on Pam's face. Her scowl made it evident whose side she was on.

"The look on your face is priceless. Did I touch a nerve?"

"Actually, you did. I had this same issue with my husband." Pam reached for the file on her desk. "Except his is an ex-wife." She gritted her teeth.

Darcy shrugged. "Well, that's different."

Her comment almost made Pam jump from her chair.

"Really? How's that?" she snapped, looking directly into Darcy's eyes. Renita had dropped by four days ago, but Pam was almost as angry about it now as she was on Sunday. She pictured the incident in her mind all over again and cringed. Although she and Conner had ended Sunday night with an intimate session, it hadn't been enough to resolve how she felt about the whole thing.

"Yikes!" Pam blurted out and made a shivering sound. A few seconds later they were both laughing.

"I didn't mean to conjure up any bad feelings," said Darcy as she opened the door.

"Let's talk later. Maybe we can help each other see both our situations through different lenses."

"Ha! Don't know about that!" Pam waved her hand as Darcy made her exit.

For the next two hours Pam worked without taking her normal 10-minute, step-away-from-her-desk breaks. She spent the time updating pertinent information in several of her clients' files. Last month, two of them successfully completed their programs at the shelter. While one had a child who also resided at the shelter, the other woman was childless. Both had substance abuse problems but after intervention and much guidance, they proved themselves ready to give living independently a go. There was still follow-up to be done with them, including two home visits a month for the next few months, but Pam and the social worker who'd been assigned to their cases felt positive about the women's progress. It was outcomes like these that made Pam's heart flutter with joy. Unfortunately, happy endings weren't always the outcome.

After returning some phone calls and setting up various appointments, Pam met briefly with one of her newest clients. It was hard to imagine that the attractive woman who sat before her hadn't decided sooner to leave her abusive relationship. How some women remained in such awful situations, Pam had no clue. They sat alone in the lounge area of the shelter and Pam imparted what she hoped was wisdom for the young woman. Instead of meeting in her office when she needed to speak with a client, Pam sometimes used the lounge, which had four comfortable chairs and a round table. The lounge was a good alternative for a place to chat one-on-one.

The vending machines, there were two, provided snacks, soda, and juice. And there was fresh coffee readily available, along with an assortment of tea bags. Once a week, sometimes twice, the women and children who resided at the shelter could select from an assortment of donuts. The rule, however, was that each person was limited to only one. But on this Thursday morning, someone on staff had baked banana bread. It must have been a hit because Pam noticed only one small slice and some crumbs left on the plate.

"It's a good thing I avoided coming in here this morning for my usual bottle of orange juice," Pam remarked, tilting her head toward the banana bread. "I don't think I could have eaten just one slice." She used humor most times to put the women at ease.

"It was very good. Tastes like what my grandma used to bake. And it *was* hard to have only one piece."

The woman was in her late 20s and had two children. She'd hoped her children would be able to stay with her at the shelter, but a judge ruled that they were to remain with family members. The oldest, who was 10, had no choice because the age limit for children at the shelter was 7. Other shelters had different restrictions but the woman had been placed in Pam's care.

"So how are you doing? Any particular issues you'd like to discuss?"

"Well, I could use a few more clothes." The woman pulled at the ends of the black, zip-down sweater she was wearing. She seemed embarrassed to ask but Pam was glad she did. The women at the shelter didn't usually arrive with too many belongings. They definitely had to mix and match what they had. Donations did come in and they were much needed and appreciated, but in the last two months it seemed that most of the donations had been children's clothing.

"I'll see what I can do," Pam reassured her. "Fridays are usually when the residents look through the items. Have you been looking to see if there were any outfits you could use?"

The woman had been at the shelter for a month now but Pam understood that it took many of them a little time to adjust to their new environment, and that they needed a little encouragement to take advantage of all that was offered. Even free clothes.

"No. But I'll make sure I look through them tomorrow."

"Please do. Three o'clock, on the second floor, in the television room."

Pam's place of employment consisted of two buildings: the shelter and the agency. So most times she referred to where she worked as an agency-slash-shelter. Fortunately, most people could easily visualize the two. Within the agency were several administrators who made sure that everything ran smoothly, but the amount of paperwork involved could send someone over the edge! With all the benefits of modern technology, paperwork still wasn't a thing of the past. And of course everyone had to work as part of a team. Communication was key between the administrators, social workers and counselors. Pam was one of two counselors. Both were licensed, which was a requirement. There was also a therapist who came in weekly, as well as a child psychologist. The agency was well prepared with whatever services were needed.

The more Pam thought about it, the more she realized how fortunate her clients were to have a reasonably nice place to call home for six months. The director of the shelter had her hands full, but with the help of a very competent assistant, she ran one of the best agencies in the city. Pam was thankful she'd landed her position.

"I hope to see my kids soon. I can't wait to live as a family again," the young woman said hopefully.

Pam had to refrain from speaking out loud. *Yeah, if you want to call living with an abuser living as a family,* she thought. "That's going to take much effort on your part. But I know you can get through the program as long as you remain focused."

Pam could sense her client's uncertainty and smiled reassuringly as she continued speaking. The women she worked with needed tough love and she gave it to them, but this moment called for something else. She'd gotten really good at striking the right balance with her clients.

"You have to work on your self-esteem. A man's hand doesn't belong on your body whenever he flies into a fit of rage. That's why boxing gloves were made."

Her last comment elicited a smile. The woman shyly put her head down but Pam instructed her to raise it back up.

"One of the ways we're going to work on your self-esteem is by having you always look at the person you're talking to. Put your head up."

The woman complied. She felt more comfortable talking to Pam than she did anyone else at the shelter. In only one month she could see that Pam really cared.

"The help is here and available to you. We're all here to help you. You just need to want to help yourself."

The young woman wondered if Pam had read her mind. Hearing her say that everyone was there to help was comforting. It would likely take a little time, though, for her to feel as at ease with the other staff members as she did with Pam.

"Thanks," was all she could say, which was fine with Pam.

The lounge started to fill with some of the residents. Pam gave the young woman a booklet to read and then headed back to her office. It was noon and she'd just remembered that she needed to call Jackie. Jackie had looked through her closets and found a few items she could donate to the shelter. Pam figured she'd try to get them before next Friday. The conversation she'd just had with her new client helped to jog her memory.

Pam called Jackie's cell phone expecting to leave a voicemail. As a high school principal, Jackie didn't really have a set time for lunch. She was surprised when Jackie answered on the second ring.

"Hello?" Jackie answered in a softer voice than usual.

"Hi, Jackie. I was expecting to get your voicemail. Are you at lunch?"

"Uh, no ... I'm not at lunch, Pam." Jackie switched the phone to her other ear.

"Okay. Well, I was just calling to remind you about the clothes you said you could donate to the shelter. I can pick them up this weekend if that's okay."

"That's fine, Pam. Uh … I'm at home, though, and Lem's home, too."

"Oh, you didn't go to work today? And Lem's back from Atlanta?"

"Uh, yeah … so, uh … we'll talk later."

Jackie sounded different but Pam didn't know why. But when she heard Jackie repeat, "We'll talk later, okay?" she caught on.

"Oooh, y'all are having relations!" Pam whispered loudly into the phone. She glanced at the clock on her office wall. "It's 12:05 in the afternoon! What married folks you know have sex at this time of day? Girl, you're the principal! You need to be at work!"

"In this household, 12:00 in the afternoon works just fine. And there's a reason assistant principals were created. Bye, Pam." *Click.*

Pam heard Jackie giggle before she hung up. "At home getting her groove on." Pam shook her head and laughed.

At 12:20 PM her cell phone rang. It was Jeff. She told him where to meet her at 1:00 PM and started getting ready for the lunch date she'd looked forward to all week. As she applied some lip gloss, Pam thought silently, *Two years ago, one could've argued that I needed help with my self-esteem.* She shrugged and put the lip gloss back into her purse. *Different deal. I wasn't involved in an abusive relationship.*

10

She's looking good, as usual. Jeff thought, standing as Pam walked toward him. He'd arrived at the restaurant just five minutes prior. He was glad she'd chosen a place that was easily accessible by Lakeshore Drive, the expressway that ran from both the north and the south side. He'd had an earlier meeting that he made sure wouldn't run past noon. And since Pam had told him that she worked on the north side, Jeff expected that she'd choose a restaurant close to her job.

Pam smiled as she removed her gray jacket. *I've never seen him in a suit before. He looks good. This is going to be harder than I thought.* She admired his manners anew when he came around the table and pulled her chair out for her, something he used to do when they were dating. At least he hadn't forgotten how to be a gentleman.

"You look really nice," he said as he sat back down.

Pam mumbled a thank you and picked up the menu. Jeff waved their server over and allowed Pam to order her drink first. She ordered iced tea while he ordered a Diet Coke.

"I'll give you a chance to look at the menu," the blonde woman said with a smile before she disappeared. Pam couldn't help but to notice her dark roots before she departed, however. It was clearly time for a touch-up. She sort of resembled the blonde who had approached Jeff at the reggae club two years ago. The expression on his face after Pam revealed that she'd seen the woman approach him had been quite comical. She wondered if he would even remember the incident. In fact, now that they were sitting across from each other, her mind began to recall all sorts of memories about him.

"So what have you—?" they spoke in unison.

Jeff laughed. "Ladies first," he said as he picked up his glass of Diet Coke. He admired the outfit Pam was wearing. Dressed casually in a white poplin shirt and gray slacks, she still looked every bit as sharp as he'd remembered. He noticed the silver pendent around her neck as well as the diamond on her left-hand ring finger. There would be plenty of time to ask questions about her life as a married woman, but for now he'd focus on other topics. Like why didn't she ever return any of his calls?

"I was just going to ask how you've been." Pam picked up her glass of iced tea although she wasn't exactly thirsty. She was nervous, though she wasn't sure why. After spending an hour chatting and eating a chicken salad with strawberries and almonds, they'd both go their separate ways.

"I've been great. Things are going well in sales though I'm no longer a vice president. I'm actually with another pharmaceutical company as a sales manager."

"Oh." Pam found herself interested and curious to know more. All Jeff had said about his job when they'd spoken by phone was that he was still in sales. Just as she was about to inquire about it, the server appeared.

"Are you ready to order?" She looked eagerly from Pam to Jeff, then back to Pam.

"I'll have the chicken and almond salad with vinaigrette and croutons on the side, please."

"Good choice. And you sir?"

"Turkey Panini, no mayo. Chips are fine for a side."

Their server nodded affirmatively, took their menus and walked away.

"So what happened with the other pharmaceutical company you were working for?"

Pam glanced at the entrance and saw two of her colleagues but they didn't see her. They picked up "to go" orders and left. She'd suggested this café because it was close to the shelter and the food was good. It did occur to her that she might run into someone from work but it didn't matter. It was just lunch with an old friend. And besides, whose business was it except hers?

"The company was bought by a larger company in Japan. Even if I had been asked to remain, the answer would have been no."

"I take it Japan was just too far away."

Pam noticed Jeff's eyes staring at her blouse. Suddenly self-conscious, she folded her arms across her chest. Jeff picked up on her nervousness and chuckled lightly. One of the things he liked so much about Pam was her boldness combined with her vulnerability. On one hand she seemed so self-assured, yet on the other she could be so defenseless.

"You're correct. I had an opportunity to work in London for a year but decided not to accept the offer. But when the opportunity in Houston presented itself to me, I went for it. It's fine for now, but who knows what the future holds."

Pam noticed a twinkle in Jeff's eye at the end of his statement. It was either her imagination running wild or Jeff was implying something else. She decided to change the subject.

"Did you sell your town house?"

Their server returned with their lunch. After asking for drink refills, Jeff began to eat. Pam bowed her head and said grace. Jeff waited until she was done.

"Sorry. I really need to get into the habit of blessing my food. My sisters and my mother get on me about that all the time."

Pam shrugged like it was no big deal, thinking, *the sisters and mother you never bothered to introduce me to.* The thought almost eased itself right out of her mouth. "I haven't always been good about it myself," she said before placing a forkful of salad into her mouth. Delicious! This salad was what she normally ordered whenever she came to this café. "So I was asking about your town house," she repeated her question.

They'd had good times in that town house. Then there was that one time in particular that wasn't so good. It was the night she'd started to inquire about their relationship. She'd asked one too many questions for Jeff and it had changed the whole mood. It had been a turn-off for him, she realized that, but there were just some things she wanted to get clearer about.

After that incident Jeff had behaved as if it had never happened. It was his ability to behave so smoothly that caused her to follow her heart instead of her head. It was an unfortunate thing many women did that caused them unnecessary heartache.

"Oh. Yes, I did." Jeff wiped his mouth with his napkin. He removed his suit jacket, displaying an upper body that obviously still engaged in regular workouts. "I actually sold it to a cousin and her husband. They're a young couple, first home purchase. So it was an ideal situation." He shrugged and laughed. "I didn't get as much as I would have liked, but money isn't everything."

Pam wiped her mouth, took a sip of her iced tea and checked the clock on the wall. Her lunch break would soon be over. She'd stay until 2:15 PM but no later. She had a group session with three clients at 4:00 PM.

Pam was sometimes amazed at the amount of work she and the other counselor—and the social workers—got done in a week. They certainly didn't have the kind of jobs that left a whole lot of room for down time. Jeff would be off to Houston in a few days and, realizing that times were different now, she felt it best to ask those nagging questions now. There were still some things she wanted to get off her chest, even after two years. Not to mention, she wanted to tell him not to call her cell phone after a certain hour.

"So tell me what you've been up to, Love."

Pam stopped eating and raised an eyebrow. "Love?"

"Sorry. Just force of habit. I guess I don't have the right to refer to you by a term of endearment anymore."

"No, Jeff, you don't. In case you hadn't noticed, I'm married." She held up her left hand. "And even if I was still single," she was on a roll, "I'd still want you to call me by my name."

"Okay." Jeff loosened his tie. "That's fair. I understand."

"Oh, do you? I seem to recall that you didn't seem to understand my feelings when we dated. It felt like everything was about you. I didn't see the arrogance when we began to date but that sure did change."

Pam tossed her napkin onto the table and glanced around the café. Most of the crowd was people who worked nearby. She did observe a couple sitting near the window. They had to have been a couple, their body language said so. And they looked genuinely happy. When she focused her attention back to Jeff, he was staring at her. Had she been any other woman going off on him, he probably would have flipped out. But this was Pam and he knew better. He waited to make sure she was done. At least for now. He tilted his head.

"What? Don't look at me like that." Pam reached for her purse, which hung from the chair next to her. She took out her credit card and got the server's attention.

"Will this be on one check?" she asked.

In unison, Jeff replied yes and Pam replied no. The server smirked, not knowing how to respond.

"You may bring one check, please." Jeff smiled at the server who smiled in return before walking away.

"I can pay for my own lunch, Jeff."

"I know," he said and removed his wallet from his back pocket.

He even made taking out his wallet look sexy. Pam pressed her lips together and Jeff continued.

"I know you can pay for your own lunch. I imagine the agency pays you a nice chunk of change. My issue is not with you paying for your own lunch. My issue is with you sisters and the passion you display. That's why so many of these white women are acting crazy. They're taking notes from sisters like you." He pointed his finger briefly at her and smiled.

His gaze held her attention. As much as she wanted not to laugh, it was impossible. Jeff was teasing her. He'd managed to make her laugh but, deep down, she knew he understood her need to vent. He might have caused her to chuckle, but her feelings were real.

"Jeff, I'm serious." Pam sat back in her chair as the server approached their table.

"Thank you. You two have a wonderful day."

Pam thought she noticed a smirk.

"And for the record, sisters are not the only ones who act crazy," Pam said as she put on her jacket.

Jeff removed his suit coat from the back of his chair and they walked toward the door.

"Oh, don't I know it," he replied and winked at her. *You women in general are just too emotional.*

Pam rolled her eyes and shook her head, but he caught the smile on her face as they left the café.

Jeff and Pam stood by her vehicle as other patrons drove in and out of the parking lot. Some of them were glancing at their watches, possibly overextending their allotted lunch times. There was a hospital several blocks away and a huge auto repair shop only two blocks from the café. It was 2:05 PM and, by now, just about everyone had taken their lunch break. The drive back to the shelter was less than 15 minutes but Pam was anxious to get back to her office. This lunch meeting had left her with some things to process.

"Jeff, I've said some of what I needed to say. There's only so much one can say in an hour anyway. Thanks for lunch. But just so you know, I am happily married. My venting doesn't change that. One has nothing to do with the other." She climbed into her Mercedes. Once inside she rolled down the window. "And one more thing," she began, keeping a straight face, "you cannot call my cell phone after 6:00."

Jeff nodded. Now didn't seem like the time to ask her to dinner. His invitation could wait. June was only a week or so away and he'd soon be back.

"Pam, I understand more than you think I do. Okay. No more calls after 6:00. I can respect that."

"In fact, it's best that you not call at all."

"Is that what you really want?"

Jeff felt certain this was not what she wanted. But he wasn't about to push the issue. He had another strategy he hoped to employ.

Pam didn't answer, she just started her vehicle. She couldn't truthfully say what she wanted. And she did have so many other things she was curious to know—his relationship status being one of them. Not that it mattered to her in any way.

"If I want to talk to you, I'll call you."

"That's fair. I fly back to Houston Sunday morning."

Jeff smiled. It was the smile that seemed to work its magic each time. He wasn't trying to come between Pam and her spouse, at least not from his perspective. He just wanted to spend time with her whenever he was in the Windy City. He saw no harm in that.

"I'm staying at the Westin on Michigan Ave. as of tomorrow night. I have to stay with one of my sisters for at least one of the days I'm here. Otherwise, I won't hear the end of it."

"Well, enjoy the rest of your visit."

"I will." *At least now you know where I'm staying*, he thought. He winked, then turned and walked to his waiting rental. Pam watched him drive away.

"The Westin Hotel, huh?" she mumbled as she pulled out of the parking lot.

Just then, Hunter came walking out of the café talking on his cell phone. He'd seen Pam talking to Jeff when he pulled into the parking lot but Pam hadn't seen him.

Must be one of Pam's colleagues, he thought silently as he got into his vehicle.

11

"I should be home before 10:00." Tricee grabbed her beige handbag. "Jackie says this minister is awesome."

Hunter nodded. He was engrossed in the 6:00 PM news. He wasn't ignoring his wife but, to Tricee, it sure felt like it.

"Did you hear me? I said I should be home before 10:00." She stared at her husband whose eyes remained fixed on the TV screen. "Jackie says this stripper's really good. He's supposed to be one of the—"

Hunter turned down the television and looked up at his wife.

Tricee gave a knowing smile. "I thought you'd hear that." She leaned down and kissed her husband on the cheek.

It bothered her that Hunter hadn't attended weekly services much in the past couple of months. He'd already missed a few Sundays, surely he'd want to at least try to make it to church during the week, she thought. He was working longer hours as a consultant, which was a good thing. It meant the economy hadn't taken much of a toll on their finances. But still, to miss church seemed a little out of character for him.

"I'm really not concerned," Hunter said, pulling his wife down onto his lap. "I know you'd never go to a strip club. It's not you." He kissed her on the cheek. "Besides, you have me to strip for you."

Tricee laughed. As attracted as she was to her husband, she'd never pictured him performing a striptease.

"Now *that* would be a sight for some real sore eyes."

"Watch it, woman." Hunter chuckled.

Hunter realized he was blessed to have such a wonderful wife. He had asked God to send him a woman just like the one from Proverbs 31. Well, no one could possibly measure up to that perfection, he knew that. But Tricee was, indeed, the woman he'd been praying for. When he saw her at the coffee shop two years ago, he told one of his friends the next day that he'd met his future wife. This was a tidbit he'd never shared with his wife, though. He didn't believe it was necessary. They had marked close to two years of marital bliss now.

There was one thing that had him bothered, however. He'd been experiencing feelings of uncertainty about a few things. But instead of discussing these things with his wife, he decided to keep it to himself for now. His plan was to pray on it and see what God said. If He told Hunter to discuss it with his wife, He'd also give him the right words to say.

"I better get out of here." Tricee eased from her husband's grip. "Jackie says the service starts at 7:00 and it's already after

6:00. The church is on 50th and King Drive. I hope I don't get stuck in traffic."

"You should be okay. I think the traffic coming north from the south side will be the problem." Hunter paused. "This is a woman minster, right?"

He did recall his wife mentioning, a few days prior, something about going to hear a minster on Thursday. She'd asked him to join her but he'd politely declined.

"Yeah, well, I don't want to miss anything. And, yes, this is a woman of the cloth."

Hunter walked his wife to the door. He looked over the beige, flared-leg pants and brown pullover top she was wearing. Because of the top's neckline, he was glad to see that his wife had chosen to wear her beige, tweed blazer.

"You don't normally wear pants to church. You look nice."

"Thanks." Tricee kissed her husband on the cheek. She turned to open the door and then paused. "Speaking of church, you seem to be missing quite a few Sundays."

She waited on Hunter to respond but he only shrugged and mumbled something under his breath.

"It concerns me, Honey," she said softly.

Still no reply. Hunter just turned and walked backed into the living room.

Feeling dejected, Tricee opened the door and left. She walked into the waiting elevator and exhaled. In the time it took her to ride down 15 floors, she'd already begun to overthink the situation. But once the elevator doors opened to the garage, she attempted to refocus. *I am going to enjoy the service this evening,* she affirmed to herself. *I cannot allow the enemy a stronghold.*

Tricee made it to Christ Redeemer Baptist Church at five minutes after 7:00 PM. The parking lot was filling quickly but, fortunately, she was able to find a space. The white, brick church was sizable, though not the largest in the area. The steeple gave the building appeal. Tricee had never been to the church before but she'd been invited on numerous occasions by Jackie and Lem. After searching for a church home, they decided that this church was where God had led them. Tricee also had a few co-workers who were members and, as far as they were concerned, their pastor walked on water. Jackie and Lem adored their pastor as well but, unlike Tricee's co-workers, they knew that pastors didn't belong on pedestals.

Tricee looked around the parking lot as she made her way toward the building. She figured Jackie and Val were probably already inside. She hadn't spoken with either of them but assumed they'd be at the service. She wasn't too sure about Pam though.

"Good evening." The greeter, an older woman with long, gray hair, smiled and handed her a bulletin.

"Good evening," Tricee said, smiling warmly.

She glanced down at the bulletin at the picture of the speaker for the evening. Realizing she'd seen the minister before on television, Tricee became even more excited. If this evening's sermon was anything like what she'd heard from this minster before, a pleasant treat was in store. Everyone in attendance tonight would leave in higher spirits than when they'd arrived.

Tricee was just about to sit in the back row until she spotted Jackie and Val sitting four rows ahead. She quickly made her way to where her friends were seated.

"Hi, Lady! We saved a space for you—barely!" Jackie said excitedly. "A lady sort of gave me the side-eye when she noticed my purse in the seat. I politely told her I was saving a spot for a friend. Besides, what did she want me to do? Place it on the floor?" Jackie laughed.

"You didn't have to do that. I should've gotten here a little earlier." Tricee took off her jacket. "Whew! Kind of hot in the Lord's house this evening." She remarked, fanning herself with the church bulletin.

Val stood and embraced Tricee. "It's not warm in here. You're having a hot flash." Val giggled and sat down. She looked over her shoulder toward the back door. "Have you heard from Pam?" Val had failed to ask Jackie if she'd heard from Pam. And

Jackie hadn't mentioned that she'd spoken to Pam earlier, when she'd unintentionally interrupted Jackie's "play time" with her husband.

"No, I haven't spoken with her at all today," Tricee said. She sat down and fanned herself again. "Whew!"

"Are you going to be okay?" Jackie teased.

Jackie admired Tricee's outfit and silently noticed that her look was different, neckline and all. She was a little surprised that Tricee was wearing pants. She figured she would have come wearing a dress or a skirt. Val was wearing pants, too, but she hadn't been surprised by that. She, herself, was dressed in a long skirt and a blouse with bell sleeves.

"You look really good." Jackie nudged Tricee's arm.

Tricee blushed. "Thank you," she whispered quietly.

The congregation was filled to capacity. The ushers, two very tall men, had to bring in folding chairs as there were still folks coming in. Other than the two ushers, there were only about 10 other men in the congregation. The women in attendance all appeared eager to hear a word for the evening. Although the majority of the women were African American, there were a few women from other ethnicities sprinkled throughout the congregation.

Soon everyone was on their feet. "Mighty to Our God," an upbeat song that made it hard to stand still was being led by a middle-aged woman. Jackie whispered that she was the lead singer for the church's choir. Standing next to her were three other women and one man. Their voices were so powerful it sounded as if there were more than just five people singing.

"Let's sing it to the Lord," the lead singer shouted out. Everyone in the congregation joined in as they clapped and swayed from side to side. Tricee, Jackie and Val were all smiles as they sang along. One woman moved out into the aisle for more space as she moved her shoulders up and down. With her eyes closed, she spun around a couple times without missing a beat.

Jackie leaned over and whispered to Tricee, "Now see that's what I'm talking about. Being able to just praise him and let go without any reservations." She then turned to Val who was moving her shoulders up and down, too. She noticed that Val's eyes were also closed and she could hear soft, muffled sounds coming from her mouth.

The next song was also an upbeat number, this time led by the only male on the worship team for the evening. It was a song Tricee had never heard before but she made a mental note to ask Jackie about it after the service. After two more songs, a very attractive, middle-aged lady from the pulpit led everyone in prayer. Dressed in an olive green dress, she resembled a younger version of the late and elegant Lena Horne. Jackie would mention later that

166

she was the first lady of the church. After introducing the speaker for the evening, she asked everyone to be seated.

As soon as the speaker, who was dressed elegantly in a dark blue dress, approached the front of the pulpit, Pam walked in and sat in the very last row, in one of the folding chairs. And just like everyone else in the congregation, she was soon lost in the words that flowed from the minister's mouth:

Oh, let us just lay aside every burden, every heartache that fills this place right now, Lord, we turn it over to you. Some of us are dealing with things, Father that we just can't figure out. We have so many questions, Father. But we don't know how to approach you because we're afraid of what you might think if we do. But it tells us in Hebrews 4:16 that we are to come boldly to the throne of grace that we may obtain mercy and find help in our time of need. We have nothing to fear, Lord, because you know all things. Lord, some of us are being tempted. But we know that you are more than able to help us through those things that come against us.

"Yes, Lord," Pam mumbled. The word "tempted" had struck a nerve. If there was anything she needed help with after seeing Jeff earlier, it was temptation. She'd tried to put on an act of strength but knew she was fooling no one, not even herself.

The speaker was, in one word, awesome!

MATRIMONY REDEEMED

After the sermon there was an alter call. So many of the women headed to the altar that Pam was able to spot her three friends. She quickly made her way over to where they were and stood in the now empty space next to Tricee.

"Oh, hey, girl!" Tricee whispered excitedly. Pam was then greeted by Jackie and Val.

"We didn't think you'd make it," Val leaned over and said quietly.

"Excuse me, ladies," Tricee said after a few seconds, "but I need to make my way to that altar."

Pam stepped back to allow Tricee to get past her. She wanted badly to follow her friend but couldn't seem to make her feet move. It was apparent to her, however, that Tricee had a strong need to get to the altar for prayer. Pam wondered if there was something going on that Tricee would share with them later.

After the service ended, the four ladies found themselves standing by Jackie's vehicle. For a May evening in the Windy City, the weather was perfect with just the right amount of a cool breeze.

"Wow, what a service!" Val shook her head. "Mmph, I needed that."

"You and me both," Jackie added. "I told you she was awesome!" She glanced at her cell phone to check the time. "It's

168

already close to 10:00. If I didn't have such a drive back to the Beverly area, I'd suggest we go somewhere for coffee."

"Girl, you and that coffee." Tricee laughed. "We," she said, pointing to herself, Val and Pam, "would have tea."

"That would be nice but I have to drive back to Forest Park." Val yawned. "Hugs, hugs," she said, reaching for each of her friends.

After Val and Jackie hugged everyone, Val headed toward her car and Jackie climbed into her vehicle. Tricee and Pam walked toward Tricee's car.

"Where did you park?" Tricee asked as she unlocked her door.

"On the street. The parking lot was full."

"I'll give you a ride to your car."

Tricee picked up a couple of books that were in her passenger seat and tossed them to the back seat. Pam's cell phone rang as soon as she got into the vehicle.

"I'm on my way home now. The service just let out," she said to her husband. After she got off the phone, she looked over at Tricee.

"May I ask you a question?"

"What's that?" Tricee replied as she turned out of the parking lot.

"What made you go to the altar—if I'm not being too nosy?"

Tricee exhaled.

"I'm sorry." Pam immediately regretted asking. "I shouldn't have asked." It was the expression on her friend's face that made her want to take her question back. But she could sense that there was something on Tricee's mind.

"I just felt the need for some prayer, that's all."

She thought about her little spat, if you could call it that, with Hunter right before she left for the service. And she had done exactly what the minister had suggested, which was turn it all over to the Lord.

"Is everything okay, Tricee?"

"Yeah, everything's fine. Hunter and I just had a small disagreement. It's no big deal."

"Okay. I'm just making sure."

"What about you? Did you enjoy the service?" Tricee pulled in front of Pam's vehicle.

"I did. It was a timely message. One I really needed to hear."

"Well, that's good. I'm glad you enjoyed it."

Pam reached over and gave Tricee a hug. "Thanks for the ride to my car. Get back to the north side safely."

Pam climbed into her vehicle. It had been a timely word, indeed. She'd wanted to share with Tricee that she had, indeed, met Jeff for lunch, just as she'd planned. She'd wanted to tell her because deep down she was hoping for a little advice. Actually, she was somewhat surprised that none of her three friends even asked about her lunch date. But after having just heard such a powerful sermon, she figured that her saga with Jeff was the farthest thing from their minds.

"Maybe I should have gone to the altar with Tricee," Pam mumbled as she drove onto the Dan Ryan Expressway.

Tricee walked into the kitchen and turned on the light. From the empty plate and glass that sat in the kitchen sink, it was evident that Hunter had made himself dinner. She glanced at the clock on the wall. She'd expected to arrive home before 10:00 PM, but the sermon had been well worth her walking into her condo at 10:30 PM. She poured herself a glass of orange juice and walked into the bedroom.

"Hey, Sweetie." Hunter sat up in the bed and turned on the lamp light. "How was the service?"

"I thought you were asleep. I was trying to be quiet." Tricee set her glass of juice on her nightstand and began to undress. "It was a powerful message." She looked forward to sharing it with him, but not tonight. All she wanted to share right now was their comfortable bed.

"I'm glad you had a good time." Hunter glanced at the glass of orange juice. "You're drinking juice this late? That's unusual." Tricee never drank orange juice in the evening.

"I was thirsty." She gave Hunter a half-smile and walked into the bathroom. The minister's words were still echoing in her mind.

"So what was the sermon about?" Hunter called out. He was interested to know if it had touched on the subject of family. He wasn't ready to adopt. In fact, he didn't know if he'd ever be ready for kids. But he couldn't bring himself to share this with his wife.

"She based her sermon on the book of Hebrews, mostly," Tricee said, emerging from the bathroom wearing an oversized red T-shirt. She noticed her husband's expectant expression but decided not to continue. It was late and she did have an early Friday to look forward to. They both did.

"Hmmm. Interesting," said Hunter. He watched his wife as she kneeled down to pray. After she slipped under the covers, he turned toward her. She planted a kiss on his lips.

"Yep, it was very interesting. Good night, Dear."

Tricee noticed that Hunter hadn't bothered to apologize for earlier, but she decided to write it off as no big deal. She reached over him, turned off the light and turned over.

"I forgot to tell you I saw Pam today." He wrapped his arms around his wife's waist. "She was with a colleague. They'd just had lunch."

"Was it a guy?" Tricee turned to face her husband. He could see the curious expression on her face in the dark. She almost looked alarmed.

"It was a guy. Why?"

"I was just wondering," Tricee replied, turning over again. "Good night."

"Is there something you're not telling me?"

"No. I was just asking."

Tricee said goodnight once more and closed her eyes. *We have our own issues,* she thought. *We need to address what's going on with you.*

12

"I'm picking up the girls tonight. I thought I'd bring them over to spend Friday evening with us." Conner's announcement caught Pam by surprise. He'd just seen his daughters on Tuesday. She'd even allowed them—well, the nice one anyway—to try on her new pair of ankle-strap knee-high boots. When she asked Pam why she'd bought boots in the spring, Pam explained the whole buy-early-for-great-sales strategy. The girl had listened intently while her sister remained quiet.

The girls were as different as night and day. While Connis was outspoken and friendly, Raneen was quite the opposite. Pam thought the child must have inherited all of her mother's traits. If she hadn't been just a kid, Pam would have referred to her as wicked. Instead, she referred to her as the little "unpleasant seed." It sounded a little better.

"It would've been nice to have known this earlier." Pam spoke abruptly. There was no mistaking her harsh tone. She was at work with only 50 things that needed to get done. It wasn't that she had a problem with him seeing his daughters, it was just that she'd made plans for them to go out to dinner. She hadn't mentioned her dinner plans because she assumed her husband would be readily available. She was already trying to keep the spark alive in their very new marriage.

"I didn't realize it would be such a big deal." Conner kept his voice low. He was in the break room at work. The last thing he needed was for the other drivers to hear him disagreeing with his wife. "What do you have against us spending time with my girls?"

"Conner, don't go there. I spent time with your girls on Tuesday."

"Yeah, all of about 30 minutes." He hadn't meant to say that out loud.

"I'm sorry, Sweetheart. I didn't mean that." His apology was sincere but Pam was not buying it.

She'd been very cordial to his daughters when he brought them by on Tuesday. He hadn't expected anything less than kindness. But he knew that his ex-wife could rub Pam the wrong way. He didn't think it was done on purpose; the two women were just very different. He and Pam hadn't spent much time with his twins together in their five months of matrimony. He always invited her along whenever he knew he'd have the twins. Pam only managed to *not have something else to do* on a couple of occasions.

He would usually take the twins to whatever place they had in mind. Garrett Popcorn Shops was a favorite. And then there was Home Run Inn Pizza on the city's southwest side. The girls only had to say a "please, daddy" and his heart would melt. Normally, he'd take them home after spending the day with them. But on Tuesday, he'd picked them up after he'd gotten off work, and brought them back to his home. He and Renita had decided that she would pick them up. She'd had an evening appointment she knew would probably run a little long.

When he and the twins arrived on Tuesday, Pam had been busily working on her laptop. She stopped what she was doing and gave the twins her undivided attention. Actually, she gave Connis her attention. Raneen hadn't wanted any. She wanted no part of Pam's and Connis' bonding, even after her father convinced her to join them. He'd heard Pam and Connis laughing and talking, and he'd had a good laugh when Connis came into the living room wearing Pam's new boots. He figured that, in time, Raneen would learn to share in the fun. He saw no reason to pressure a 10-year-old girl who was obviously shy. Pam didn't agree. She thought Raneen's behavior was meanness, not shyness.

"Conner, I need to go. I have a lot of things to do."

"I am sorry," he apologized once more, "look, why don't we all go out to dinner? And then we can watch a movie."

"I'll have to see. We'll talk later."

After ending the call with her husband, Pam thought about the sermon from the previous night. During her drive home, she'd listened to a CD that her aunt had given her. The topic was what to do when the enemy strikes and what to do when you feel your marriage is under attack. Two powerful messages in one night couldn't be a coincidence. She decided to call Conner back and apologize, and to tell him she'd made reservations at one of his favorite restaurants. The call went straight to voicemail.

"Conner, it's me." She paused and looked up as her colleague, Darcy, walked into her office. *I need to start keeping my door closed,* she noted to herself. She released the call but kept her cell phone in her hand. "Can you excuse me a moment? Personal phone call."

Her colleague whispered an "I'm sorry" and backed out of her office. Pam redialed her husband's number and left her voicemail message. When she stepped outside of her office, she saw Darcy chatting with one of the other social workers. She excused herself when she saw that Pam was free.

"I'm sorry. Your door was open so I assumed it was safe to enter."

"That's quite alright. I should close my door when I make private calls. What's going on?" Pam observed a stack of folders in Darcy's arm. That was a good sign. It meant she had a lot of work to do, which meant the chat would be brief.

"I've just been assigned a new case. A client who's just gotten out of a bad situation," she began explaining. She looked more tired than usual. Pam couldn't help but wonder if she and her husband had resolved the issue with the ex-girlfriend's visit. Knowing Darcy, she probably threatened to leave her husband if the issue didn't resolve itself.

"They're all cases where the situation is bad, Darcy. That's why we're here." She gave her colleague a warm smile. In some ways, Pam felt that she and Darcy had more in common than they'd realized.

"You're right. But I just feel really bad for this woman. She's been attending church on a semi-regular basis, so my guess is that she's really trying to get it together."

"Well, that's why we're here. Have you met her?" Pam laughed, realizing she'd just repeated herself.

"What's so funny?"

"I can't believe I said that's why we're here twice. That sounded very bad."

"I hadn't even noticed." Darcy yawned. "Excuse me. I didn't get much sleep last night." Her cell phone rang but she ignored it. "No I haven't met her. I will on Monday, no I mean Tuesday, Memorial Day holiday is on Monday. I don't know yet if she will be staying at the shelter," she adjusted the folders she was holding, "anyway, I came to ask if you wanted to go to lunch."

frustrated. "I do understand," she said and left it at that.

Pam was more than willing to have lunch with Darcy, but only if she had a productive morning. She'd already planned to eat at her desk for lunch and she'd wanted to ensure that her newest client made her way to the second floor this afternoon to look through the clothes. Not only that, she now had to consider whether to join Conner and the twins for dinner after canceling the dinner reservations she'd already made. And then, of course, there was Jeff. Two powerful spiritual messages and an invitation from her husband hadn't been enough to erase him completely from her mind.

Pam decided to try to reach her husband once more. Realizing his break was over, she knew she'd probably get his voicemail again. She was just about to dial his number when her cell phone rang. She looked at the name displayed above the number: Tricee Hatchett.

"Hi, Tricee. What's up?"

"Oh, nothing. Just had a few minutes and thought I'd give you a call."

"Is everything okay?" Pam raised an eyebrow. While it wasn't unheard of for her to receive calls from her friends while she was at work, it was a rare occasion.

"Everything's fine." Tricee paused. "Pam, Hunter mentioned to me last night that he saw you with a guy. He said it was a co-worker."

"Okay." Pam raised the other eyebrow.

"Well, I remembered you said you were meeting Jeff for lunch. It's not my business, I was just wondering, that's all."

"It was Jeff. You're correct in your assumption, Tricee."

"Okay. I just thought I'd tell you that Hunter saw you. No biggie."

There was a brief silence. Pam broke it first.

"Thanks for telling me. I guess I need to be more careful, huh?"

She chuckled lightly but Tricee sensed a bit of awkwardness from her friend.

"Pam, what you do is your business." Tricee didn't know what else to say. "We'll chat later, okay? I need to get to a meeting."

Pam got off the phone with Tricee and sat still at her desk for several minutes. Hunter didn't know Jeff. It could very well have been a co-worker. But it wasn't. This could get complicated. Even though she knew Tricee wouldn't be a blabber mouth—at least she didn't believe she'd be one—it didn't feel right. Hunter knew and liked Conner.

Pam picked up her desk phone and dialed her colleague's extension. "Hi, Darcy," she began, stapling the stack of papers that lay before her. "I think having lunch with you will do me some good. It'll help to take my mind off some things."

13

"You tried to call me back." Conner spoke into his earpiece as he turned onto the street where his ex-wife resided with their two daughters. He hoped Pam had changed her mind and decided to hang out with him and the twins after all. He had the evening all planned—the twins would stay overnight. He hadn't yet shared this piece of information with his wife.

"Yes, I did try calling you back. I left you a voicemail."

"Yeah, I got the message. But there was a 'missed call' from you shortly after your first call."

"Well, I saw no need to leave another message."

Pam walked over to one of the kitchen drawers in search of some aspirin. She kept Advil and Aleve in her desk drawer at work. It seemed to come in handy for her co-workers. Conner didn't believe in taking aspirin of any kind, so they rarely kept any in the house. That would soon change. She wasn't one to suffer headaches frequently, but after her brief chat with Tricee earlier, she had a bad one.

She needed to just put an end to all this drama with Jeff. She certainly didn't need any drama, but that was what it was starting to become. A simple phone call that lasted for all of five minutes had caused her great stress. Being told that Hunter had seen her with another man wasn't exactly the outcome she'd been looking for. Pam found herself wondering if anyone else they knew, other than Hunter, had also seen her and Jeff together.

"So are you with the girls?"

"Yes." Conner unfastened his seat belt. "I just pulled in front of their house so, technically, I am."

"Have a fun evening." Pam removed the small packet of Aleve from the drawer. *Perfect!* she thought. She swallowed the capsules and then chased them with a swig of water. "I actually had dinner plans for us," she said, setting the glass in the sink. "I guess I should've told you, but I was hoping for it to be a surprise."

"Aw, Babe, you should've just told me."

She could hear the disappointment in her husband's voice, but figured that this, too, shall pass.

"I was hoping you'd change your mind and join us. We could still have dinner. It would be the four of us. It would be fun."

Yeah. Lots of fun hanging out with one happy twin and one evil one. The thought almost escaped her lips. "Maybe next time. You go ahead and enjoy your quality time."

"I'm starting to think you don't love my daughters," Conner laughed. It wasn't a serious comment. It was meant to elicit a giggle from his wife before he shared the next piece of information. "Uh, Babe? The girls are spending the night. I plan to take them home tomorrow afternoon, or maybe first thing in the morning. Renita has something to do this evening."

"Uh …," Pam stammered. Conner waited to see if she would finish her thought. When she didn't he spoke again.

"I was going to tell you, actually." He looked up and saw that his ex-wife had opened the front door. She was probably wondering who he was talking to and figured it must have been an important call.

"Hey, look. I'd better get the girls. I'll call you once I get back in the car." Conner got out of his vehicle and walked to the front door.

"It would've been nice to know Conner, that you were bringing your girls back here this evening." There was no missing the irritability in Pam's voice. And any time she inserted his name into the middle of a sentence, he knew she was serious.

"Yeah, I know. Let's talk about it later, okay?" He gave Renita a smile as he heard the click in his ear. *She hung up on me. Oh, boy. It's going to be an interesting evening back at the Buckner household,* he thought.

"Daddy!" the twins squealed in unison.

"Can we have pizza?"

"Try 'may we have pizza?'" Renita corrected Raneen's grammar. She was so fond of her daughters and hoped they'd

184

never have to endure the trauma she'd endured when she was younger. Though she believed her daughters looked like both her and Conner, most people thought Raneen was the spitting image of her mother.

"*May* we have pizza?" Raneen looked up at her dad and smiled.

"I don't want pizza. I have my taste buds for something else." Connis spoke with such authority. Conner thought she was a lot like her grandmother—his mother—who was strong and in charge. For a 10-year-old, the girl knew exactly what she wanted.

"So your taste buds want something other than pizza?" Conner asked. He and Renita smirked at their daughter's comment. They both wondered how she even knew what taste buds were.

Connis nodded in response to her father's question while Raneen made another plea for pizza.

"I want pizza and lemonade," she said, then turned and headed for the bedroom she shared with her sister. "Daddy, can I—may I bring my princess movie?" she called from down the hall.

"Sure, Sweetie," Conner answered and turned to Renita. "I need to change out of this uniform." He held up his gym bag.

After changing into a navy blue gingham shirt and a pair of jeans, he and Renita chatted briefly. They agreed that he'd drop the girls off by 11:00 AM tomorrow morning, then he and the twins were out the door.

The twins had been invited, sort of last minute, to a birthday party on Saturday at noon. From what the parent who was throwing the party had shared, the party had been a last minute decision. The phone call had come right before Conner arrived to pick up his daughters.

Renita had already promised her daughters that they could spend Friday night with their dad—well, with their dad and Pam. And she figured she could use some time alone after her Friday evening session. Twice a week she attended a counseling session with a trained psychiatrist, a 60 year old black woman, who helped those with unresolved issues. Renita often said that had it not been for the woman's pleasant and caring demeanor, she'd have ended the sessions a long time ago. But this woman had been a Godsend.

After the twins left, happily trailing their dad, Renita brushed her hair, pulled it back into a bun and grabbed her purse. *Friday evening and I'm off to discuss my problems with a woman I don't know well but whom I can trust,* she thought bitterly. *Some life.*

"Mom, Pam let me try on her new boots," Connis had shared enthusiastically in the car Tuesday evening during the drive home. Renita and the twins resided in the Beverly area, on the south side of Chicago. The drive from the Buckners' Hyde Park home was about 30 to 40 minutes. She didn't know if she could tolerate her daughter going on and on about Pam's new boots. Renita did notice that Raneen, on the other hand, never really talked about Pam. Oh well. No big surprise there, since Connis was the outspoken one. Renita brushed it off as normal. But the "Pam this" and "Pam that" from Connis could get old really quick.

Conner dialed his wife's cell phone only to get her voicemail. He left a message informing her of his whereabouts: Dave & Busters restaurant. It had been a while since he'd been there and the twins had never been there, at least not with him. The games and the variety of food offered would be a perfect way to spend a Friday night. His only regret was that Pam hadn't joined them. Maybe once they got back home, she'd be up for watching the princess movie. But he doubted that very seriously. For him, an action movie would be a better way to unwind. Pam could keep the girls company while he enjoyed the DVD he hadn't yet gotten around to watching.

Pam listened to her husband's message as she climbed into her vehicle. The night was still young at 7:15 PM and there was plenty of time to do something enjoyable on a Friday night. She'd spoken to Jackie right after having talked to Conner earlier.

"He could have told me his daughters were spending the night. I need to be prepared."

"Oh, Pam." Having a daughter herself, as well as two stepdaughters, Jackie showed no sympathy. "You inherited the man's kids when you said 'I do.'"

"That's not the point," Pam retorted, eager to express her views. "It's a matter of consideration."

"Mmm hmm," was all Jackie would say. She had learned over time that it was best to just allow Pam to vent. She would say what she had to say, though. That wasn't about to change.

Before they hung up, Jackie got around to asking Pam about her lunch date with Jeff. Pam simply replied, "It was nice." There was no way she was going to share with Jackie what Tricee had told her. The conversation would have taken a whole other turn.

Well, Jackie and Lem had plans, as did Val and Cory, so Pam decided to take a drive and possibly go somewhere for takeout. Calling Tricee was out of the question. She wasn't ready to chat with her just yet. Besides, she and Hunter probably had plans of their own as well.

Pam found herself parked in front of her favorite place for fish and chips and paused before getting out of her car. Fish and chips—along with a slice of peach cobbler she knew she didn't need—while sitting in front of the television sounded good. It would be at least a couple of hours before Conner and the twins came home. It would make for a relaxing evening alone. She could pretend to be asleep as soon as she heard Conner put the key in the front door.

He'd said in his voicemail message that he'd be taking the girls home by 11:00 AM. This was good. This way, she'd only have to spend breakfast with them, at best. Pam thought about how she'd said recently to Tricee that she wanted to bond with Conner's daughters, and she did. But her feelings went back and forth. It seemed it was going to take effort, and she hadn't realized it until now.

She reached for her cell phone. *I could have fish and chips or I could drive downtown to the Westin Hotel,* she thought, scrolling through her phone until she reached Jeff's number—she hadn't deleted it this time. He answered on the second ring.

14

"When was the last time you spoke with Annette?" Hunter asked Tricee before taking a sip of his iced tea. It was a little weak but it would have to do. He was certain the food would be prepared to perfection.

He'd heard a lot about the fairly new restaurant in the south loop from a couple of his colleagues. "You have to try the grilled pork chops! And get the grilled corn salsa to go with it!" a young female colleague raved after he mentioned he was thinking about checking the place out Friday evening. She was a young lady who'd just become an education consultant and she was forever talking about the various restaurants she frequented with her fiancé. Hunter wondered if the young couple's goal was to hit every restaurant in the Windy City.

Though his other colleague, a recent widower in his late 50s, had shared that the food was good, his level of excitement was nowhere close to the young lady's. In fact, he had shaken his head when he heard her excitedly discussing several of the dishes with Hunter. "Young folks these days don't believe in home-cooked meals," he'd said under his breath.

Tricee sipped her raspberry lemonade, which was tasty, but a little too sweet.

She frowned before she responded. "I talked to her last week. She's fine and the family's fine—though she did say Niesa had come down with a terrible cold."

"How old are her kids, again?" Children wasn't exactly what he wanted to discuss, but it seemed a fitting question to ask since Tricee had mentioned the girl.

"Niesa's 6 and Nelson is 7. They're getting so big! I can't wait to see them again."

Learning two years ago that she and Annette, her best friend since third grade, were half-sisters had been plenty stressful. While Annette had taken the news better than Tricee, other than her desire to go off on their father J.P, she still had so many questions for him. Unlike Tricee, who still had two living biological parents, Annette had only J.P. to unload upon. Her mother had passed away several years ago. The news had, indeed, been a shocker, but Annette didn't believe it would've been fair to dump on Ruby, Tricee's mother. So after hearing the shocking news via a telephone call, the only question Annette had asked was, "Are you 100% certain?" To which Ruby had replied, "Dear, I wish it wasn't so. But, yes, I'm certain."

It had taken Tricee a couple of weeks to finally call Annette and have a much-needed chat. The whole situation felt weird. But after being on the phone for close to three hours, Tricee led them in prayer and they both decided to lean upon God for understanding.

Annette had even joked before they hung up the phone, "Now pray that the Lord gives me the strength to hold my tongue when I call J.P. to ask him why he helped to create such a mess! And if his answer doesn't make sense, which I'm sure it will not, I'm on the next thing out to Louisville to personally hit him upside his head with my new pumps!"

Tricee had saved her frustration with her father for last, dealing with Ruby first. Her relationship with her father hadn't been strained like her relationship with her mother. Although she let her father know she was none too happy with the turn of events and the part he played in them, it was Ruby who'd caused more of the pain. It seemed unfair, yes, but that's just the way it worked out.

Annette and Tricee had decided, a couple months after learning the well-kept secret, to visit J.P. in Louisville, Kentucky, where he still resides. It started off as a very tense visit, with J.P. apologizing profusely, but by the time they left, all was well— well, as much as it could be—between them.

"I think I might make a trip to St. Louis this summer," Tricee stated as she picked up the menu. "I think we should plan a trip there together since you've never been."

"Yeah. I enjoyed meeting Annette and her kids when they were here," Hunter replied, without looking at his wife. He was studying the menu hard even though he already knew what he wanted to order.

Tricee looked across the table at her husband. Maybe the thought of visiting St. Louis, her hometown, and where Annette still resided, wasn't very exciting to him. She suddenly blurted out, "You seem distant. Are you okay?"

Hunter set his menu back on the table. "Yeah, Babe, I'm fine." He smiled, showing the dimple in his left cheek that had hooked her when they first met.

A few seconds later, the server, a white woman with black hair, approached their table. She looked to be in her early 30s, but the obvious tan she got from a tanning bed made her skin look a little rough, especially around the eyes.

"I'll have the grilled pork chops and the spinach penne salad." Hunter decided to forego the grilled corn salsa.

"And I'll try the chicken paillard with cherry sauce and parsley rice," Tricee ordered, feeling adventurous.

Hunter nodded at his wife's choice. "You're letting your hair down, I see."

"Yeah," Tricee laughed. "I think I should stop being so boring."

She'd wanted to ask Hunter this morning why he hadn't apologized to her last night, for basically ignoring her when she'd commented on him missing church. But then she remembered deciding to blow it off as no big deal. Well, it *was* a big deal, despite what she'd decided. When Tricee awoke this morning it was still on her mind. To her it had felt like a couple's spat. But maybe to him it had simply been a few words exchanged that didn't warrant an apology. He'd asked this morning, after an early-morning session of intimacy, if she was okay. She'd grinned and responded, "I'm fine. It's just funny how our disagreeing doesn't seem to affect our lovemaking." There had been some truth in her statement. The man saw no reason to apologize but still wanted to feel good before going to work.

Their food arrived and, after saying grace, they dug in. Hunter's young colleague had been right. The grilled pork chops were delicious, as was the spinach salad.

"How's your chicken paillard?" Hunter asked his wife, though by the faces she was making, he already knew the answer.

"Oh, my! It's sooo good. I'm glad you suggested we come here."

"Anything for the woman I love." He took a sip of his water before speaking again. "Actually, my colleague recommended that I order the grilled corn salsa, but the spinach penne salad seemed to go better with the pork chops."

"Oh," Tricee waved her fork at her husband as she spoke, "I can make grilled corn salsa for you. I have a recipe for that."

Hunter raised his eyebrows. "Really? I've never even had that. Is that a black person staple? It sure doesn't sound like it. But my colleague's black." He shrugged.

Tricee chuckled at her husband's assessment of the dish and its popularity among ethnic groups. If it didn't sound like something black folks ate, he was quick to point it out. He kept her in stitches with his humor.

"You are too funny, Honey. One of my co-workers gave me the recipe a few years ago. And, no, she's not black. She's from El Salvador." Tricee paused. "But her fiancé is African American. But that doesn't matter—a delicious dish is a delicious dish."

Hunter nodded. He loved the cute way his wife would explain things.

"Anyway," Tricee continued, "I made it once before we met. You use a few ears of sweet corn, a yellow squash—maybe two depending on how much you are making—a red sweet pepper, some red onions and a tomato."

Hunter listened intently while he continued to shovel food onto his fork and then into his mouth. Tricee stopped talking long enough to take a few sips of her raspberry lemonade. Then she helped herself to a few more bites, wiped her mouth with her napkin and continued.

"You use olive oil, white balsamic or cider vinegar, some basil leaves, salt, garlic powder and dried oregano."

"Wow. Sounds like it takes a while to prepare." Hunter was impressed.

"You just have to remove the kernels from the cobs and cut the squash, pepper, and onions into bite-sized pieces." Tricee shrugged. "But that's all there is to it."

Hunter sat back in his chair. "Woman, is there anything else about you I don't know?"

Tricee responded in a deep voice, "Yeah, uh, I used to be a man."

Hunter almost choked on his water, laughing. It wasn't so much of a shock that she'd never mentioned the dish, it had just been interesting to learn yet another thing about his wife that he didn't know. She was a good cook, no doubt. But he just assumed he'd sampled and eaten all of her dishes.

"Well, again, I still say that no black person—other than you—would make a dish like that. Your co-worker's fiancé is one lucky brother."

"Excuse me?" Tricee gave her husband the no-he-didn't expression. "What does that mean?"

Hunter laughed. "Aw, girl. You know I don't mean it like that. I'm just saying he has the benefit of tasting probably a lot of interesting and delicious dishes, that's all."

"Okay. I thought that was what you meant."

Hunter adored his wife. He knew when he saw her at the coffee shop two years ago that she was the one. The fact that she hadn't been wearing a ring on her left hand is what prompted him to ask her to meet him back at the coffee shop the following Saturday. Paul, Tricee's friend who'd met her at the coffee shop that evening, had posed no threat to him in any way. And now that they were married, he was comfortable with his wife's friendship with Paul. They only spoke every now and then, and that was fine with him.

Now, as his wife sat across from him wearing the outfit he'd helped her pick out—a knee-length light blue dress and matching shrug—he thought back to this morning when he sensed there was something bothering her. They were having a relaxing dinner, the environment was cozy and he wanted to know what it was. He still didn't want to get too deep into the other conversation he knew would have to take place soon.

"Sweets?" He rarely called her that. "What was wrong with you this morning? You had an expression on your face like something was bothering you."

The server reappeared. After ordering a slice of lemon cake to go, Hunter asked for the check. The server smiled and disappeared. She looked very tired by now. Tricee wondered if the woman's shift was ending soon.

"It wasn't my lovemaking was it?" Hunter teased.

"You're crazy." Tricee shook her head and giggled. "I can gua-ran-tee you it wasn't that." She said it slowly, emphasizing the word guarantee.

Hunter laughed. "Good. For a minute I was worried."

Tricee took the bait. Now was a perfect time to ask him why he hadn't bothered to apologize. If there was one thing she told herself she'd try to do in her marriage, it was wait for the right opportunity to bring up anything that was bothering her.

"You didn't even bother to say you were sorry when I got home last night. I mean, we did have a disagreement, that much was obvious. The fact that you didn't say you were sorry just bothered me," she admitted, reaching into her purse for her lip gloss.

"Oh, Babe. Why didn't you just say that then?" Hunter hadn't realized that his failure to apologize had caused his wife distress. Maybe it was unintentional selfishness on his part, but he hadn't thought anything more about their disagreement.

Tricee applied the gloss and placed the tube back into her purse. "I just don't want to make a big deal over a thing, that's all. But from now on, when something's bothering me, I'm going to tell you." She frowned, unaware of her expression.

"I'm sorry. Really, I am." Hunter reached across the table and took his wife's hand. "Now stop frowning," he said and kissed the back of her hand.

"I didn't even know I was frowning. One more thing," Tricee began, just before noticing the server approaching again. "I'll tell you later," she whispered.

After Hunter paid the bill, they grabbed their light jackets off the backs of their chairs and headed for the door. Hunter excused himself to go to the men's room. As Tricee waited for him, she was shocked to see Pam and Jeff enter the restaurant through a set of double doors. She immediately turned away, hoping to avoid eye contact. Though she wasn't exactly sure why, her action had been for Pam's sake, not hers. Unfortunately, she'd been standing too close to the door.

"Uh, Tricee, hi." She could sense the awkwardness in Pam's greeting.

"Hey. Just had dinner with Hunter." *This feels really awkward for me, too.*

"Oh. Well, this is Jeff. Jeff, Tricee." It was a quick and awkward introduction. A few seconds later, Hunter emerged from the men's room.

"Right this way, please." The hostess led Pam and Jeff away.

Once Tricee and Hunter were inside their vehicle, it was Hunter who spoke first. "I think that was Pam's co-worker. The one I saw her at lunch with yesterday." Hunter wasn't so sure that this guy was actually a co-worker but he chose not to say anything, at least not now.

"Oh, okay," Tricee responded, thinking that this was a perfect time to change the subject. "So what I was going to say before our much-tanned server appeared was, the next time you fail to apologize, don't even think about asking for any. I'm serious." She *was* serious but it was hard not to laugh.

"Okay. I get that." Hunter smiled, then reached over and placed his hand on his wife's knee. They could have so many of these moments together *without* children. Being able to come and go when they pleased sounded perfect to him. *Surely, this thing will work itself out,* he thought silently. *I'll just let you lead me, Father. But please tell me something before we meet with these folks from the adoption agency. I'm just not feeling this.*

He also thought about Pam and that guy. Surely, there was something else going on. He'd been willing to believe the guy was a co-worker when he'd seen them yesterday during lunch hours, but this evening was different. It didn't add up. And he was certain his wife knew some details. He would ask her when they got home.

It's going to be so great having kids around. Hunter is going to make a great father. I can't wait to meet with the folks at the agency. Tricee was willing to overlook her husband's imperfections—after all, everyone had them. But she did feel better after telling him how she felt about him not apologizing. If they were going to add little ones to the household one day soon, it was imperative that they work on these things. It was imperative that they worked on them anyway.

Now the church thing—that still needed to be discussed and she'd get to that soon. Only one thing at a time, she reminded herself. But Hunter was sadly mistaken if he thought he was going to just stop attending church. No way was he going to set that kind of example for their children.

Tricee was lost in her thoughts on the way home: *I was going to ask Hunter what he thought about Pam getting together for lunch with a guy she used to date, but it seems like Pam is getting together for more than just lunch. I don't even want or need to know what he thinks now. I hope he doesn't even bring it up.*

She smiled as her husband turned their SUV into their parking garage. Tomorrow, after she completed her Saturday errands, she'd give Pam a call and maybe invite her to lunch. She felt the need to discuss some things with her friend without making it appear as if she was prying. Pam had to have known how awkward she felt seeing her with Jeff instead of her husband of five months. Tricee was afraid that things were about to become more complicated for Pam. In fact, they already were.

15

That was awkward, Pam thought as she and Jeff followed the hostess to their seat. When she decided to meet Jeff this evening, she had no idea she'd run into one of her friends. It was funny that it had been Tricee, too. She'd just called Pam this afternoon to inform her that Hunter had seen her with Jeff yesterday. And now here she was with Jeff again running into both Tricee and Hunter. This wasn't a part of the plan.

"Your server will be right with you." The young lady smiled and walked away.

Pam gave the establishment a quick once-over. It was nice. The artful décor on the walls caught her attention. One piece was an image of a café with the word France written across the bottom. Now that was someplace she'd always wanted to visit. She'd suggested a city in France to Conner for their honeymoon. She felt Paris would've been the ideal place. But Conner's heart had been set on a cruise in the Caribbean, so they spent five wonderful nights in Jamaica.

Pam had loved it! She'd been to Mexico and Puerto Rico and loved those places, as well, but being in Jamaica with the man she'd just taken as her husband had been a perfect picture. Now, as she sat across from Jeff in this restaurant, she couldn't resist asking him about his favorite places. Besides, it would help take her mind off the awkward moment she had a little while ago with Tricee.

"I like that artwork." She tilted her head in the direction of the picture. "I would love to go to Paris someday. Where's the one place you've always wanted to visit?"

The server appeared, set two glasses of water on their table and proceeded to take their orders.

Pam ordered the crusted salmon with lemon sauce and grilled corn salsa, while Jeff chose the chicken and Andouille gumbo.

"Good choices." The server smiled as he walked away.

Jeff resumed their conversation. "South Africa is on my list for early next year." He drank from the tall water glass. "And I guess Paris would be nice. I hear all about how romantic it is," he said, smiling warmly, the twinkle in his eye hard to miss.

Pam turned her head slightly and rubbed the back of her neck. *Here we go, again.* She knew she'd have to try her best to ignore any of his flirting this evening. This wasn't like two years ago when she was single. But to say she wasn't enjoying the moment would've been completely untrue.

When she'd called him and suggested they meet for tea or coffee, Jeff suggested the new restaurant in the south loop. He'd made plans to fit it into his schedule before flying back out to

Houston, so having dinner there with Pam was an ideal opportunity. On the drive over to his hotel, Pam contemplated what she'd say if he invited her up to his room. A simple "no, just meet me in the lobby" was what she'd decided to say. But to drive both cars didn't seem necessary, so the rental car remained at the hotel. Having to drive him back to the hotel could become an issue if he kept up this flirting.

"I would love to visit the Ivory Coast," Pam said, choosing not to acknowledge his flirtatious comment. "My cousin has been there twice and she loved it."

Pam gave Jeff the once-over. Dressed in dark slacks and a black shirt, he looked very casual and relaxed. Dressed in black pants and a fitted, green, V-neck top, she felt a little underdressed. But, of course, Jeff had commented on how nice she looked as soon as he'd seen her.

"Well, I'm sure you'll visit there in the future. If memory serves me correctly, you're a woman who knows what she wants."

The server arrived with their food and Pam processed his last statement. *Is he trying to imply something else?* she wondered. She thought back to two years ago. She overanalyzed then and she was overanalyzing now.

"Shall we bless the food?" Jeff's offer interrupted her thoughts.

"Sure." She bowed her head and recalled what he'd said during lunch yesterday about needing to get into the habit of blessing his food.

There was still so much she wanted to know, or felt the need to know. Jeff seemed to have changed some but he also seemed to have remained the same. This would likely be the last time they'd see each other for a while, so this was a perfect time for her to probe even more deeply than she had during lunch.

"How's your meal?" Jeff asked as he placed his fork on his plate.

"Oh, it's delicious." Pam wiped her mouth with her napkin, being careful not to speak until she'd swallowed. "I'm glad you suggested this place."

"So you've never been here before?"

Pam shook her head before sipping her too-sweet iced tea. "But I can see coming here again."

"Your friend, Tricee—was that her name?" The question caught her off guard. "I take it that was her husband?"

Pam sighed.

"Is there something wrong, Love—I mean—Pam?" He remembered her reaction yesterday when he'd called her that. But he figured her perplexed look now was likely due to them running into her friend, but he still had some questions of his own, too.

"Yes, that's her name and, yes, that was her husband."

A brief silence followed. The server appeared and refilled their glasses of iced tea and water. After informing the server that they didn't need anything else, Pam spoke as soon as the young man left the table.

"Jeff, I'm married as I'm sure you've realized by the ring."

"I know, and what a lucky man he is. How long have you been married?"

"Five months." She put a forkful of food into her mouth. She wondered if he'd ever get around to asking her that question in particular. Knowing him, he probably thought the whole thing through first. He was just that thorough in how he operated.

"You're happy?"

"Of course, I'm happy." Pam was almost offended.

"What about your position at the agency?"

"I enjoy it on most days," she admitted before finishing the rest of her iced tea.

"Tell me more about what you do." Jeff was genuinely interested. He was hoping, too, that she'd join him later at the hotel, just to chat.

Pam gave Jeff a few details about what her day at the agency/shelter consisted of and how she felt good at the end of the day. Unlike sales and the nice salary that had come with it, being a counselor helped her to really see a contribution to others.

But discussing her life and how things had worked out for her wasn't what she'd wanted to talk about all evening. It was time to turn the conversation around.

"Let's not talk about me. What about you? Is marriage a part of your plans for the future?"

Wow, she's direct, Jeff thought and chuckled.

"What's so funny?" Pam was half frowning which only made him chuckle some more.

"You really have a way about you when you ask questions," he answered. "But I don't mind." He finished his water before answering her initial question. "I'm not sure but it's a strong possibility."

His plate was empty with the exception of a few crumbs and Pam had consumed most of her meal with the exception of the grilled corn salsa.

"Hmph. Well, I can recall you being a bit commitment-shy when we dated." She couldn't believe she'd gone there but it felt good. Jeff gave a half-smile.

"Is that bad that I don't wish to rush into anything?"

"Of course not, as long as you're up front about it."

That might have sounded like the wrong thing to say given that they were both in different places, but it was obvious that there were still things Pam wanted—no, needed—to express. She glanced down at her watch.

"I need to get going soon. My life doesn't allow for staying out past midnight anymore."

"I see." Jeff picked up on the sarcasm. "I don't want to get you in trouble." *That's not the full truth,* he admitted to himself, knowing he still planned to ask if she would stick around after dropping him off at the hotel.

In spite of her plea that they split the bill, Jeff insisted on paying and leaving the tip. Once inside Pam's vehicle, he turned to face her.

"I know running into your friend and her husband was unexpected. I could sense that it was awkward for you."

Pam let out a deep sigh. "Well, what made it very awkward is the fact that her husband saw us at lunch yesterday." She wasn't going to mention it but it seemed fitting considering his comment.

"Oh, I see. I can understand that." He sat back against the leather interior as if pondering what to say next.

"I'm glad you understand. I'm not trying to get into anything complicated. I shouldn't have to say that. It should go without saying."

"It was lunch yesterday, tonight it was dinner," Jeff said simply as he fastened his seat belt.

"Yeah. Both you and I know that," said Pam as she thought the rest to herself. *But folks will reach their own conclusions.*

Pam fastened her seat belt. The time on her dashboard read 9:30 PM. Surely, she needed to get home as Conner and the twins were likely already there. She knew he'd called her cell phone earlier because she'd felt it vibrate.

Neither of them had said much on the drive back to the Westin Hotel. When Pam pulled in front of it, she left her engine running. Jeff had to have known that parking here on Michigan Avenue for more than 10 minutes was out of the question. That and she wanted to check her voicemail and call her husband.

"Thanks for dinner. Have a safe flight back to Houston."

Pam expected Jeff to smile and nod, thank her for joining him and make his way up to his room. But, as usual, Jeff had other thoughts.

"Can you spare another 15 minutes? I was hoping we could chat a little more. I might be leaving tomorrow afternoon and not Sunday as I'd originally planned."

"And what does that have to do with me?" Pam's expression and tone were serious. She knew exactly what his statement meant. Translation: Tonight will be my last chance to see you until my next visit.

"I just really enjoy your company." Now he was facing her. "And there's a parking garage only a block away."

It was as if he'd read her mind. Pam hesitated. *Does he really want me to believe that he wants me to park my vehicle in some expensive garage for only 15 minutes?* She wondered. "I need to make a phone call." Pam hoped her tone sounded as if she was in control.

"Okay. If you decide to hang out some more I'll meet you in the lobby. I'll wait for about 10 minutes." He winked as he climbed out of her car. Jeff knew exactly what he was doing and, though she didn't want to admit it, so did Pam.

16

Pam listened to her husband's voicemail message. He'd sounded slightly annoyed but it could have been that he was just very tired. *The girls and I are on our way home. I called home and you didn't answer so I assume you're still out. I'll see you later.* She was sort of surprised that Conner had attempted to reach her only once on her cell phone. When she tried to call him back, the call went straight to voicemail. She hadn't tried to reach him on their home phone.

When she finally arrived home after 11:00 PM, her husband and the twins were asleep. Conner was a deep sleeper but when Pam tiptoed into their bedroom, she saw his body move under the sheets. Not wanting to wake him, she dimmed the light switch on the football lamp that sat on the dresser. She stood still and waited to see if he would make another move but he lay motionless. She took a long, pink nightshirt from her top dresser drawer and headed for the bathroom.

As the warm water trickled down her body, she thought about the evening she'd just spent with Jeff. He still had a way of making her feel as if she was all that mattered. But she knew she had to resist his charms. If she had let her guard down totally tonight, there was no telling what would have transpired between them. It had taken all of her strength to not allow things to go any further than they had already. She'd stayed in his suite much longer than she'd planned. Fifteen minutes had been the plan— well, her plan at least—but that 15 turned into 45.

She was relieved to find her husband sound asleep. It was late, after all, and having to explain why she'd strolled in after 11:00 PM would have required too much energy. Actually, the more she thought about it, having to explain it any time of the day would have required more energy than she had to expend. She wasn't up for having to explain anything. She dried herself off with her big, blue bath towel and slipped the nightshirt over her head. She paused before leaving the bathroom. What if the shoe was on the other foot? What if it had been Conner strolling in after 11:00 PM and she had been the one asleep? How would she have responded? Pam shuddered at the thought. "Okay, Pam," she mumbled to herself. She closed her eyes and shook her head. "Don't go filling your head with crazy thoughts."

Pam's and Conner's master bedroom, with its spacious (depending on who you asked) bathroom, was one of her favorite spots in their home. When Pam's cousin, Maureen, visited shortly after Pam and Conner got married, she was quick to voice her opinion. "This is a beautiful home. I love the master bedroom. But the bathroom seems a little small to me." Upon hearing Maureen give an account of all she liked and disliked about their home, Conner had been about to respond until he looked at his wife.

Pam was shaking her head, mouthing, *Just let it go*. Then as soon as Maureen was out of earshot, Pam whispered to her husband, "That's just her way, Baby. I've learned to let it be." Conner's reply had been simply, "Okay. But if she keeps it up, this will be her last invite to the Buckner home. Who does she think she is? Our *personal* interior decorator?" Pam couldn't help but to laugh at her husband's reaction to her cousin. While Maureen enjoyed professional success as an interior decorator, Pam sometimes wondered if, perhaps, Maureen's attitude about her success was the reason she was still single.

Pam tiptoed into the bedroom and reached over to turn off the football lamp. As soon as she slid under the covers, she was startled by the sound of her husband's voice.

"Where have you been?"

Silence.

Conner sat up and turned on the small lamp on his nightstand. "I tried to call you here at home. I assumed you'd be in at least by 10:00, Pam."

"I got your message. I was on the way home and when I tried to call you back, you didn't pick up." *Now let me go to sleep,* Pam pleaded mentally. This was the answer that made the most sense to her and it was the truth. But she knew Conner wasn't done. She could feel the tension filling their bedroom.

"Okay. But you didn't answer the question." Conner was sitting with his back against the headboard. "Were you out with your girlfriends?"

A 'yes' would have ended the discussion. Conner trusted his wife and realized that an occasional girl's night out was a very normal occurrence. But when he'd asked Pam earlier to join him and the twins for the evening, she'd revealed that she had originally made dinner plans for just the two of them. So it was highly unlikely that she'd gotten together with her girlfriends on such short notice.

Pam quietly exhaled, being careful not to show any hint of annoyance with the late-night interrogation. "I was not with my girlfriends." *Although I did run into Tricee, for crying in a bucket!* she added silently. "I had dinner since my plans to have dinner with my husband backfired on me." *Now let this answer suffice so we can both get some sleep.*

Deep down inside, Pam knew it was unfair to try to throw a guilt trip on Conner but she surely couldn't admit who she'd gone to dinner with. Besides, it's not like she *intended* to have dinner with Jeff. But it definitely wasn't worth the hassle. Pam decided right then that there would be no more lunches or dinners with Mr. Jeff. He had his life in Houston now. There was no reason to make things any more complicated. If he called, and surely he would, she would tell him it was best that they no longer speak. She would give him her best wishes and that would be it.

Conner was almost willing to accept that answer from his wife, but it sounded like a half-truth. And he didn't appreciate Pam's poor attempt at turning her unaccounted absence around and making it seem like he was to blame.

"You had dinner, I got that part. But you're leaving out some other details. And don't try to make me feel bad because of your dinner plans gone awry."

Pam was lying with her back to her husband and the last part of his comment made her raise an eyebrow. *Gone awry? You've never used that term before,* she noted. But before she could respond, Conner snatched at the light green blanket covering them, practically pulling it completely off his wife's body.

"So you're not going to explain to your husband why you came in close to midnight?" He abruptly stood up. "I'm going to ask you one more time." His voice was rising. "If you weren't at dinner with your friends, are you telling me that you were at dinner alone?"

Conner rarely showed anger or raised his voice. She should've just admitted that she had dinner with an ex. Knowing Conner, he would've been upset but just brushed it off until he was ready to discuss it further. Watching his reaction now, however, was unsettling and Pam couldn't bring herself to admit the truth. To say that this was becoming complicated was an understatement. Pam repeated in her head what she'd decided only seconds ago: This was so not worth it.

"I came in before midnight! You're exaggerating." Pam sat up in the bed and angrily tugged the sheet back over her. "I had dinner, Conner—alone! Now can we please get some sleep?!"

The look in her husband's eyes was one she hadn't seen before. She almost felt frightened. But then he told her to stop raising her voice when he was the one behaving as if he was auditioning for a Tyler Perry play. Her apprehension turned to indignation.

"*You* are raising *your* voice! Don't tell me not to raise my voice when yours can be heard all over Chicago!" Pam pounded her fist on the bed and pulled the blanket over her as she lay down again.

Conner walked around to Pam's side of the bed and grabbed the blanket. This time he pulled it completely off of her. He then made an attempt to pull the matching green sheet from her body as well. If Pam thought she was going to lay there and have a peaceful sleep, she was sadly mistaken. No one was going to sleep until the matter had been resolved to Conner's satisfaction.

Pam sat up again. "You better not grab this sheet off me!" she warned, her quick reflexes snatching the sheet before Conner could get a good grasp. "Jeff, you need to calm down!" She heard herself call her husband Jeff and tried to play it off. Maybe he hadn't heard her. "We're not here in this house by ourselves! Your daughters are in the next room!"

"My name's Conner." Suddenly Conner's voice was eerily normal and he was glaring at her.

Pam sat motionless on the bed. *Oh, goodness,* she thought. She started conjuring up every possible reason as to why they were arguing in the first place: His daughters were one reason. Had he joined her for dinner and not agreed to spend his Friday frolicking around the Windy City with two 10-year-olds, they'd likely be making intense love right about now. He could have spent all day Saturday with them or some other time. But no, he just had to choose the Friday night she'd tried to surprise him by making dinner reservations.

Pam got up from the bed and angrily picked up the blanket that had fallen to the floor. Conner grabbed it in an attempt to snatch it away from her but only succeeded in snatching Pam closer to him. Now they stood only a few feet apart, each one pulling the blanket toward their chest. Surely, the blanket had seen better days.

"You know you act like you're crazy at times!" Conner gave up the tug of war and angrily let the blanket fall from his hand. "You come waltzing in at odd hours of the night and expect for your husband not to question your whereabouts?!" His voice was loud again. He was very upset with his wife, more upset than he ever imagined he could be.

"You must not have cared that much, Conner, or you would have tried to reach me on my cell phone more than once! So don't try to pretend you're all upset now!" Pam realized that she probably wasn't making much sense though she couldn't help but wonder why Conner hadn't tried her cell phone, again, after not being able to reach her at home. Had it been her, she'd have tried to reach him until she was successful. Apparently they had different approaches when it came to handling certain things. And quite frankly, Pam wasn't feeling her husband's approach.

Conner continued to glare at his wife. He wasn't clueless as to what was going on. She was trying her best to turn this whole thing around any way she could. It was her way of not dealing with her mishaps. He was about to tell her about herself when there was a light knock on their bedroom door.

"Now see what you've done!" Pam tried to keep the frustration out of her voice. Conner grabbed at the blanket again before proceeding to their bedroom door. "Stop grabbing this blanket!" she said as forcefully but as quietly as she could.

"Daddy, what's wrong?" Raneen stood before her father wearing her princess nightgown. She looked over at Pam who attempted to crack a smile.

"It's nothing, Sweetie. Daddy and Pam are fine. We were talking and we just got sort of loud, that's all. Go back to bed, okay?" Conner reached for his daughter's hand and glanced at Pam before leading her back to the bedroom she was sharing with her sister.

"Yeah, go back to sleep, Evil Twin," Pam murmured under her breath. *Okay, forgive me, Father, that wasn't nice. But I'm upset right now,* she thought shamefully.

Raneen looked over her shoulder at Pam as she and her father left the room. Pam gave her a half-smile but it looked to Pam like Raneen rolled her eyes.

Conner tucked his daughter back into bed and then planted a kiss on her cheek. He crossed the room to where his other daughter, Connis, was sleeping soundly and planted a kiss on her cheek, too.

When he returned to his bedroom, Pam was sitting up in bed, her legs under the sheet. She'd put the blanket back on the bed. Conner removed the blanket, leaving Pam with only the sheet. She would have to go and get another blanket because Conner was taking this one.

"You sleep by yourself tonight. I'm too upset to be next to you. I'm not even going to ask you who Jeff is, Pam, because I know I am *not* going to like the answer." He grabbed his pillow and headed for the door.

Pam waved her hand at her husband. "Whatever."

"I'm taking the girls home in the morning and when I return, you should be prepared to talk to me like you have some sense."

Pam ignored her husband's statement. Then he paused and turned back before leaving the room. What he said next caught her by surprise.

"And if I'm still not satisfied with what you have to say, I suggest you have a bag packed."

That statement had been a hard one to ignore. Pam closed her eyes and a few moments later, wiped away the tear that was making its way down her cheek. The only thing she could think to do was whisper a sincere prayer: *Lord, this might be a premature request, but I am asking that you redeem my marriage as I need your direction. Surely, you can redeem matrimony just as you can redeem our souls. Amen.*

What a difference an hour made. One hour ago she'd put up a brave front. Now she was crying and hoping her husband's last statement had been made out of anger and hadn't been genuine. Only time would tell.

17

"Is it June 22nd yet? I'm ready for the school year to reach its *end*." Jackie sipped a hot cup of black coffee.

Tricee glanced at the menu before responding. "Why the extended school closing dates? Does it have anything to do with school days lost during the brutal winter?" Tricee smiled realizing she'd answered her own question.

"That would be correct. You're so smart, Tricee," Jackie teased.

Tricee had called her at 8:00 AM this morning, a little earlier than usual for a Saturday. But she had opened her eyes at 5:45 AM and couldn't go back to sleep. She carefully eased herself out of Hunter's still sleeping embrace and got out of bed. After going into the bathroom to freshen up, she drank a hot cup of peach tea while reading the Word. She opened her Bible to the book of 1 Corinthians and read the verse from chapter seven, the same verse she'd read one week prior. By the time 7:00 AM rolled around, she'd completed the remainder of 1 Corinthians and part of the second book. She wrapped up her Bible time with Chapter 121 from the book of Psalms.

Hunter woke up long enough to go to the bathroom and peek into the kitchen at his wife. He smiled warmly and retreated back to the bedroom. As she watched her husband walk away, she thought about seeing Pam and Jeff at the restaurant the previous night and the conversation she'd had with her husband over dinner. They had resolved their issue as far as the disagreement they'd had but Tricee's mind was still a little out of focus. Not to mention, her mother, Ruby, and her husband were coming for a visit next weekend. She made a mental note to call Pam and invite her to lunch. Though Pam's private affairs were her business, Tricee felt they really needed to chat.

"When does your teaching position begin?" Tricee asked after they placed their orders. She ordered a vegetable omelet while Jackie opted for waffles and turkey bacon.

"I have orientation on June 23rd, I think. The class starts the end of June and goes for about five weeks."

"You never know, you might decide to trade in your principal position and teach full time. The field of higher education can be quite rewarding, you know."

"Yes, Tricee, I know." Jackie smiled. "You remind me of that often." She mocked the sentiment she'd heard from her friend more than once. In her best Tricee voice, she said, "Jackie, with your Ph.D. in educational leadership, I can easily see you in a position at a university." They both laughed.

"You do sound like me." Tricee was well aware of how much Jackie enjoyed her position as a principal. And she realized it was a very rewarding career for her dear friend. But she still enjoyed ribbing her every now and then.

Their server, a young white male in need of a haircut, placed their meals before them. "Enjoy, Ladies. Let me know if I can get you anything else."

"How about the winning numbers for the lottery?" Jackie responded.

The young man tossed his head back and laughed. "Ma'am, if I had the winning numbers, I'd be as far away from here as possible." He gave a conspiratorial glance around the café. "But before I left, I'd tell my boss a few unkind things," he said quietly.

Tricee and Jackie chuckled as he winked and walked away. They blessed their meals and began to feast.

"Delicious!" said Jackie, "almost as good as the banana pancakes at our favorite restaurant on Broadway, Pancakes 2 Go."

"I started to ask you to meet me there but I figured it was only fair that we meet halfway. I didn't want you to have to drive all the way to the north side," Tricee replied, before taking a bite of her omelet.

"We could've met at that café near your job."

"They don't serve breakfast sandwiches, remember? We'd go there more for lunch or an early dinner."

"Oh, okay." Jackie swallowed before continuing. "Remember when the three of us met there that day two years ago? When Pam was complaining about Career Day?"

"How can I ever forget?" Tricee shook her head at the thought. Now, two years later, it was interesting that Jeff was still on the scene. The day Pam had complained at the café had also been the day Tricee had asked Pam to reconsider her relationship with Jeff. Now, to have seen them together last night seemed odd and a little ironic.

"Well, I like this café. So thanks for the invite. You didn't mind driving to Hyde Park?" Jackie wondered briefly if there was something wrong when Tricee called earlier. But she dismissed the thought and figured her friend was just up for one of their like-old-times moments.

"You're welcome. I just needed to get out this morning and treat myself. And, no, I didn't mind driving south. Had you not been available, I would've just gone to someplace up north. I had to clear my head though, so it's good that I didn't have to spend the morning talking to myself." Tricee smiled and Jackie decided to take the bait.

"Is something on your mind?" Jackie took a sip of water and waited for Tricee to reply.

"Not really. Well, there were a few things but I've already taken it to the Lord in prayer. I was up before 6:00 this morning, asking Him to prepare me for my mother's visit next weekend."

"Oh, that's right! I'm sure it will be a nice visit."

"It better be. I even washed my face and brushed my teeth before getting into the Word. I normally just climb out of bed and pray. But I didn't want to approach the throne of grace with morning breath."

Jackie laughed and practically spit out her mouthful of waffle. She composed herself as Tricee began to laugh at her friend's reaction.

"Girl, you are crazy! But I can just hear the Lord's voice now: *Uh, Tricee can you take care of your morning breath before you call on me?*"

"You know," Tricee continued, already feeling much better, "sometimes we don't consider Him like we should." She was near tears from her own joke.

They finished breakfast and Tricee paid the bill. She didn't tell Jackie she'd seen Pam and Jeff last night when Jackie asked her how she and Hunter spent their Friday night. She saw no reason to divulge that piece of information about their friend. But as they proceeded to their respective vehicles, she did bring up her husband.

"I think something is bothering Hunter but I don't know what it is."

"Oh?"

"Yeah." Tricee paused briefly. "But God has it under control. Keep me in your prayers, as I know you will."

"You know," Jackie suddenly remembered what she'd wanted to ask, "I wanted to ask you, Pam, and Val if you ladies would be up for our first Bible talk session early next week."

"Oh." Tricee looked puzzled. "Bible talk?"

Jackie gave her friend the side-eye. "Remember what we discussed at your place? When we were over for dinner?" She kept her gaze fixed on her friend. A few seconds later, Tricee responded, almost embarrassed.

"Oh, yeah, that! Sorry! I had a senior moment." It was now very obvious to Tricee that she had much on her mind these days.

"It happens." Jackie said, smiling. "But if it starts happening too much, I want you to promise you'll go and see a doctor."

"I will." Tricee shook her head. "Wow. Focus, Tricee, focus." She had been all for the idea and felt certain that Val and Pam would, also. She and Jackie agreed to discuss it more in detail and to share it with their other two friends. They embraced and promised to chat again before the weekend ended.

They headed home, Tricee driving north and Jackie driving south. Both of them were looking forward to the four of them meeting up again soon.

When Tricee pulled into her parking space back at her building, it was a little after 10:00 AM. She dialed Pam's number and left a voicemail message. A few minutes later, Pam returned her call but she was crying so hard, Tricee could barely make out what she was saying. *Bible talk is sounding better and better,* Tricee thought silently.

18

"Pam, what's wrong? I can barely make out what you're saying."

Tricee immediately regretted not calling her friend sooner. She wished she'd invited Pam to breakfast instead of Jackie. Maybe then whatever had her friend in tears could have been avoided. But instead of jumping to conclusions, she attempted to calm her friend down so she could find out exactly what was wrong. She thought back to last night when she'd seen Pam with Jeff at the restaurant and realized that might have something to do with her friend's tears. Tricee had been waiting for the elevator but decided to continue their conversation in the lobby.

Pam took a breath and started over. "Conner and I had an argument last night and he wants me out." The crying immediately started up again.

Tricee's mouth flew open. This was not what she'd expected to hear. What had happened when Pam arrived home last night? Did Conner find out about Jeff? Was her dear friend's marriage coming to an end after only five months? A series of questions flooded her mind. She felt badly for Pam. Conner wasn't just some guy she was seeing, he was her husband! Tricee smiled a greeting to a resident who lived in the building. As soon as the woman passed her, she turned her attention back to her friend.

"Try to calm down and tell me what happened. Do you need for me to drive over? I can be there in less than an hour."

Pam pondered her friend's request. That might not be such a bad idea. After all, she was home alone. Conner and his daughters had gotten up early, too early, for a Saturday morning. Pam knew that, had they not argued, there was no way he and the twins would have been up by 7:00 AM. By 7:30 AM, the three of them were eating cereal. She lay in her bedroom, where she'd slept alone. She'd awakened fairly early herself after tossing and turning for most of the night.

When Conner entered their bedroom this morning, she was awake, but neither of them said a word. He showered, got dressed and proceeded to go wake up his girls. By 8:00 AM, the three of them were walking out the door. The only thing he'd said to his wife was that he'd be home sometime in the afternoon. As much as Pam wanted him to stay so that they could talk, she just couldn't bring herself to say it. Instead, she just sat and cried off and on before deciding to call her sister Lynn.

Lynn, seven years younger, was the sister Pam called whenever she was in distress. It had been Lynn whom she called when she found out two years prior that Jeff had lied. He'd told

Pam he was going to Atlanta for the weekend but Pam and Tricee had seen him with Karen, an acquaintance of Tricee's who Pam was not particularly fond of. Tricee had introduced the two women at an earlier occasion and, for whatever reason, their personalities had clashed. So for Pam to see Karen with Jeff was very upsetting.

When Pam called Lynn crying over Jeff's dishonesty, Lynn had tried to convince her to drive back home and not waste any time confronting a man who obviously didn't care enough about her to be truthful. But her advice had fallen on deaf ears.

Though Pam was certain that her sister would, once again, give her sound advice, she chose not to leave a message. She figured Lynn would likely see her missed call and call her back. But until she did, Pam allowed her tears to be her source of comfort. That is, until her phone call with Tricee a couple hours later. Hearing her friend's voice had been just what she'd needed.

Tricee could hear Pam sniffling as she explained the shorter version of what had happened.

"I came in sort of late last night and Conner got all upset. He asked me who I was at dinner with …" Pam paused.

Tricee remained silent. She glanced at her watch and walked toward the elevator. If she was going to drive to the south side to see Pam, she wanted to do it in the next half hour. She and Hunter had no plans this Saturday morning. At least none she knew about.

"He left this morning to take his daughters home. I could see just how upset he was. Tricee, I don't know what to do." More tears.

Tricee inserted the key into her front door and hoped that Hunter was still asleep. She wanted to talk to Pam without having to answer any questions he might have. And besides, she still didn't know all of the details. She walked into their bedroom and saw an empty bed. She shook her head when she spotted Hunter's underwear and white T-shirt on the floor. Hearing the running water, she knew that he was now up and in the shower. She picked up his clothes from off the floor and tossed them into the laundry basket in the hall on her way to the kitchen.

"I can come right over. What time do you expect him back? Can you meet me somewhere? Maybe that will be better." This was the solution Tricee had come up with. Although she felt that Pam hadn't been completely truthful with her husband, now wasn't the time to judge whether she had done the right or the wrong thing. She had intended to invite Pam to lunch at some point to discuss some important things anyway, so her plans were working out after all. Except her plans didn't involve Pam crying over what appeared to be her own undoing. But, of course, Tricee would keep that thought to herself.

"We could meet somewhere, that would be fine," Pam said softly. "I heard your message earlier."

Tricee waited for another response. When Pam remained silent, Tricee asked her to meet her at the coffee shop in Hyde Park.

"We can meet at that café-slash-coffee shop near my job. We can have lunch or just tea." *I just ate*, Tricee thought as she rubbed her belly.

Tricee giggled softly as she recalled Jackie's mention of the café earlier. She thought about the current situation with Pam and Jeff and was going to suggest another place to eat. She didn't want the Small Plate Café to conjure up any unpleasant memories for Pam. But Pam didn't seem to mind.

"Yeah, we can meet at the *café-slash-coffee shop*," Pam said through a chuckle.

"I was wondering why you were laughing." Tricee smiled, glad that she had made her friend laugh, however unintentionally. She was standing at the kitchen sink when Hunter approached her from behind. "Man, you scared the living daylights out of me!" Tricee jumped then turned her attention back to Pam. "I'll meet you at what? Say, 11:45?"

Pam glanced at the clock on her nightstand. "Yeah, I can be there by then. Thanks, Tricee. I really appreciate it."

Hunter started with the questions as soon as Tricee's call ended. "You're meeting your friends for lunch? I thought you had some errands to run? Do you want me to start a load of clothes? And what exactly does it mean to 'scare the living daylights' out of somebody?"

Tricee walked past her husband while he was talking. She stopped where the laundry basket sat. "Yes, my nosy King, you may start a load of clothes," she began, spreading her hands toward the basket. "And, yes, I'm meeting Pam for lunch. I already met Jackie for breakfast while you were out cold. I do have a couple of Saturday errands to run but they can wait. And you know full well that 'scare the living daylights' is just a figure of speech."

Hunter, who was dressed casually in jeans and a thin, blue, long-sleeved T-shirt, grinned as he began to reply to his wife's reply.

"Okay, my turn." He pointed at the laundry basket. "I would be honored, my princess, to wash your clothes—"

"My clothes?"

"Yeah. I don't have anything in there."

"Uh, you do. And could you not leave your underwear and stuff lying all on the floor, please?"

Tricee walked into the bedroom and her husband followed.

"Anyway, before I was so rudely interrupted," he began, "I woke up to use the bathroom this morning and saw that you weren't in the bed. I figured you were at the coffee shop on Sheridan, right down the street. Jackie drove all the way to the north side to meet you for coffee?" Hunter shook his head. "You women have a special bond, I tell you."

Tricee changed into a white, cotton, button-down shirt but her khaki pants would remain. "No. I drove over by Hyde Park. We met halfway, well sort of." She said sort of because Jackie lived closer to Hyde Park than she did.

"Wow! You've already had a breakfast date, you just set up a lunch date and I'm just now starting my day. You sure you're not seeing some dude?" Hunter raised his eyebrow.

Tricee grabbed her purse and rummaged around in it as she headed out of the bedroom. "Yeah, I'm seeing Sidney Poitier now. He finally decided to give me some play. He's kind of old, but I think he might be able to hang." She winked at her husband and walked toward the door. "I'll be home shortly. Kiss?"

Hunter turned his face away in a pout. "Naw, no kiss. Get your kisses from Mr. Poitier."

They both laughed as Tricee reached over and kissed her husband on the lips.

"So what's on your agenda for the day?" she asked, glad that he hadn't mentioned seeing Pam with another man.

"I'm going by my mom's in a bit. She wants me to look at her air conditioner. I'll do the laundry first. Call me on my cell."

"Okay." Tricee was just about to walk out the door when Hunter spoke again.

"So Pam and that guy from last night—would that be a possible topic of discussion at today's lunch?"

"Maybe. Right now she just needs me to listen."

Hunter nodded. He kissed his wife on the cheek and watched her walk toward the elevator. *I'm so glad we don't have that issue in our marriage,* he thought. *But we do have this issue with me not wanting kids.* He closed the door and, seeing his wife's Bible on the kitchen table, began reading where she apparently left off.

The home phone rang several minutes later. Tricee's cell phone number was displayed on the caller ID.

"Hey, Babe. What's wrong?" Hunter asked, concerned.

"Nothing. I just thought I'd call and say I love you." Tricee turned onto Lakeshore Drive.

"Aww, Babe. I love you, too. A lot! More than any man ever could. Remember that, okay?" Hunter smiled and felt his heart skip a beat.

"Okay. Duly noted." Tricee smiled as she pushed the button on her head piece. Then she had a quick conversation with the Lord: *I'm so thankful we're not dealing with the issue that Pam and Conner are dealing with. Lord, I know there's no such thing as a perfect marriage. Just give us both guidance to deal with whatever issues might arise. And help me, Lord, to say all the right things as I prepare to meet Pam for lunch. The enemy is surely busy.*

19

"Hi, Pam." Tricee reached out and gave her friend a hug, noticing the redness in her eyes. "Uh, this might be the time for some Visine." Tricee smiled, hoping her attempt at humor worked.

"Do you have any?" Pam gave a half-smile, grateful for the company of a friend.

"No, I actually don't." Tricee sat in the chair across for Pam. "But I'd be happy to get you some." She smiled as she touched Pam lightly on the arm.

Tricee looked around the very familiar café. She assumed the tables for two were all taken upon Pam's arrival. The two empty chairs at the table for four where Pam was seated caused her to reminisce briefly. *I remember how we would all come here for lunch every now and then.* She wished that being here now was one of their happier times.

Although she frequented the café for lunch at least once or twice a week, Tricee enjoyed the atmosphere better when she was there with her friends. During the week, the place was filled with students and staff from H&P University, where Tricee was employed. She couldn't recall when she'd ever been to the café on the weekend. It seemed like the place to be on a Saturday at noon, though, as every table was taken.

"You know, I met Jackie this morning for breakfast and she mentioned this café. The four of us don't come here like we used to," Tricee said, looking over at the counter. "It looks like we might have to go to the counter and order. There are only three people working and it is pretty busy. What would you like?"

"Oh," Pam began, picking up the menu but not looking at it. "I don't know. I don't even know if I can eat anything." She placed the menu back on the table. A few seconds later, a tear made its way down her cheek. She took a tissue from her purse.

"I'll order us both a turkey sandwich," Tricee said, standing and walking toward the counter.

She glanced at Pam and realized just how tired her friend looked. Neither Pam, Val, Jackie nor Tricee wore much make up. A little powder and some lip gloss was usually all, if that much. But this afternoon, Tricee noticed that Pam wasn't wearing any makeup at all. She was still every bit as attractive without it, but there was no mistaking that what transpired between her and Conner last night had left her physically and emotionally drained. Tricee returned to the table carrying two glasses of peach iced tea.

"So you said you met Jackie for breakfast?"

Pam's question was unexpected. Tricee nodded as she sipped from her glass.

"Did you tell her you saw me with Jeff last night?" Pam's voice was a mere whisper.

Tricee looked her friend in the eyes and wrapped her hands around her glass of iced tea. Surely, Pam didn't think she'd share such private information with Jackie. Yes, they were like sisters, but still. This was a rather personal situation. Tricee realized then just how vulnerable Pam must feel.

"Pam, you know I wouldn't share that with anyone. Not even Jackie or Val."

"I know. I guess I'm just dealing with so many emotions. I don't know what to think right now."

The server who brought them their sandwiches smiled as she looked from Pam to Tricee. Tricee thanked the young lady, a college student she'd seen before on campus, and

would've just told me sooner that you weren't ready to adopt, it would have lessened the pain."

"I don't know if it would have, Babe. But I understand what you mean. And I do apologize for waited until she was out of earshot before she spoke.

"For a minute, I thought she was waiting around so she could hear our conversation." Pam smiled weakly and looked down at her sandwich. "Well, it sure would give her something to tell her friends."

Tricee took a small bite of her sandwich. She felt it best to try to keep the conversation as light as possible. Not only for

Pam's sake but for her own. If she could use humor to keep the mood light for the rest of the afternoon, it would be all the better. She wiped her mouth with her napkin and chose her next words carefully. She didn't know all of the details but she didn't want to ask too many questions. She knew that words of encouragement were a good place to start.

"Pam, maybe you shouldn't be so hard on yourself. I mean, I know you feel horrible that you've made a huge mistake, and you should, but—"

Pam eyes grew wide.

"Oh." Tricee picked up her glass of iced tea. "I'm sorry. I guess that came out wrong."

Pam exhaled before picking up her sandwich. Tricee was right and she knew it. And it *was* difficult to hear the truth. But she also realized that she needed someone to talk to, and next to her sister Lynn, Tricee was the best person.

They ate the rest of their meal in silence. Well, Pam managed to eat her meal; Tricee, still full from breakfast, had only eaten a few bites of her sandwich. When the server removed their plates, Tricee ordered two more glasses of iced tea. It was only a little past 1:00 PM and she still had some time left to discuss Pam's dilemma. She knew Pam well enough to know that there were still things left to discuss. But Tricee also knew she didn't want to spend *her* whole Saturday at the café.

She wanted to ask Pam why. Why did she feel it necessary to meet Jeff for dinner after having met him for lunch? She wanted to tell her friend not to get caught up in a situation that would only lead to ruin. But the distress on Pam's face told her not to give a lecture right now. Tricee refused, however, to give in to the enemy's trick. She decided to share what she felt had been placed on her heart.

"Pam, you have to pray and ask God to give you the strength to be truthful. I mean, I just don't know how else you're going to arrive at a place of peace."

"I don't know what to do, Tricee. Five months into our marriage and he wants me out. How did I get myself into such a mess?"

Tricee remained silent, not sure she understood Pam's statement. Did she think that getting together with Jeff would have been acceptable if she'd been married longer than five months? And she was talking as if she'd played no part in any of it. Well, she did admit to getting herself into this mess. But how could she not know how she'd gotten into it? It was *she* who agreed to meet an ex for lunch and dinner! Conner, as far as Tricee knew, wasn't the one who'd crossed any boundaries. Indeed, *that* was how she'd gotten into such a fine mess.

Tricee took a deep breath. She knew that, right now, honesty had to be the best policy. *Okay, here goes. I hope she receives this in love,* she silently hoped. She drank the rest of her iced tea before she spoke.

"Pam, I'm going to tell you what I think because we're friends." She fingered the straw in her empty glass. "Maybe you should just be honest."

Silence.

"I mean, just tell Conner …" she paused as she searched for the right words. "If it were me, this is what I think I would do. I would admit that I did have dinner with another man and ask my husband to forgive me. And I would promise not to make that mistake again."

Tricee wanted to say much more but first she wanted to give Pam a chance to process what she'd said and respond. But Pam remained silent.

"Okay." Tricee leaned forward and placed her hand on Pam's arm. "It was just dinner, right? And lunch was just lunch. You chatted with him and that was it. Okay, you might have stayed out longer than you expected to, but that happens with a lot of conversations. I doubt if Conner will throw away his marriage over an extended conversation."

Pam inhaled slowly. For a second, Tricee thought her friend was experiencing breathing problems.

"We chatted in his suite." Pam looked away as soon as she'd said it.

Tricee sat back in her chair. "Oh. Okay. I don't even think I want to ask—"

"Thanks for meeting me, Tricee." Pam cut her off. "I really did need to have this chat." Pam took out her cell phone and placed it on the table. Before Tricee could stop her, she picked up the check and proceeded to the counter to pay the bill. When they left the café, Tricee's head was filled with more questions than when she'd arrived.

Outside the café, Pam called her husband's cell phone. She left a message on his voicemail and hoped he'd call her right back. She thought about Tricee's advice and wasn't completely convinced it was the answer. She also thought back to something she once heard a popular minister say: Many times, we want God to bless the mess that we have created. It was certainly fitting for her situation. But she knew prayer was still the best option.

Tricee and Pam reached Pam's Mercedes.

"Well, thanks again, friend. I feel better." Pam gave Tricee a hug. "You do understand why I sort of cut you off when you asked me if it was just dinner."

"Uh, no." Tricee again decided that honesty was the best policy. "I don't know. But I have a pretty good idea."

"You're drawing your own conclusions," Pam said, coyly. "We'll chat later, okay?"

"Yeah, let's talk later. Oh, by the way, did Cassie tell you that she and I had lunch a couple weeks ago? I forgot to mention it when you ladies were over for dinner last weekend."

Pam's youngest sister, Cassie, was in her second year of college at H&P University on a full academic scholarship. During lunch with Tricee, Cassie mentioned the time, two years ago, when Pam made Tricee suffer because Jeff and Karen got involved. Cassie had made it her business to call Tricee a few days after the incident happened to apologize for her big sister's lack of judgment.

"Yeah, she did mention that to me." Pam shook her head. "She also told me she still couldn't understand why I'd treated you so horribly."

"She had me laughing so hard I couldn't even finish my lunch!" Tricee laughed again as she recalled hers and Cassie's conversation:

"Tricee, I don't like to relive the past, but I still haven't totally forgiven my old crazy sister for how she treated you a couple of years ago."

"Well, Cassie, I understand, but Pam's only human. She apologized and we got past it."

"Yeah, but it was so not called for. I mean, no one had ever even met this Jeff." Cassie said his name as if she was spitting out something nasty from her mouth. "Does he even exist?"

"Oh, yes. He exists. We've just never met him. It happens." Tricee shrugged.

"But how does a woman meet and date a man—and do who knows what else—without even introducing him to any of her friends or family? The only way I can see a woman doing that is if the man is downright ugly!"

"That could be," Tricee chuckled. "But sometimes there are other factors. There could be a multitude of reasons."

"Hmph!" Cassie grunted. "I believe he had a multitude of things wrong with his face, and that's why my sister kept him hidden!"

"Cassie is Cassie. Sometimes I think my parents picked up the wrong baby from the hospital," Pam smiled. "She did tell me how she called you to express her feelings about me."

"Yeah. And she also told me that you used a few not-so-pleasant words when she tried to tell you that you were in the wrong." Tricee and Pam both laughed.

"Why didn't you tell me back then, Tricee, when my baby sister called you?" Pam was curious, even though this had all taken place two years ago.

Tricee shrugged her shoulders. "I didn't see it as relevant. Besides, it was just a small misunderstanding."

Pam got into her vehicle and drove away, promising to call Tricee later. Tricee walked one block farther to her own vehicle. She thought about the discussion she'd just had with Pam about Jeff and wasn't sure if it had helped at all. Yes, she was drawing her own conclusions because Pam had been rather vague. And it was funny how the issue with Pam and Jeff from two years prior had resurfaced only two weeks ago, via Pam's own sister.

Geez! Jeff is like a bad virus that just won't go away, Tricee thought with amusement. Her cell phone rang just as she was fastening her seat belt.

"Hi, Babe. It's me." Hunter exhaled.

"What's wrong?" Tricee felt her stomach tighten. His voice sounded different.

"One of the women from the adoption agency called the house a little while ago."

Tricee smiled. "Great! I didn't expect to hear from anyone on a Saturday. Was it Ms. Rous? She's nice."

Hunter exhaled again and spoke before Tricee could go on. He had a hand on his forehead.

"I'm just not feeling this whole adoption—"

Those were the only words Tricee heard before she pulled the phone away from her ear and let it drop onto the passenger seat.

20

"Pam, look. I can't talk right now. I'm visiting with my mother." There was no mistaking the aggravation in Conner's voice. At least this time he'd answered his phone.

"Conner, please." Pam sighed. "You're not making this any easier."

"*I'm* not making this any easier?" Conner couldn't believe she'd just said that. "Have you forgotten that you're the spouse who strolled in close to midnight? So if there's anyone who's not making this any easier, it's you!"

"Conner, please." Pam tried to defend herself, again, but her husband was through talking.

"I'll talk to you when I get home." *Click.*

Pam stared at the phone. He'd hung up, just like that. She fought back tears as she got up from the kitchen table.

After meeting with Tricee, Pam stopped by Lynn's home but her brother-in-law informed her that she'd just missed Lynn and their 7-year-old son by 10 minutes. When he asked Pam if everything was okay, she said yes, but he wasn't fooled. He could tell that she was upset about something. Pam decided she'd better say something in case her brother-in-law made his own assumptions. She didn't want him to tell Lynn that she'd stopped by and looked as if something was wrong. It wouldn't have mattered much since Pam's intention was to talk to her sister, anyway, but she figured she wouldn't leave her brother-in-law completely in the dark.

"Conner and I just had a disagreement." She forced a smile as she spoke. "It's no big deal. I guess I'm just being too sensitive."

Her reply had gone over well because her brother-in-law chuckled and replied, "Yeah, you women are known for being too sensitive at times." Pam knew he would still ask Lynn if things were okay with her and Conner. He was a very caring person in that way.

After visiting briefly with her brother-in-law, Pam went into the nearest coffee shop and called her sister Terri. They chatted briefly as Terri was out with her husband and 6-year-old daughter for a late breakfast. She invited Pam to join them but Pam declined. When Terri asked if she was okay, Pam said yes, she just didn't feel up to driving out to Matteson, Illinois. Matteson, where Pam's parents and where Terri and her family resided, was less than an hour's drive, but to Pam, her excuse made perfect sense. Her sister probed a little deeper and Pam relented somewhat, pretty much telling her sister what she'd told her brother-in-law. "Disagreements are normal. It's a marriage, it's not designed to be perfect," Terri had said. Pam forced a laugh, thinking, *If you only knew*.

Once she got off the phone, she ordered a tall cup of iced caramel latte and headed for home. During the drive, Pam couldn't help but notice how happy her two sisters appeared to be in their marriages. Then she thought about Tricee and Hunter. They were happy along with Jackie, Val and both of their spouses. She remembered Jackie mentioning having a disagreement with Lem over pork chops. She wished she and Conner were disagreeing over food. She'd take that any day.

It was now past 3:00 in the afternoon, and instead of doing household chores or running errands, Pam was in distress. This had to have been the worse Saturday afternoon she'd experienced. After changing into sweats and a sweatshirt, she decided to look through a few documents for work. But after 10 minutes, she couldn't focus. She tossed the documents back into her work bag and went into the living room. Her mind wandered as she sat on the leather sofa in the quietness of her home. What had Conner told his mom? What had been his mother's response? Pam liked Mrs. Buckner. They got along fine. She wondered if that was all about to change after today, though.

Her cell phone rang and interrupted her thoughts. She hurried into the bedroom to answer it, hoping it was Conner. It was her sister Lynn. As soon as Pam heard her sister's voice, the tears started up again.

"Pam, what's wrong? Barry said you'd stopped by and I saw your missed call. Why didn't you leave a message? Do you need me to come over?"

"No, that's okay," Pam managed to say through her tears. "Conner and I had an argument. I had dinner with Jeff last night—"

"Jeff?" Lynn's face turned into a frown. "That guy, Jeff, you were seeing a couple years ago?"

Lynn immediately thought back to that Sunday night, two years ago, when Pam had called her, upset that Jeff had been less than honest. Before Pam could answer, her sister went into a rant.

"Pam, when on earth did you start seeing him?! Please don't tell me you've allowed this man back into your life! Isn't this the same man who lied to you when you were dating him?! Gee whiz, Pam! It was bad enough that you dealt with him when you were single! You're married, now, to a great man! Why would you even allow yourself this drama, Pam?! Why?! Gee whiz! What am I missing here?!"

Pam counted the number of times Lynn said her name, and the number of times she'd said gee whiz. There was no mistaking that Lynn was trying to get her point across. And as much as Pam

252

wanted to come back with a retort of her own, she knew it was useless. Her sister had every right to react the way she did, even if she didn't know all of the details.

Pam grabbed the box of tissue off of her nightstand. She wiped her face and blew her nose. Her sister managed to keep quiet as she waited for Pam to explain.

"Lynn, it's not like that. I'm not *seeing* him. We had lunch once. And he asked me to have dinner, that's all. I just stayed out longer than I should have." Pam chose not to go into too many details. But no matter what she said, Lynn, like Tricee and Conner, would draw her own conclusions. "I have no intention of seeing him again. I'm not looking for any trouble. I tried to explain to Conner …" Pam paused as this wasn't exactly the whole truth, but she planned to explain as soon as he came home.

Lynn sat and listened, still frowning. This wasn't what she expected from her oldest sibling. Surely, Pam had to have known better than this. But instead of scolding Pam again, she stayed calm. Maybe this was just a mistake Pam would learn from and not make again. She sure hoped so.

"Conner said I should be prepared to leave if he's not happy with what I have to say. We were too busy arguing for me to explain, and his daughters stayed overnight." She took a breath to help fight the tears. "I met with Tricee for lunch and she says I just need to be truthful."

"You already know being truthful is the best thing, Pam. Gee whiz, sis! Please explain to your husband that it was just dinner and ask him to forgive you."

"I know. I called him but he's over at his mom's. He hung up on me."

Lynn shook her head. "Pam, good grief! The man has reason to be upset!"

Pam pulled the phone away from her ear and looked at it. *Why does she keep saying my name in every sentence?* she almost wondered aloud. She knew one thing for sure. None of them—not Lynn, Jackie, Val or Tricee—were fans of Mr. Jeff.

"Look, Pam," Lynn blurted out. "I don't want to be harsh or to judge you. I just never really cared for him, anyway. I didn't even meet this Jeff when you were dating him. But from what little you did say about him, I just felt like you deserved better. Ugh!"

Yeah, so did my three friends. "I know." Pam sighed.

She wasn't surprised by her sister's words. Neither Lynn nor Pam's three closest friends had ever met Jeff, so they didn't know him like she did. As far as Pam was concerned, he really was a nice guy in his own way. But that bit of information wasn't likely to change what her sister felt.

Lynn held up a finger to her son and mouthed, *One moment, Sweetie.* The 7-year-old repeated his mom's "Ugh!" then laughed and left the room.

"Is that my nephew I hear?" Pam asked. She almost felt herself smile.

"Yeah, that was him mocking me. I try to keep from saying too much around him, but I didn't expect for him to come into the room."

Pam and her sister chatted for another few minutes before ending their phone call. Lynn and Barry had had their fair share of disagreements in the few years they'd been married, but according to Lynn, it was usually about something very trivial. So much so, she told Pam, that they usually ended up laughing about it afterward. Well, unless Pam was able to provide an acceptable explanation when Conner came home, there was no telling when the laughter would commence in the Buckner household.

Pam rose slowly from the sofa. She picked up the remote and turned on the television. She stopped channel surfing when she reached the food channel. Not really interested in watching television, she sat back down on the sofa. *Maybe I'll try Conner again,* she thought. *He can't stay at his mom's forever. When he gets here, I'll just tell him what happened. I had dinner with a guy I used to date—if you can call it dating—and lost track of time.*

When she got her husband's voicemail, she let out an exasperated sigh. *I wish he would just talk to me*, she thought. She chose not to leave a message. She then scrolled through her cell phone until it reached her mother-in-law's home number. She paused after dialing the first six numbers. "No, I'm not going to call over there. In fact," she mumbled, "I am not going to try Conner again. He knows I'm trying to reach him." Pam tossed her cell phone onto the coffee table and proceeded into the kitchen. The home phone rang and she rushed to answer it. Not looking at the caller ID display, she assumed—she hoped—it was Conner.

"Hello?" she said excitedly into the phone.

"It's me, Lynn. Calling back."

"Oh." The disappointment was clearly audible in her voice.

"I was calling to make sure you were okay," Lynn said in a tone Pam knew was one of genuine concern. But they'd just spoken and she wasn't expecting her sister to call again so soon.

"Lynn, I'm fine," Pam said softly. Then she smiled. "What? Did you think I was going to do something stupid?" Both she and Lynn chuckled.

"No, I know it's not that serious. I was just calling to check on you."

"Thanks, but I'm okay. I think I'll go and see what I'm cooking for dinner." *That is, if I still have a place to call home,* she half-joked silently.

"Let me clarify my statement," Lynn remarked. "I'm not saying your issue is not serious, I just meant—"

"Lynn, I know what you meant." Pam smiled, thankful for the close relationship they shared.

After chatting for a second time with her sister, Pam grabbed some blue corn chips from a kitchen cabinet and some bottled water from the fridge. Dinner could wait; the corn chips and water would make do for now. After her snack and after trying to watch a movie that failed to hold her interest, Pam fell asleep on the sofa. Close to three hours later, she was awakened by her cell phone. The nervousness in her mother-in-law's voice caused her to jump up from the sofa.

"Pam, I'm at the hospital with Conner."

Pam grabbed her keys and made a fast dash to the door.

21

"I don't want to discuss it right now, Hunter. I just need to be left alone." Tricee held back tears as her husband followed her into the bedroom.

Hunter was intent on trying to explain why he didn't feel ready for children. But whatever his reasons, they didn't matter to a very upset Tricee. His words had stung, cut her to the core. And they had taken Tricee by surprise. As much as they'd discussed having children, Hunter had never expressed disinterest. So when she heard the words 'I'm not ready,' she was dumbfounded.

"Look, Honey—please. I know you're upset. But at least give me a chance to explain."

Hunter watched his wife grab a light jacket from the closet. It was after 7:00 PM, just the right time for a nice breeze off Chicago's lakefront. Hunter knew Tricee was likely going for a stroll as she sought time away from him.

After meeting Pam for lunch, instead of coming straight home, Tricee stopped at the Harold Washington Library on State Street. The place was huge and had become one of her favorite destinations. The research she had to conduct for her classes was divided between the internet and the H&P University library, her place of employment as well as her choice for pursuing her Ph.D. But the downtown library also had great resources.

But earlier, as she sat in a corner on the sixth floor—the floor she called "my social sciences resources"—the last thing she'd wanted to do was read. The library closed at 5:00 PM on Saturday. Had it stayed opened later, Tricee would have likely still been sitting on the sixth floor.

It had only taken a couple minutes to walk back to the parking lot on Van Buren Street once she left the library, and her mind had conjured up all sorts of thoughts in that short time. What she was feeling didn't seem real. It was as if someone had taken a sharp object and was turning it into her back. With her mother's upcoming visit, Tricee didn't need or care to have to deal with any added stress.

Hunter followed his wife to the front door. "I don't think you need to leave here all upset. Please let me at least walk you downstairs."

Tricee gave Hunter the evil eye. *Walk me downstairs?!* she thought, incredulously. Rolling her eyes, she shook her head and opened the front door. Hunter exhaled, realizing his wife had nothing more to say.

Tricee hurried toward the elevator. She unintentionally left her cell phone upstairs but going back to get it wasn't an option. She didn't want to look at her husband's face. Once downstairs, she walked through the side door, which led to the back doors, which led to the lakefront path. She slowly began to walk north, whispering a few prayers to God. He had fixed everything else in her life in the past. Surely, He had already fixed the issue that had arisen between her and her husband.

Hunter plopped down on the sofa. He put a hand to his forehead and massaged his temples. He regretted not discussing his feelings about parenting with his wife sooner, but the right time just never seemed to present itself. When the woman from the adoption agency called—Hunter believed she said her name was Ms. Rous—he started not to answer. She had likely called from a cell phone as he hadn't recognized the number. The only other time he'd spoken to her was when she'd called from her office. And in that instance, he knew from the caller ID that it was the adoption agency.

Their lives just seemed too full right now. Of course, he'd like to see his wife pregnant with their child one day. Tricee had gone on and on about not wanting to wait too much longer. Because she was 37, she said they didn't have much time. Okay, he understood that. He also understood, after much discussion between them, that there were many children who needed a home. So why not adopt, she'd said. And, perhaps, within the next three years, they could ditch the birth control and work on Tricee getting pregnant. For now, he was truly enjoying their time without kids.

With Tricee pursuing her Ph.D. and his already very busy schedule as an education consultant, when would they have the time? Not to mention all of the places he wanted to visit with his wife. A life minus children was looking better and better. But he knew from Tricee's enthusiasm that she was ready now. Like, yesterday.

"Okay, I guess I messed up this time," Hunter uttered quietly to himself as he threw his legs across the sofa. He placed a throw pillow under his head and lay there for several minutes, hoping Tricee would walk back through the door. When her cell phone rang, he hurried to the bedroom where he knew she'd left it.

"Hello?" Hunter said as he walked back into the living room.

"Hi, Hunter. It's Val. Is Tricee around?"

He could tell from Val's voice that something was wrong. "Hey, Val. Tricee stepped out for a bit. Is everything okay?"

"No. Conner's daughter Raneen is in the hospital. She fell and hit her head. I think she was at a birthday party. She's unconscious. Pam called to tell me. Of course, she and Conner are at their wits end."

Hunter sat down on the sofa. "Oh, wow. I'm sorry to hear that. I'll, uh, go see if I can catch up to Tricee. She went for a walk. What hospital is she in?"

"South Shore. But if you guys can't make it tonight, that's okay. Conner's mom, his ex and one of his relatives are there. I just wanted to call and let Tricee know."

"Ok, Val. Thanks. Keep us posted, please."

"I will."

Hunter grabbed his keys and quickly left their condo. He prayed for Raneen as he rushed out the door, hoping to run into Tricee. Suddenly, their problems didn't seem so terrible.

22

"You go on home. I'll stay here with my granddaughter. You need to rest." Conner's mother spoke softly to him. They'd both been at the hospital with Raneen pretty much all day Sunday and Monday, which was Memorial Day. Conner had called in to work and his supervisor at the Chicago Transit Authority had been more than understanding. She'd told a distraught Conner to take as many days as he felt he needed.

His mother, a paralegal for a small law firm in Wilmette, a Chicago suburb, had requested Tuesday and Wednesday off. But since Raneen was now conscious, Conner had convinced his mother that tomorrow, she needed to go in to work. He was well aware of how many cases she had been working on over the past couple of months and saw no reason for her to miss another day.

He asked her, "Aren't Wednesdays your busiest days and when you normally conduct conference calls with the clients?"

Viola had replied, "Yes. But Conner, we're talking about my granddaughter here."

The current situation had opened up a conversation between Conner and his mother about whether there would be another grandchild any time soon. It was Viola's way of easing the tension while nervously awaiting the doctor's update on Raneen. Unfortunately, that conversation was only added tension for

Conner. He had, indeed, told his mother that, yes, another grandchild was in her near future. Now he wasn't so sure.

When Conner arrived to his mother's home on the far north side of Chicago, the day after he and Pam had argued, he'd told her he was out and thought he'd visit. But Viola sensed from her son's facial expression that there was more behind his visit than that.

She didn't probe, only asked if everything was okay. Conner said yes, but something in his mother's eyes told him she wasn't so sure he was telling the whole truth. He admitted to her that he and Pam had had a small disagreement but decided not to share any more than he thought was necessary. He thought briefly about the time Pam had referred to him as a mama's boy, the most untrue statement he'd ever heard about himself.

Conner and his mother ended up talking about a lot of things from the past, much of which had to do with his now deceased father. Viola shared with Conner that she had been so in love with his father that she doubted seriously if remarrying was an option for her. She said even if she met a man who seemed to be the perfect Mr. Right, he would only be "the perfect Mr. Right Now until I say enough is enough." Conner laughed at his mother's way with words. He told her, "As long as you're happy, mom. That's all that counts."

They ended up having dinner. Viola had whipped up her famous chicken and dumplings earlier in the day. Along with her lasagna, her chicken and dumplings were Conner's favorite. They had eaten and were watching the 6:00 PM news when they received the phone call about Raneen from Renita, who was crying uncontrollably.

On the way to the hospital, Viola had taken it upon herself to phone Pam. Pam had been so nervous that she hung up the phone upon hearing the words "I'm at the hospital with Conner." Her first thought, of course, was that Conner had been in some sort of accident. Once she'd grabbed her keys and hurriedly climbed into her vehicle, she realized she needed to call Viola back to find out more information. It was then that she learned that it was Raneen who'd been taken to the hospital and not Conner. She'd been taken to South Shore hospital but, on Monday, was transferred to Rush on the city's west side.

Pam learned as soon as she arrived at the hospital that Raneen had slipped and fallen while at her friend's birthday party. Conner thanked the very distraught mother of Raneen's friend for acting immediately. She had called 911 and accompanied Raneen to the hospital. Fortunately, the woman had two friends assisting her with the party and she left the other children in their care. But the party had to be cut short.

The woman's husband got to the hospital as soon as he was able. He was a doctor, though not at the hospital Raneen was in. On Sunday morning, Conner, Renita and the birthday girl's parents spoke over coffee in the hospital cafeteria. The father tried to insist that he would cover the expected medical bill but Conner wouldn't hear of it. It was an accident and he saw no reason to make the girl's parents suffer any more than they already were. He explained to the father that his employment insurance would cover it and he assumed they had homeowner's insurance, which of course they did.

When the four of them finished their coffee and prepared to leave the cafeteria, the father pulled Conner to the side. He told Conner to expect a check in the mail soon. He and his wife had already discussed it. They'd suspected that Conner and Renita would decline their offer to pay the bill, so they felt that a personal check deposited into a savings account for Raneen was the next suitable option.

As Viola prepared to leave, she kissed Raneen on the forehead with a promise to return the next day. Conner shot his mom a look. "I'll be here tomorrow," Viola said and smiled, looking at Conner this time. She knew her son well. He wasn't only concerned about his 10-year-old daughter's complete recovery. He was concerned for his tired mother, who he could tell needed to rest.

"If I don't make it tomorrow, Pumpkin, you'll see me on Thursday. But until then, you eat and do what the doctors tell you so you can come home."

"Okay, Gransi." Raneen smiled as she lifted herself up to give her grandmother a hug.

Gransi, Pam repeated silently as she entered the room. She walked over to her mother-in-law and embraced her. Conner merely gave her a nod as he walked over to the window and looked out.

"I like how your grandkids refer to you as Gransi." Pam smiled at her mother-in-law and stole a quick glance at her husband.

Viola chuckled. "I wasn't feeling that granny stuff," she said, patting Pam on the arm. "Gransi sounds better. At least for me it does."

Viola walked over to the window and gave Conner a hug, then left the room. She called to Pam as she attempted to strike up a conversation with Raneen. Pam removed a cute white teddy bear with a bandage on its forehead out of a bag she was carrying and gently laid it on Raneen's bed. She then joined Viola who was standing in the hall just outside the room.

Viola spoke softly. "Pam, I don't believe in getting in my son's business, you know that." She adjusted her purse strap on her shoulder. "But I could tell from Conner's reaction when you came to the hospital Saturday night that something was going on with you two. That and the fact that he told me you two had a slight disagreement."

Pam folded her arms. But not wanting to appear defensive, she quickly unfolded them. She wanted to ask Viola exactly what Conner had told her. She hoped he hadn't shared everything with her. Viola didn't need to know any details.

No one needed to know that Conner had slept in the spare bedroom when he arrived home from the hospital early Sunday morning. He'd missed church but had called the pastor to have Raneen added to the prayer list. Upon returning from the hospital late Sunday night, he slept in the spare bedroom again. On Monday, he insisted that Pam spend the night at her parents' house. He just couldn't talk to her about much of anything still and he needed some space.

As much as Pam pleaded with him to just talk to her, he wasn't ready. Pam prayed fervently, even asking God to explain how her husband, an assistant pastor, could be so stubborn. She told her sister Lynn, who had stopped by their parents' Monday night, that God must have still been out to lunch or something, because he had yet to supply her with an answer. Lynn just laughed. But before she left, she told Pam, "This is a really difficult time for Conner, sis. You're going to have to do all you can to find some patience in dealing with this. You have to try to understand what he must be feeling right now." Pam informed her sister that she *was* trying to understand. This was why she wanted them to talk about it, so things wouldn't get even tenser between them.

Pam prayed specifically for God to give her patience. She also asked God to help Conner understand how unbearable it was for her to have spent Monday night at her parents' house. Her mother had asked all sorts of questions while her father sat-munching on barbeque chicken-and just nodded his head. Pam told her mother that every marriage, even hers, had its fair share of disagreements. She even went so far as to bring up one of her parents' legendary arguments from years past. Mrs. Rhodes tried to insist that the disagreement Pam was talking about had been a different situation altogether, and when she looked to Mr. Rhodes for help, he simply picked up his glass of Diet Dr. Pepper, and his newspaper and headed for the bedroom. When Mrs. Rhodes stood up, as if trying to block her husband from leaving the kitchen, Mr. Rhodes gently swatted his wife on the behind and then planted a kiss on her cheek. Pam was a little embarrassed at her father's flirtatious behavior. She put her head down and smiled as she excused herself and went into the extra bedroom. She hoped that when she and Conner were her parents' age they'd share the same flirtatious moments.

As much as Pam loved her parents, she didn't wish to go through another hundred questions with mother Rhodes. So no matter what Conner said or felt, she was set on telling him that tonight, and for the remainder of the week, she was spending her nights in *their* home. She'd spoken to her cousin Sondra but hadn't shared any details, so spending the night there wasn't really an option. Besides, she had only shared what was happening with Tricee and her sister Lynn, though she'd shared more details with Tricee. And spending money to stay at a hotel wasn't going to happen either.

Now, as Viola stood before her, not asking a ton of questions like her mother had done, Pam almost wanted to ask her mother-in-law for some advice. But she decided against it, feeling that a hospital wasn't the best setting and the timing wasn't the best.

"Conner knows he can talk to me without me giving him unsolicited advice," Viola said. Her voice was soothing. Pam realized how fortunate she was to have a mother-in-law she really liked. "But he knows that, if he asks me, I will only tell him what I believe is best."

"I guess I'm curious, Viola, as to what he shared." The words eased out as Pam felt a sense of comfort, at least for the moment.

"He said you two had a disagreement." Viola reached into her handbag and removed her car keys.

Several seconds passed before either she or Pam spoke. It seemed to Pam that Viola was waiting for her to respond, but something in her mother-in-law's light brown eyes said only that she cared. Pam could see the fatigue on Viola's face and, not wanting to keep her much longer, nodded her head.

"It was just that: a disagreement. I came to the hospital to see Raneen and to see if Conner has become less stubborn," Pam glanced at her watch, "in the last hour."

Viola laughed. "I'm sure that, whatever it is, you two will work it out. But Pam," Viola said, taking her by the hand, "sometimes we all have to bend just a little." Viola squeezed her daughter-in-law's hand, smiled, then turned and walked away.

Bend a little. Pam thought about those three words as she walked back into Raneen's room. *I wonder exactly what I was supposed to get from that?*

23

"Val, that was one heck of a birthday celebration!" Jackie scrolled through the images in her cell phone, gushing over all the pictures she'd taken of the 1-year-old Ashlyn. Last week, on June 8th and 10th respectively, Ashlyn had turned 1 and Cory, Val's husband, had turned 38. The celebration had taken place at their home, complete with a clown and a magician for the children. While friends and family—the adult crowd—returned later in the evening to celebrate Cory turning a year older, he'd felt the day was more about his baby girl, and he was elated that so many had shown up for the party.

Tricee had arrived without Hunter and only stayed for about 45 minutes. Pam, Conner and his daughter Connis were in attendance, but Raneen had stayed home. With all that had happened to her recently, Conner and Renita felt she needed to rest. There would be plenty of other parties for her to attend. Conner was cordial to his wife at the party, even though he and Pam hadn't said more than three words to each other the entire time. That had been his doing, of course.

"Yeah, it took my mind off my marital troubles, somewhat," Pam said as she buttered her wheat toast. She'd met Val and Jackie at Foster's diner on the north side. Located on the corner of Broadway and Sheridan, the diner was only a few blocks from Tricee's building. While unable to join her friends for breakfast—too much homework had been her reason—Tricee asked her three friends if they cared to meet up at her condo afterward. They agreed. And all four women felt it would be a good time to finally hold their first Bible talk session.

It had been at least three weeks since Raneen's accident and Conner was spending a lot of time with his daughters at his ex-wife's home. He'd even phoned his cousin to inform him that he needed to cancel preaching the sermon at his church. He just didn't feel up to it, as bad as it might have sounded it was true. His cousin understood and they agreed that, perhaps, sometime later in the summer would be better.

It wasn't just Conner spending so much time with his daughters at his ex-wife's home that had Pam's panties in a bunch. It was the fact that he was also spending so much time around his ex-wife. She knew Conner had no romantic interest in Renita, but due to her recent mistake, her insecurities were messing with her mind.

"He still won't talk to you?" Val asked as the server poured her another cup of Chai tea.

"No," Pam answered. "Wait—I take that back. He says good morning and good night, I'll be home later and I'm going to see the girls after work. The kind of talking I want him to do with me isn't happening."

Val shook her head. Pam had only shared a few details with Val and Jackie. She told them, on separate occasions, that she'd come in later than she should have and Conner had become incensed. They both knew she had been out with Jeff but no other questions were asked and no other details were shared. Jackie felt Conner was well within his right to be upset and so did Val, and they shared how they felt with Pam during that particular chat. Pam had not, however, shared with them that Conner had asked her to leave.

The Tuesday evening last month at the hospital, when she had spoken briefly with Viola, Pam had slept in her home. She told Conner that, even though he was very upset, she was not spending another night at her parents'. She reminded him that it was still *both their homes*. He'd mumbled "fine" and slept in the spare bedroom, where he'd been sleeping ever since. And that was after he would arrive home after 10:00 PM from his ex's house and spending time with their daughters.

"Well, he can only be silent for so long," Jackie remarked, placing her cell phone back in her purse. "But, Pam, you have to admit—the man has every reason to be upset."

Jackie waited for Pam to respond. She was curious to know if Pam had spoken to Jeff since their dinner so she decided to just come right out and ask.

"I'm just curious. Have you spoken to Jeff in these past few weeks?"

Val was all ears as she bit into her ham and cheese omelet. It was an interesting way to spend this particular Saturday morning. With so much going on—planning for the party and Cory studying for a final exam—it felt as if more than just a few weeks had gone by since she had a chance to catch up with her friends. And on top of everything else, a cousin from New Jersey had arrived last weekend and was staying with her and Cory for a while.

"I mean, you have to know," Jackie said as she finished her turkey bacon, "that when you share something with us, it leaves us—"

"Inquiring minds want to know," Val blurted out. She looked quickly from Pam to Jackie as she held her toast to her mouth and nibbled on it, her shoulders hunched.

"Girl, you look like a house mouse," Jackie said and began to laugh.

Pam joined in. She knew it was Val's intent to use humor to ease any awkwardness in the conversation, especially after Jeff's name was mentioned.

"I have talked to him. But have I seen him? No." Pam waved the server over. Only crumbs had been left on their plates and breakfast was over.

The three ladies left the diner and stood on the corner of Broadway and Sheridan. They each had driven their own vehicles and were parked at least three blocks away.

"It's after 10:00. I'll call Tricee and let her know we're on our way," Jackie said, reaching into her purse for her cell phone.

"I called her this morning, on my way here, to confirm that we were still on," said Val. "I asked her if she was sure she couldn't meet us for breakfast and she said yes. She was up very early working on a paper."

"Okay." Jackie put her phone away. "Then I guess we should just head on over and not even try to find a closer parking space."

"This north side and the parking," Pam added as the women began walking east toward the lake. "Tricee has been on the north side long enough that I'm almost used to the parking—lack of parking, actually."

"It's the beautiful lake and the convenience of the shopping," said Jackie, mocking Tricee's voice. Val and Pam laughed.

"Yeah, well, to each his own," Val giggled. "It works for her just like living in Forest Park works for me."

Jackie made a face that indicated she had something on her mind. Pam noticed it as they turned onto Sheridan and Glenlake.

"What are you thinking about?" Pam looked directly at Jackie.

"I don't know. It just seems like something is going on with Tricee. She was so quiet when she and Hunter came to the hospital that night."

"She was probably just concerned about Raneen. You know how sensitive Tricee is at times," Val added.

"I know. But in the past couple weeks, I haven't spoken to her much. And she didn't stay long at Ashlyn's and Cory's party."

"She's really busy with classes and work," Pam said. She'd seen Tricee only once, briefly, since meeting her for breakfast that awful Saturday, but she'd spoken with her via phone on several occasions.

"Well, I'm just glad we all had this Saturday free to meet up." Jackie turned to Pam. "We could use some serious Bible talk."

Pam noticed the way Jackie was looking at her and stopped walking.

"Why were you looking at me when you said that? I mean, I know I have issues in my marriage, but do you have to look at me and make it so obvious?"

"Stop being so overly sensitive, Ms. Celie," Val teased as they reached Tricee's and Hunter's condominium.

"Yeah, you did kind of resemble Ms. Celie when you made that face," Jackie said, chuckling, as they stopped at the front desk. The doorman smiled as he phoned Tricee to inform her that she had guests. The three women boarded the elevator and a few seconds later, they were walking into Tricee's condo.

Hunter spoke to his wife's friends and smiled as he left, but it wasn't the warm smile they were used to. Jackie knew then that there was definitely something going on. She sent up a silent prayer as she walked toward the bathroom: *Lord, you know all things. We just thank you for your presence right now in this place.*

24

"I'm about to go off on one of these white folks." Darcy caught up to Pam just as she was entering her office. "I know what my job description is and I don't need a reminder."

"Who are you upset with now?" Pam shook her head and smiled. She hung her purse on the hook behind her office door. As she sat down at her desk, she noticed the small paperback in Darcy's hand along with a manila folder. "Malcolm X's autobiography?" She tilted her head as she looked at the front of the book. "You plan on whipping one of these white folks with the words from that book, do you?"

Pam couldn't help but to chuckle internally at Darcy's militant nature. It came out every now and then and that only made it more comical to Pam. She watched as Darcy began to flip through the book. She chose a page at random and began to read with passion.

"Whew, that's deep!" Pam commented. "He sure had a way with words!"

"Yes, he did," Darcy agreed.

Darcy gave Pam a once-over, admiring her beige skirt suit. She'd paired it with an orange top, which wasn't too bright, that made the suit look even better. For the middle of June, it was a nice outfit.

Pam had seemed a little distracted. She and Darcy had gone to lunch once more since their lunch the month prior. Pam shared with Darcy what had transpired at home. It felt good to be able to vent and to talk to someone at work, that she felt she could trust. Pam was a little surprised, initially, that she felt comfortable sharing some of the details with Darcy before she'd shared them with Val or Jackie. As a result, Darcy opened up even more about some of what she was dealing with at home.

"I've read it a couple times," Pam said, nodding toward the book. "Gee, it's been about 10 years now." She opened the file that was on her desk.

Darcy glanced at her watch. "I read it about 10 years ago, too, but only once." She held up the manila folder. "Well, let me get to my office. I'm meeting with my newest client this morning. I tell you, when I see the issues these women have, mine pale in comparison."

"Hmm, that's a true statement. So true." Pam looked off toward the wall briefly. Darcy's words had given her pause.

Darcy adjusted her purse and the manila folder. "Want to have lunch? How was your weekend? Have things resumed a sense of normalcy at home?"

"Lunch, maybe. My weekend was fine and, as for back to normal, I'm going to keep the faith and believe we're almost there.

I've been praying. I went to church yesterday and felt a tug from the Holy Spirit. And I got together with my three girlfriends on Saturday for a Bible talk."

Darcy listened intently but her expression was one of confusion.

"Bible talk. That's what we decided to call it. When you meet and chat about Bible stuff, just like a Bible study session. Anyway," she clapped her hands together, "it was such a powerful session that all four of us caught the Holy Ghost. Whew!"

"I know what Bible talk is, Pam," Darcy laughed. "I might not be the holiest of women, but I get it. And while I'm glad you caught the Holy Ghost at your friend's home, please—this is the workplace. Try not to catch it up in here."

Pam laughed and reached into her oversized handbag to remove a jar of black olives. Darcy turned and walked toward the door.

"Let me know if you want to have lunch," Darcy reminded Pam and looked over her shoulder. "What's with the olives?" Her mouth turned down in a small frown.

"Oh, I stopped at the grocery store—at Dominick's—and picked up a salad. I like to add olives. Why are you frowning?"

"There's something about a jar of black olives that rubs me the wrong way," Darcy explained, pointing her forefinger. "There's something racial behind it." She squinted, still pointing.

She started to leave again, then got to the door of Pam's office and hesitated. "A quote from the late brother Malcolm just came to mind."

Pam stared at Darcy in anticipation of what she would say next.

"When white America catches a cold, black America catches pneumonia."

All Pam could do was shake her head and chuckle as Darcy left her office.

After a 10:00 AM meeting and a 1:00 PM court hearing, Pam met with her newest client. She was glad to see that the young woman had taken her advice regarding the clothes that were available. She'd worn a cute outfit this day: a black skirt with a red, button-down blouse. Pam thought the outfit made her look quite professional.

In the past month, Pam had seen some progress. She only hoped that this client would continue along this path. Pam had even heard from one of her co-workers, who taught one of the classes, that the young woman would soon interview for a position at the Walgreens pharmacy. It was a step in the right direction. And it made Pam proud. Though she had her own set of unpleasant issues at home, she was able to keep her emotions in check and focus on the women she worked with. But as soon as she left the shelter at the end of the work day, her mind would focus right back on her troubles at home.

Lunch ended up being her store-bought salad after all and she ate at her desk. She decided to phone her husband. The call went straight to voicemail. She left her usual message and hung up. As she closed the lid on her jar of olives, she couldn't help but chuckle. The more she thought about it, the more she realized that Darcy had been a blessing in disguise.

With only an hour left in the work day, Pam returned three phone calls and set up an appointment for next week at the library. She was hoping that something would have been available sooner but knew she'd have to take what she could get. Thankfully, the shelter's computer system was up and running again. The technician had said something about a possible virus that left the shelter without use of its computers for about three hours this morning. Pam decided to use what was left of her last hour at work to enter data into the system and prayed there would be no other "malfunctions."

She picked up her water bottle to refill it before getting started with her last project of the day. When she stepped into the lounge, she noticed a woman sitting with Darcy. It had to have been the new client Darcy mentioned last month. Pam still hadn't seen nor met her until now. Darcy looked up and waved Pam over.

"Pam, this is Janae Mays-Morrison. She'll be staying here at the shelter."

Darcy immediately noticed the frown on Pam's face. Pam looked at the woman's green dress and braids and realized it was the same woman she'd seen at church last month. Her fingernails, however, were polish-free today. This was the same woman she'd judged for wearing a form-fitting dress to church, Ms. Tight Green Dress who'd flirted—or tried to flirt—with Conner that Sunday.

"Oh, nice to meet you," Pam greeted the woman and forced herself to smile.

The woman smiled, mumbled a soft hello and then quickly turned her attention back to Darcy. She didn't recognize Pam and had no idea why she looked so sour.

"Have a good evening, Darcy. See you tomorrow." Pam turned and walked away. She refilled her water bottle at the cooler and went back to her office.

Now that's interesting to see her here. I haven't seen her back at church. I wonder what the deal is? Pam thought silently to herself. She logged on to her computer and then a thought suddenly occurred to her. *Wait, her last name, Mays-Morrison.*

The woman's hyphenated name, the Mays part that is, was the same as Jeff's. *Could they be related?* she wondered.

It was already 4:15 PM, which left only about 45 minutes for entering data. Pam had hoped to get it completed today to free up some time on Tuesday. She opened her first manila folder and entered the data into a spreadsheet. After entering the data from the second folder, she paused, still curious about the woman's last name.

Information on every client could be accessed by all of the staff members at the agency. And Darcy was really good about entering her clients' information a few days prior to their arrival; once it was determined they would become temporary residents. Pam knew this and there was only one way to put her curiosity to rest.

She minimized the program she was in and clicked on the "open client file" icon. The clients' names were listed alphabetically by last name. She scrolled quickly down the list: *Lindsey, Lockett, Marshall, Mays-Morrison.* There it was: Janae Mays-Morrison. She clicked on "open file."

Pam immediately took note of the Schaumburg address. She didn't remember the exact address of the town house Jeff owned in Schaumburg but the street name was very familiar. And so was the apartment number: 2B. Janae Mays-Morrison resided in Schaumburg, Illinois, in the town house that Jeff used to own, the

town house he'd told her he sold to his cousin and her husband.
Now this is interesting, Pam thought silently as she logged off her
computer.

25

"Tricee, are you okay?" Jackie asked as soon as she emerged from the bathroom.

"No, Jackie. I'm actually not okay." Tricee's words were sharp. "My husband has changed his mind and doesn't want to proceed with the adoption process."

Pam and Val, who had been headed into the living room, stopped and turned around simultaneously.

"I'm sorry," Tricee placed her hand on Jackie's arm. "Charge that one to my head and not my heart. I didn't mean to sound so abrupt."

"It's okay," Jackie replied as she and Tricee proceeded into the living room. "I understand."

Val and Pam glanced at each other as they continued into Tricee's living room. They had allowed Jackie and Tricee to pass them in the hall after Tricee's outburst. They almost tiptoed into the living room, both looking as if they were afraid of making a wrong move. Tricee noticed their expressions and pointed to the sofa, indicating that they should sit.

"It is okay, Ladies. I promise not to bite." Tricee gave a half-smile. "It's just one more thing in my life that I need to deal with."

"Whew! You had me worried for a minute. I was about to break up out of here!" Val fanned her face with her hands as she sat down.

"I know, right? I thought I saw fire in them there eyes," said Pam as she joined Val on the sofa.

"Them there eyes?" Jackie swung her head around to look at Pam. "You must've watched *Lady Sings the Blues* when it was on last night."

"I did!" Pam began to sing the lines from the movie, wiggling her head and shoulders.

"But we know Diana Ross wasn't singing that she saw fire in Billy Dee's eyes," Val added.

"True," said Jackie. "But can we get back to the topic." She pointed discreetly at Tricee, her finger close to her belly, and spoke out of the side of her mouth.

"Jackie, I'm sitting right next to you," Tricee uttered. "And why are you talking like that?" A few seconds later they all laughed.

It had been tense in the Hatchett household the past couple weeks. Tricee phoned Ruby with an excuse as to why her visit needed to be canceled. Her mother had asked a ton of questions and tried to insist on paying her only daughter a visit, but Tricee wouldn't change her mind. She even asked Tricee if she was canceling because of Boyce, her husband of the past year. While Tricee had been slightly taken aback when Ruby announced her plans to marry the brother of her best friend, Bev, she had nothing against the man, personally. In fact, two years ago, when Ruby and Tricee had gotten together for dinner, Tricee sensed there was something more to her mother's friendship with Bev's brother. But admittedly, on that evening two years ago, Tricee hadn't been ready to meet Boyce.

He had driven to the Italian restaurant on Bryn Mawr to pick up Ruby, but Tricee had remained a safe distance away as Ruby climbed into his vehicle. That particular dinner had to have been one of the most awkward meals either of them had ever had. Tricee was just glad that all of the issues from the past were just that—in the past. So now, as she dealt with this issue between herself and Hunter, she wondered if this was to be her lot in life, dealing with one issue after another.

Tricee brought out four glasses and a pitcher of peach iced tea. She set the tray on the coffee table. She'd awakened this morning before Hunter and allowed the tears to flow. But, afterward, she prayed and asked God to let His will be done. She was still very upset over her husband's decision—which they both agreed he should have made her aware of long before now—but she was determined to remain strong in the midst of their adversity.

"Well, we've finally gathered for our first official Bible talk," Val said, setting her glass on the coffee table. She turned to face Tricee. "Is this something you want to discuss further? I'm so sorry that things have come to this for you and Hunter."

There was no mistaking the sadness in Val's eyes. She could only imagine the pain Tricee was feeling, having given birth to her first child a year ago. It had been such a joy having a child around and she knew how badly Tricee wanted that for herself.

"I am, too," Pam chimed in. "You know, with Conner and me and this thing between us," she shook her head, "I mean, it's serious. I feel we—meaning Conner and me—will get past this. I hope. I admit I'm partly to blame for where we are right now. But a couple's decision to have children is deep. I mean, I am so hurt over how things are with Conner and me, but … Tricee, I feel badly for you. When did he tell you?"

Jackie listened as Pam described how she was *partly* to blame. Pam didn't seem to realize just how big her part was. Jackie hoped that after this Bible talk session, they'd all walk away with a greater peace.

"Before she answers," Val jumped in, "let's pray."

The four women slowly bowed their heads. Val reached for Pam's hand, which caused Pam to jump.

"Ooh! Girl, you scared me!"

Jackie and Tricee opened their eyes.

"Sorry," Pam apologized, "I guess I'm just a little jittery."

Jackie and Tricee smiled as they shook their heads. They all closed their eyes again. Tricee reached for Jackie's hand as Val started to pray:

Lord, we gather here in your awesome presence. We ask for your guidance as we seek you concerning our trials and tribulations. We know that you are king over all. Help us to know your voice as we ask you to show us what you will have us do in circumstances that have spun out of our control.

There was a brief silence. "Does anyone else want to lift up a prayer?" Val asked as she glanced over at Jackie and Tricee.

"I'll go," Jackie cleared her throat:

Lord, now you know I am grateful for all you've done. I thank you for each and every blessing and every breakthrough. I thank you for my three closest friends as we gather together once more to sing your praises. We know that even though things look dim ...

Jackie opened one eye and stole a peek at Pam.

... we can rest and feel assured that you have it all figured out. Lord, you are a forgiving God, not a God who holds our mistakes against us. So give us that peace that only you can provide as we come to you open and honest ...

Her voice got louder.

... about everything, Lord!

This time it was Pam who opened one eye and stole a peek at Jackie.

And, Lord, I just need to ask you to help me in a situation I've been holding inside ...

Jackie squeezed Tricee's hand, causing her to flinch.

... I know you said to love our enemies and to bless those who persecute us. But Father, ...

Her voice got even louder.

... if that principal at Hope High School—and you know who he is—keeps getting rude with me during our meetings, I'm going to go off on him and I just want to tell you this, Lord, before it happens.

By now, Tricee, Val and Pam were all staring at Jackie who kept right on praying. She was oblivious to their stares.

Lord, I try to be nice, you know that. But you know folks don't always make it easy. I'm trying to raise a God-fearing daughter, I'm trying my best to be that loving wife like the one in the book of Proverbs. So, Lord, you know I'm trying to walk right. I love my career and I look forward to engaging in a new skill, teaching, this summer.

But if, during this last meeting for the year, this principal
gets out of line with me, look out!

Jackie was almost shouting at this point.

Tricee interjected. "Jackie." She nudged her friend gently with her elbow. "Jackie, are you okay?"

None of them had known of any issues Jackie was dealing with at work. They were all aware of how much she enjoyed her job as a high school principal, so they were a little stumped by her prayer request. Not to mention, they'd never heard Jackie pray with such fervor before. Were it not for the fact that she was praying, they would have laughed at her.

"Oh." She glanced at Tricee and then looked over at Pam and Val. "I guess I got a little carried away."

"Yeah, just a little," Val said with a smirk. "But that's okay. Father knows our hearts."

"You were really going," Pam remarked. "Do you need to discuss it?"

Jackie immediately waved her hands. "Oh, no. No, I'm good now. Besides, there are far greater issues we need to address."

Pam felt Jackie glance at her but decided not to comment.

"So," Pam began, looking over at Tricee, "your mother was supposed to visit right?"

"Yeah, she was, wasn't she?" Jackie recalled. "Is she still coming? I thought she was coming two weekends ago?"

Tricee shook her head. "She was supposed to visit, yes, but I called and told her that now just wasn't a good time."

Jackie, Val and Pam were silent as Tricee spoke. The sadness in her voice reminded them of two years prior when Ruby revealed to Tricee that her best childhood friend, Annette, was actually her half-sister. Tricee had experienced so much anguish. They could only imagine how she must have felt. Now here they were witnessing her deal with yet another unpleasant circumstance.

"You know, if I didn't know any better, I'd think I was doomed for problems," Tricee said and reached for her glass of iced tea.

"That's not true." Val went over and sat between Jackie and Tricee. Jackie moved over a few inches to allow Val some room.

"Are you gaining weight, Val?" Jackie asked, but the expression on her face indicated that she was only teasing. Val swiped her on the arm anyway.

"I asked because I had to move over to give you some room." Jackie laughed, which caused laughter to rise from the other three women.

They spent the next couple of hours talking about whatever issues they felt needed to be discussed. And there were quite a few scriptures read, mostly from the New Testament. Tricee and Pam found scriptures from 1 Corinthians very helpful, while Jackie shared a few verses from the book of Proverbs. Jackie felt that what she really needed was wisdom from on high to help her deal with unpleasant people. Val just went with whatever her three friends wanted to talk about. At the end of their session, she did ask for prayers for her and Cory as she prepared to return to work full time in a few weeks.

It was 2:30 PM by the time the ladies were gathering their purses to leave. Tricee felt a little better but her heart was still sad. She had a paper due by Wednesday so she knew she'd have to keep her emotions in check. Whatever issues she had at home would have to be dealt with through a lot of praying. She had no intention of stopping the Ph.D. program she was in.

"Tricee, let me say this," Val said as they all stood by the front door. "I know you can't see it now because your heart is too heavy, but I sense a tug in my spirit. There's a reason you and Hunter aren't supposed to adopt right now." She closed her eyes and began to shout, "Thank you, Jesus! Thank you, Lord!"

Soon Jackie and Pam were shouting, "Oh, thank you, Lord! Yes, Lord! We hear you, Lord! Hallelujah!"

Tricee was speechless. She watched in silence as her three friends had a shout-fest right at her front door. She felt something tugging within but was unable to release any words. Pam threw up both her hands, closed her eyes, and bowed her head. Tricee continued to look on as Pam began to send up her praises.

"Lord, I thank you for what you're doing right now in my marriage." Her words were followed by Val's and Jackie's *Praise you, Father! Yes, Lord!* "I know you have already redeemed my marriage because you are the creator of all things good, Lord. So whatever it is I need to do, Lord, show me, just show me."

When Pam began to jump up and down, Tricee bowed her head and began to speak softly. "Yes, Lord. Thank you, Lord."

When Pam ran into the living room, still shouting, Val and Jackie followed suit. Tricee's dwelling felt more like a church. Her friends were having a hallelujah good time right in the middle of her living room. The Holy Spirit had not only visited their Bible session but his presence had decided to stick around even after they all thought it was over.

"Praise you, Father. We sing your praises, Lord." Jackie stood in front of Tricee's sofa waving her hands back and forth.

"Oh, Father, restore broken marriages. Let your peace reign, oh, Lord, in every situation." Val was walking around the coffee table with her hands on her hips. Then she bent over and rocked back and forth.

Still standing in the entry way, and watching her friends, Tricee prayed quietly, "Lord, please don't let Val fall over my coffee table. Thank you, Lord. Thank you for this day and giving me peace."

Pam was standing by the entertainment center marching in place. "Oh, glory! Glory!" she shouted.

Tricee locked her front door and then joined her friends in the living room. With her head bowed and standing by the recliner, she continued to pray quietly, "Oh, Lord, I hear you now. In Jesus' name, I hear you now, Lord."

None of the women heard Hunter when he unlocked the front door and came inside. And since they all had their eyes closed, they didn't see him either. He stopped in the entryway and watched his wife and her three friends having church right in his living room. His eyes grew wide as he slowly made his way through the foyer.

"Hmm, sweet Jesus!" Val's shouting came to a halt as she rocked her head back and forth.

"Yes, Lord," Jackie said softly. She exhaled as she sat down of the sofa. "Whew, precious Lord."

Jackie reached into her purse, removed some tissue and wiped her forehead. It was then that she saw Hunter. He mouthed,

What the heck? Jackie just shook her head, closed her eyes again, and resumed praising Him softly.

Pam shouted one more hallelujah before her voice became a mere whisper. "Thank you, Lord, for your mercy, because without you I'm lost."

Hunter waited until he sensed that all four women were done getting their praise on. He wasn't bothered by it, just really surprised. He had never witnessed this before. He cleared his throat as he walked over and stood by his wife.

"Are you okay, Dear?" he asked as he glanced at Pam who was taking the tissue Jackie had offered.

"The Lord showed *up* and showed *out!*" Val said as she walked past Hunter and into the bathroom.

"I've never seen you like that before, Babe. What happened?" Hunter asked later on during dinner. "I mean, you were praying quietly, unlike your girls who were hollering and whooping all over our living room. But I could tell that you were really in the spirit."

"Well, we had our first Bible talk session. We prayed and discussed whatever we felt we needed to pray about. Pam and Conner and their issues, you and I and our ..." Tricee paused. She reached for her glass of water and took a sip before continuing. "It's not easy to go through these sorts of things. I mean, I was—"

298

she stopped and drew in a breath, "I'm still so hurt, Hunter, over the bomb you dropped on me. If you being the cause of your pain." Hunter's apology was sincere.

Hunter pushed his plate away from him. There wasn't one speck of food left on it. He had enjoyed dinner but wished the tension between him and his wife would end completely. He'd been looking forward to Ruby's and Boyce's visit, especially since he'd only seen them a couple of times since he'd married Tricee. And even though Tricee and her mother were still mending a strained relationship, he knew Tricee had been looking forward to seeing her.

Hunter had even arranged to take Boyce to a White Sox game. Boyce had gone on and on about how much he missed living in Chicago and watching his favorite teams. He'd adjusted well to his new surroundings in St. Louis, but informed Ruby— more than she cared to hear it—that Chicago would always be the best city in the world to him.

"I know you were looking forward to seeing your mom. I'm sure they can still visit sometime this summer." Hunter nodded when the server approached and asked if he'd like more iced tea. "I feel as though I've really added more stress to your plate, but that wasn't my intention."

Hunter took his wife's hand and held it in his. The last thing he ever wanted to do was cause her pain. But he felt he had to be honest about the whole adoption thing. She would've discovered his true feelings sooner or later. He wasn't saying he would never want to adopt, he just didn't want to adopt right now.

"I know you wouldn't hurt me intentionally, Hunter," Tricee said. "I just wish you had handled it differently." Tricee removed her hand from her husband's grip. She shrugged and continued, "As for Ruby and Boyce visiting, we'll see how things go this summer." Ruby and her husband were the last people on Tricee's mind at the moment.

Hunter and Tricee had decided to have dinner at Mia Francesca's Italian restaurant on Bryn Mawr. It was one of Tricee's favorite places to go for Italian cuisine.

Hunter had hoped they could sit and talk after her friends left, but he knew that giving her some time alone to finish her paper was a better option. Once she was done, with the exception of the bibliography page, she was all too willing to accept her husband's invitation to dinner.

Tricee placed her fork on her plate. They'd both ordered the Pollo azza Fiorentina: sautéed egg battered chicken breast on a bed of spinach with a lemon sauce. It was so delicious, Tricee was tempted to lick the fork.

After ordering one tiramisu dessert to go, Hunter paid the bill and they left the restaurant. They had taken the Red Line train to the restaurant, which was only two stops from where they lived but, due to Chicago Transit Authority rail repairs, the trains were bypassing certain stops. Tricee and Hunter boarded a southbound train at the Loyola station, which was just a couple blocks from their condo, but it went express to Wilson. So they had to get off at Wilson and ride a northbound train four stops to the Bryn Mawr station to get to the restaurant. It was a little inconvenient for the time being, but not intolerable. But both Tricee and Hunter were glad they didn't rely on the train during the week.

As they walked the one block to the station, Hunter took his wife's hand, hoping she wouldn't pull away. He could tell that, even though she was a little warmer toward him, he still wasn't completely off the hook. The train was arriving as they reached the top of the stairs.

"I like how they're redoing the train stations, don't you?" Hunter asked as they stood by the double set of doors. The renovations were making a big difference to the appearance of the stations.

"Yeah, I do," Tricee said softly. "But for those who ride the trains during the week, I'm sure they have to allow extra travel time."

Tricee took in her husband's appearance. He looked handsome in his dark blue slacks and light blue, button-down shirt. The evening air was crisp and cool. She'd brought a jacket with her but Hunter had said he wouldn't need one. Tricee almost wanted to laugh when she saw him shiver when they left the restaurant, then she remembered she was still sort of miffed.

Hunter leaned over and whispered in his wife's ear, "Are we going to make love when we get home? It's been a few days, you know?"

This was his attempt to ease the tension between them and make his wife laugh. When he saw her grin, he grew hopeful that things would soon be back to normal.

"I don't know about all of that." She smiled, though she was trying her best not to. "Besides, it hasn't been that long."

The prior week, Tricee had brought up the fact that she was upset that he'd missed church on several occasions. As much as she'd been trying not to bring it up, she felt she had every right to vent. After Hunter revealed his disinterest in adopting, she felt vindicated in bringing up his willingness to forego the Lord's house. She wanted him to suffer just as he'd made her suffer.

"Why are you missing church?!" she'd shouted one day last week as Hunter was taking off his clothes. It had been a long and tiresome day for them both but that didn't stop Tricee from venting. "It's been about six Sundays now! You have some nerve missing out on God's Word when *you*," she'd pointed directly in his face, "are the one bringing discord into this marriage."

Before Hunter could respond, Tricee had walked out of the bedroom and into the living room where she'd slept that night on the sofa. Hunter had tried to provide an explanation the following day but Tricee had dismissed him with a wave of the hand.

The train reached their stop at Granville. Once they made it down the stairs, Hunter stopped walking.

"It's been a whole week, Babe. That's long enough."

They walked toward the lake and toward their building. Once they arrived home, Tricee showered, and then proceeded into the living room, where she stretched out on the sofa. Hunter lifted his wife's legs as he sat down and laid them across his lap. He began to massage her feet.

"You know, Babe, I guess the reason I was missing church was simply because I was trying to work through my feelings, and how to tell you what I was feeling."

Tricee could hear the sincerity in her husband's voice. But his reasons for missing church didn't seem to matter to her now as much as they had before. The fact that he wasn't yet ready to adopt, when he knew how much she'd been looking forward to it, had taken precedence over all else.

"I just felt I had to spend some alone time with the Lord," he said.

Hunter stopped massaging her feet and stood up. He turned to go into the bedroom and Tricee got up and followed him.

"So you feel better now? Now that you have that off your chest?" Tricee's tone was a little sarcastic but Hunter decided not to entertain it.

An hour later, they were both fast asleep—Tricee on the sofa where she'd fallen asleep watching the original movie *Sparkle* and a disgruntled Hunter in the bedroom. No intimacy had taken place—*again*.

When their home phone rang at 3:00 AM, it was Hunter who jumped up to answer it. Startled and groggy, he grabbed the cordless phone from its base.

"Hello?" he said as he looked at the digital clock on the nightstand. "What? When did this happen?" Then he gasped. "Oh, no! Oh, man!"

His voice woke up Tricee who came running into the bedroom. "What, Honey?! What?!"

This phone call would alter both their lives in a way they never would have expected.

26

"So what do you know about your new client?" Pam asked Darcy as she looked suspiciously around the fast food restaurant. The only information Pam had on Janae Mays-Morrison was personal data. No notes had been added to her file as of yet.

When Pam got to work on Wednesday, two days ago, she logged on to her computer and opened the program the social workers used to take notes and assessments. Darcy had always been an efficient worker who prioritized her tasks, so Pam was disappointed and almost offended when she saw that Darcy hadn't input any information on the woman, and that she'd have to remain curious about the woman she'd presumed was Jeff's cousin for a few extra days.

"I know quite a bit, I guess," Darcy answered in a quiet voice as she glanced around like Pam had done. "And why are we looking around like we're spies?"

"I'm just trying to keep my voice down. You never know who might decide to eavesdrop."

Pam and Darcy had agreed to a late lunch at 2:00 PM. Besides, it was Friday and they'd both accomplished quite a bit during the week—with the exception of Darcy not entering her notes as promptly as Pam had expected.

"Well, of course I know quite a bit about my new client," Darcy confirmed, wiping her mouth after a couple of bites of her juicy burger. "After all," she smirked, "she is my client."

"Okay, Smarty Pants." Pam smiled. "I realize that. It's just that I noticed there were no notes added to the assessment file." She looked toward the door and softened her voice. "That's all."

Darcy watched Pam take a small bite of her burger. It seemed to her that Pam was almost afraid to eat it even though she'd commented on how good it tasted. She was really beginning to enjoy talking to Pam and felt that her mannerisms at times were quite amusing, like now.

Whether they were working or having lunch, she sensed something unique about her colleague. She sensed that Pam had a big heart and that she wouldn't intentionally cause harm to anyone. She also believed, judging from the times they'd spoken, that Pam was the type of person who really wanted to do right in every aspect of her life. She could tell from their conversations that Pam loved her husband dearly and that she wouldn't trade him for anything in the world.

Darcy could tell that Pam had been hurt in past relationships, as was the case with most people. But in Pam's case it caused her to keep her guard up, sometimes a little more than was necessary. She believed that after today, she and Pam would be more than just co-workers who occasionally had lunch together. She'd made a mental note to ask Pam where her church was located, as she was interested in visiting.

"May I have that packet of ketchup, please?"

"You know," Darcy said as Pam bit into another french fry, "You're going to have to stop with all this whispering."

Pam stopped chewing and looked at Darcy as though she was speaking a foreign language.

"You are too funny!" Darcy laughed and slapped her hand on the table. "Why are you looking at me like that? And, um," Darcy cleared her throat, "there are only three other people in here and they're not interested in our conversation."

"Well," Pam said, before drinking the rest of her lemonade, "that older white guy over there," she tilted her head in his direction, "keeps looking over here every time I open my mouth."

"Girl, please. That man looks like that all the time," Darcy said with a wave of her hand. "I've seen him a couple times before, I think he lives in the area. He has to be in his 90s so looking at other people might be the highlight of his days."

"Well, still. You know, in our profession we have to be careful." Pam stood up. "I need some water."

Pam and Darcy had never been to this particular fast food restaurant, at least not together, and when Darcy mentioned that she had a taste for a burger and fries, Pam agreed that it would be a self-indulgent change from her usual semi-healthy lunches. And just about everyone else from the agency agreed that Ian's, located on Montrose, was the place to go for great-tasting fast food. Ian's even had menu selections for those who didn't want to totally blow their healthy eating habits. Turkey burgers, tuna on rye and Caesar salads were three of the options available. The place was also walking distance from the agency, which made it an excellent choice.

After Pam returned to the table with two glasses of water, they resumed their conversation. "Why are you asking me about my new client?" Darcy asked after taking a few sips of water. "By the way, I did enter my notes this morning. I hadn't gotten around to it because, you know, I was in court all day yesterday and Wednesday." She began to eat what was left of her burger as she waited for Pam to respond.

Pam had to constantly flick her wrists to keep the long, flared sleeves on her red blouse from falling into her food. She exhaled before she began.

"I saw her at my church last month. She was wearing that same tight—well, form-fitting dress that she had on Monday. I was just surprised to see her at the shelter."

Pam took another small bite of her hamburger. Darcy finished what was left of her meal and glanced at the round clock on the wall. They still had about 20 minutes left to their lunch break and it took about 10 minutes or so to walk back to the shelter. But Darcy could tell that Pam was in no hurry to get back. Neither was Darcy for that matter. Pam continued.

"Her nails—her long nails, that is—were the same color as her dress. But I see that she had those removed."

Darcy was now curious, wondering exactly where Pam was going with this conversation. It wasn't unlikely or unheard of for a client to attend church. And it certainly wasn't uncommon for a woman to have long nails.

"Please don't think I'm being petty because I'm discussing the woman's personal taste," Pam said. "It's just that she sort of stood out."

"Okay, now let me ask you a question," Darcy said as she folded her arms.

For a second, Pam thought she'd offended her colleague, but Darcy, noticing the way Pam was looking at her, chuckled.

"Pam, you can relax." Darcy unfolded her arms. "I was just going to ask if your church had a certain dress requirement."

"You're joking, right?"

"I am," Darcy replied. "By the way, I don't think you're being petty, I'm just wondering where—"

"You're wondering where this conversation is going," Pam completed her colleague's sentence.

Darcy nodded as she reached into her purse for a tube of lip gloss. The color, ginger spice, was a perfect match for the light orange and beige blouse she wore with a pair of black, flared-leg slacks. When it came to fashion, Darcy did not disappoint. Small gold earrings were the only accessory needed to complete her outfit, other than her watch. Pam had wondered earlier, whether her colleague was going out after work.

"I spoke with Janae last week, actually—via telephone, a day before she arrived at the shelter. Things had suddenly gone from bad to worse for her. She left an abusive husband and went to stay with some relatives. They live somewhere on the far south side, I think."

Pam was all ears. She hadn't even gotten a chance to finish what she'd started to say about Janae. And Darcy must have gotten distracted because, as interested as she seemed in hearing why Pam was so curious about this woman, she started sharing information before allowing Pam to explain.

Darcy glanced at the small gold watch on her wrist this time instead of at the clock on the wall and announced that they'd better get going. "We need to go," she said and tapped her watch. "It's close to 3:00 and we don't want folks looking at us cross-eyed for coming back late."

That was more of a joke and both women knew it. No one at the agency was given a hard time if they strolled in a few minutes late after their lunch break. This was because it rarely happened. The counselors, social workers, and administrators all worked very hard given the great deal of stress that often came with the job. And since the staff staggered their lunch breaks so everyone wasn't out of the office at the same time, there was always someone on hand to handle any issue that might arise, even a major crisis, which has been known to happen every so often.

Pam drank the rest of her water and tossed her napkin on top of what was left of her burger. It had been delicious but the abundance of fries that came with the order made for more than she could finish. Darcy teased her as they made their way out of the restaurant.

"Did you not enjoy your lunch?" she asked Pam as they walked down Sheridan Road headed to Montrose Avenue. "I noticed you were taking very small bites out of that burger. For a minute, I thought you were afraid it was going to bite you back."

"Oh, no, it was really good," Pam replied with a laugh. "It was just way too much. They give you so many french fries."

"Yeah, I'm full," Darcy replied. "My husband and I are going out tonight with some friends to listen to some blues. Afterward, he and I are going to dinner. I'm sure I'll be very hungry again by then. Anyway," Darcy tapped Pam lightly on the arm, "we had a chat about that ex-girlfriend of his showing up unannounced." She frowned, which made Pam laugh.

"Oh, I meant to ask you how that was playing out."

Pam was genuinely interested in hearing how that issue had been dealt with between Darcy and her husband. She and Darcy hadn't really discussed it since the first time Darcy mentioned it. Pam hoped that she would give her the short version because she still wanted to hear more about Janae.

"I told him I had run into an ex-boyfriend—which was a lie—and that he might be stopping by sometime unannounced."

Darcy laughed as they stopped at a crosswalk. Pam thought it was comical how Darcy had gone from a frown to a laugh. It was obvious she felt vindicated in using that strategy.

"He didn't really believe that, did he?" Pam asked.

While walking back to work, Pam noticed that there were a lot of children outside, some with adults and some with other children. The school year was over but the summer session had begun. When a boy and his friend—they looked to be around 12—rode past Pam and Darcy on their bikes, Pam thought about the boy she encountered two years ago, when she and Tricee spoke at career day.

The school where they'd spoken was only a few blocks in the opposite direction. Pam recalled how a sixth grader stated that he would hire women to be his secretaries. She'd given the student a quick lesson on how "administrative assistant" was the more appropriate term—at least for her it was—and how women weren't groomed to only be support staff. Though she hadn't used those exact words, she'd gotten her message across. She'd also given the young man the evil eye for having the nerve to be a male chauvinist at 11 years old.

Darcy spoke as they crossed the street. "I don't know if he believed me or not, but it worked." She chuckled. "Men. They can dish it out but they can't take it."

Things in the Buckner household were still a little shaky, although she and Conner had been intimate two nights ago. Pam was amazed at how she and her husband could make such beautiful music in bed and then—Bam! An hour later, Conner was back to being grumpy. But the way Conner had made love to her the two times they'd been intimate since their disagreement—not that she was counting—convinced her that all was well between them. And Pam knew her husband well. She could sense that his focus had been completely on her. His mind hadn't been elsewhere during the most beautiful act shared between two people who were married.

Now, as she and Darcy arrived back at the agency, her mind drifted from her husband back to Darcy's client.

"So that's pretty much it about the client?" Pam asked.

When Darcy mentioned that Janae had stayed with relatives, Pam automatically assumed it was one of Jeff's sisters.

Darcy responded quietly as they walked into the building, "I'll walk to your office with you."

They spoke to the security guard as they passed his desk on the way to Pam's office. His bag sat atop his desk and he wore an expression that said he was ready for the weekend. His shift ended at 3:00 PM and it was now 3:05 PM, mere seconds, he hoped, before his relief would take over.

"Ready for the weekend, Harlan?" Darcy asked the middle-aged guard. Though not considered very handsome, he had smooth brown skin and his personality made him very likeable.

"You know I'm ready," he answered and smiled. "You ladies enjoy the weekend."

Once inside Pam's office, Darcy sat down and took a pack of Trident gum out of her purse along with her cell phone. Pam sat down at her desk and logged on to her computer. Darcy began to

314

open the pack of gum as she spoke, keeping her voice to a whisper because Pam's office door was open.

"Janae's husband is still living in their town home but her relatives are working on that. That's pretty much it."

"Interesting," said Pam, placing both hands on her hips.

"Has your curiosity been satisfied now?" Darcy asked. "And for the record, my sharing information with you about my client wasn't gossiping. You could have found out anyway and I trust you."

"I know you're not gossiping and, yes, I'm sort of satisfied."

Pam figured she could share with Darcy that she knew a relative of Janae's, even though she had no intention of seeing him again. Her marriage meant too much to her for her to risk ruining it. This time it would be for good when she told Jeff goodbye. She would mention it to Darcy on Monday, but for now it was time to get back to work.

Darcy stood up and remembered she wanted to ask Pam about her church. "Pam, I meant to ask—where is your church located? I'd like to attend."

Pam could see the sincerity in Darcy's eyes. "Oh, Darcy, that would be nice. In fact …" Pam grabbed a yellow Post-It note from her desk drawer and wrote down the church's address. "My husband is giving the sermon this Sunday. There's been a lot going on in the past month with his daughter and, well," Pam sighed, "with us. He canceled speaking at his cousin's church last Sunday, but he told me he's still on for giving the sermon at our church." Pam shrugged. "I really hope that things get back to normal with us soon. That's going to depend all on me."

Darcy adjusted her purse on her shoulder. "Honesty is the best policy. As long as you're honest, you guys will be just fine."

"I know. I've heard that one before."

Pam glanced at her watch. She wanted to meet with one of her clients before 5:00 PM rolled around. More than likely, the young woman was on the second floor with some of the other clients going through the clothes that had been donated. She decided to wait until 4:00 PM. The clients were usually done by then and watching television.

Pam's mind was filled with several things but at least Darcy had expressed an interest in attending her church. That was a good thing. What Darcy said next, however, caught Pam off guard.

"Pam, you know, I wanted to tell you that I've been thinking about becoming saved, and I have you to thank for that."

"Oh?" Pam raised an eyebrow.

"It's true. I know it might seem like I'm all harsh, and I know I sometimes come off like Ms. Militant, but I want to live in a way that pleases Him, you know?"

"I'm really glad to hear that, Darcy," Pam responded with a smile.

"I would love to introduce my husband to yours," said Darcy. Then she remembered Pam's "issues" with her mate. "Well, you know when the time is right."

Darcy placed the yellow Post-It in her purse. She hoped that Pam felt the same way she did, that their friendship was slowly developing past the co-worker stage. From Pam's expression, Darcy felt that she did, indeed, feel the same way, even if she hadn't come right out and said it.

"That would be fine. And hopefully your husband will come with you this Sunday if you can make it." Pam really hoped they would.

Darcy smiled as she turned to leave, but suddenly turned back.

"Janae did mention that her cousin and his wife will be visiting her this summer from Houston. The relative she was staying with only allowed her to stay for a short time. That's why she's here." Darcy shrugged. "I guess some relatives will only help so much. She says she's really close to this particular cousin and that he's not happy at all with the situation, and wants her husband out of that town house. But what can he do? It belongs to both Janae *and* her husband, and her husband is paying the mortgage."

Darcy finished the last part of that last sentence very slowly when she saw the horrified expression on Pam's face.

"What's wrong?" she asked Pam.

Pam's neck did a swirl. "Her cousin and his *wife*? Did she happen to mention his name?" She already knew the answer but needed to hear it for confirmation.

"Yes, his name is Jeff. Jeff Mays."

Not exactly sure why Pam was looking at her as if she had two heads, Darcy raised an eyebrow as she turned to leave Pam's office.

27

The enemy will use anybody to do his dirty work. And let me remind you that Satan doesn't show up wearing a red suit and holding a pitchfork in his hand. He will use a co-worker, a boss, a friend—even a family member. That's why it's so important to stay rooted in the Word. You know what it says over in Hebrews, chapter four, verse, uh ...

Conner flipped through the pages of his Bible, then glanced quickly at his watch.

Well, you know what it says. I don't have time to show you right now. If you don't know, just see me after the service so I can take you there.

There was laughter throughout the congregation.

I want you to hear me this morning. You need to get this. The enemy knows which buttons to push. He knows our weaknesses. Why do you think there are so many failed relationships? He knows that as soon as you take your eyes off the Word and start relying on your flesh, he has you exactly where he wants you. For those of you who are single—wait on God to bring you your spouse. Stop being in such a hurry. Slow down.

He stepped down out of the pulpit and stood in front of the congregation.

*And for those of you who are married—you know, don't be
so quick to think that just because you're married, you no
longer need that quiet, solo time with the Lord. I had a guy
tell me once that he prayed and asked God for a wife. Then
after his request was granted, he said now he can focus on
other stuff.*

Mmm hmm, a few of the women in the congregation
murmured. Conner could see a few heads nodding.

*That was one of the dumbest things I'd heard that day. I
almost told him that but the Holy Spirit caught me. I know
this man had to have known what I was thinking because
I'm sure my facial expression gave me away. This was a
saved man. He went to church on Sundays and paid his
tithes regularly.*

Conner turned and climbed the few steps back up to the
pulpit.

*See, we have to be careful and prayerful at all times. It
amazes me how folk run around claiming to be Christian
folks, but then their actions show something totally
different. They get mad at a loved one because they're not
behaving the way they think the person ought to behave.
Instead of going to the Lord and asking Him to help you
with your issues—and we all have issues—you want to get*

*all mad and allow Satan to have you all put out with
somebody.*

Half of the congregation was on their feet with their hands
raised. The other half sat and nodded their heads, letting everything
Conner had to say sink in. Darcy and her husband sat and listened
intently as Pam's husband delivered what Darcy felt was a very
thought-provoking message. She'd already made up her mind that
New Hope was going to be her church home.

*I don't know how I got off on that. That wasn't even part of
my notes.*

Conner shared in the laughter of the congregation.
*Saints, we have to lean on Him. We have to stop trying to
do things on our own. Let me take you to one more place.
Sit down.*

He looked at the people in the congregation and smiled.
Go with me to Proverbs, chapter one, verse five ...

He read from the King James Version:
*A wise man will hear, and will increase learning; and a
man of understanding shall attain unto wise counsels.*

He paused and closed his Bible.
*Folks, the Lord is waiting on you, you're not waiting on
Him. He already knows the beginning and the end. Just
seek Him and tell Him what you're going through. I*

guarantee you, you will find your answer. Now give the
Lord some praise.

Pam smiled as she observed the body language of the folks in the congregation. She was pleased that her husband had preached a sermon that brought many to their feet. His message had even made her flinch a time or two. There were at least 10 people waiting to chat with him briefly after the service.

Aunt Polly placed her thin arm around Pam's. Her smile almost lit up the church. Pam smiled back at her Aunt Polly who was wearing a green dress with a long, green, beaded necklace. The white flats she wore reminded Pam of the kind of shoes hospital staff wore. As she stood arm-in-arm with her aunt, she noticed just how much her father resembled his older sister.

"Pam, I tell you, that husband of yours really allowed the Lord to use him this morning," Aunt Polly commented as she and Pam looked toward the pulpit.

"Yes, Aunt Polly, I have to agree with you," Pam replied just as Darcy and her husband made their way to where Pam was standing.

"Darcy!" Pam exclaimed and carefully extracted her arm from her aunt's. "Aunt Polly, this is my colleague, Darcy, and her husband." Pam extended her hand to Darcy's husband. "I'm sorry, I don't even know your name."

The few times Darcy spoke about her husband to Pam, she'd never mentioned his name and Pam had never bothered to ask. It wasn't a big issue, but it would have made the introductions less awkward had she known his name.

"That's quite alright," said Darcy's husband as he smiled, displaying a nice, even set of white teeth. "I'm Sedric, with an 'S.'" Then he turned to Aunt Polly. "It's a real pleasure to meet you."

"Oh, it's a real pleasure for me, too, Sedric." Aunt Polly blushed and then lowered her eyes, behaving as if she was a teenager with a crush. Had Pam not known any better, she would have thought her aunt was flirting. She and Darcy exchanged looks. Pam could see that Darcy was trying her best not to laugh.

"So did you enjoy the service?" Pam was looking at Darcy but the question was meant for Darcy and her husband.

"Oh, I sure did!" Darcy responded with enthusiasm. "That message was long overdue." She glanced at her husband. He smiled but remained silent, not exactly sure what his wife expected him to say. He had, indeed, enjoyed the sermon, but he wasn't making any plans to return next Sunday. He knew his wife well enough to know that she was definitely planning on coming back, though. He also realized that she might have already had an outfit picked out. It amazed him, sometimes, how detailed most women were.

Darcy had mentioned on at least two separate occasions that she and Sedric needed to go to "somebody's church." She was beginning to feel as if something was missing from their lives. Sedric had said to her, "We can do like my mom and go to our bedside church." But Darcy failed to see the humor in her husband's statement. In fact, whenever he mentioned his mother at all, Darcy cringed.

Sedric thought it was funny how his wife and his mother were cordial to each other, but neither woman liked being in the other's presence. He did not, however, think it was funny when Darcy informed him that she'd run into one of her exes. He ended up putting a stop to the visits from his ex-girlfriend, even though the woman was nothing more than a friend. Not only did he believe women were detailed but they also seemed to be one step ahead of the men in their lives. But Sedric would never admit this to his wife.

"You know that's Pam's husband who gave the sermon," Aunt Polly announced proudly.

"Oh, yes," said Darcy, even though Aunt Polly was speaking to Sedric. "Pam told me her husband would be preaching."

Conner joined his wife and extended his hand to Sedric. He acknowledged Darcy with a smile. He spoke before allowing Pam to make the introduction.

"I'm Conner, Pam's husband. Is this your first time with us?"

Aunt Polly cleared her throat. Conner laughed and immediately bent over and planted a kiss on the older woman's cheek.

Unbelievable! This woman wants all the attention, Pam thought and shook her head to keep from chuckling. Darcy liked Aunt Polly already.

"Yes, it is," Darcy replied, "but it certainly won't be our last."

Sedric gave Conner a half-smile and Conner immediately picked up on the thought behind it: *She might be coming back but don't count on me.* Conner smiled back and decided that Sedric was more than likely a very nice man who was married to a woman who called most of the shots in their marriage. The tension he'd experienced in his own marriage over the past several weeks had allowed him to see things from a different perspective. Perhaps the incident with Pam occurred so his eyes would be opened to the plight of other married people. This, he believed, would allow him to serve others even better.

He was still not at all happy with the choice Pam had made to stay out later than was expected last month, and he realized they still needed to discuss how to move past it in order to move on. Being an assistant pastor had not made him less human. He had feelings just like everyone else.

"I'm glad you guys could make it. I sure did get something from my husband's message." Pam gave Conner a warm smile. "I think he needs to preach more often."

Conner shrugged. He smiled at Pam but quickly turned his attention to Aunt Polly. Pam would be mistaken if she thought that all was totally right between them, even if they were standing in the house of the Lord. She wasn't off the hook just yet.

"Aunt Polly," Conner addressed her warmly and extended his hand to her. "May I have the honor of walking you to your car?"

"I would be honored to have both you handsome men escort me to my car."

She grabbed Conner's arm as well as Sedric's, and the two men chuckled as they led the older woman out of the church. Darcy and Pam laughed. Aunt Polly's shorter stature and thin frame between the two taller men was, indeed, a sight to see. And the way Aunt Polly turned and looked over her shoulder at Darcy and Pam made it even more entertaining.

"I like that lady," Darcy laughed.

"Yeah, she's something." Pam shook her head as she and Darcy headed for the set of double doors. Pam stopped just as they reached the lobby.

"What?" Darcy asked. "Did you forget something?"

"No," Pam said, a smile forming on her face. "I just thought of a great idea for the OWN network."

"Really?" Darcy asked.

"Yeah." Pam smirked. "Seventy-five-year-old woman steals younger woman's husband after church service."

"Oh, stop!" Darcy laughed and lightly tapped Pam on the arm.

Pam and Conner rode home in silence. The only time they spoke was when Conner's cell phone rang.

"It's the girls calling. I told them I would stop by after church. I'll call them back as soon as we get home."

"Would you like for me to go with you?" Pam asked, hoping her attempt at being nice would succeed. But when Conner uttered, "No, that's okay," she realized it was going to be another long Sunday afternoon alone.

Once home, Conner climbed out of the car and walked quickly to the back door. As soon as he put his key into the double lock, his phone rang again. Pam exhaled as she followed her husband inside. From his end of the conversation, she could tell that he wasn't speaking to his daughters.

He walked into the bedroom to change out of his suit and Pam was only a few steps behind him. Conner ignored or was oblivious to the fact that his wife was so close to him. They were practically wearing the same shirt.

"I'm on my way. I promised the girls I would stop by. Do you need anything?" Long pause. "Okay, well I don't see that as being a problem at all. But we can talk about it some more when I get there."

Conner switched his cell phone to the opposite ear and went over to the closet to retrieve a pair of tan slacks. As he stood in front of his wife in boxers and a T-shirt, Pam thought about something her sister Terri had said.

"Sis, you might want to learn a few bedroom tricks to get Conner speaking to you again."

Pam and her sister Lynn had laughed upon hearing Terri's advice. It had been one day last week during a three-way call that Terri had so freely offered her wisdom.

"Terri, sexual favors don't always work on husbands," Lynn had offered.

"And it's not like we're not talking at all. He *is* speaking to me some," Pam said.

"Yeah, but you want things to be back to normal, don't you?" Terri asked. She winked at her husband who appeared in their bedroom. "I'm telling you, sis. Learn a new trick. Turn a flip, swing from the ceiling fan, do *something*. And I guarantee you, he'll be back to his regular self."

Pam chuckled as she recalled that conversation. But she wondered if maybe her sister was right. What if she tried something different with her husband? She'd already decided to ask Conner if they could, perhaps, go out to dinner later on, and try to talk about those things that had yet to be discussed. She only hoped he hadn't planned to spend the entire Sunday with his daughters.

"I'll see you in a little while. Tell the girls I'm on my way."

Conner ended his conversation and placed his cell phone on his nightstand. Just as he zipped his pants, Pam walked over and stood in front of him.

"I think we need to—" They spoke in unison. Pam had removed her skirt but was still wearing sheer, off-black pantyhose and an off-white blouse.

"You first." Conner looked his wife from head to toe. The scent of her vanilla body spray filled their bedroom. It was his favorite scent among the 10-plus small bottles that lined Pam's dresser. Unlike many women who seemed to bathe in perfume,

Pam had always applied just a dab behind each earlobe. That had been one of the things he'd noticed when they first met.

There had been times when the bus was crowded and Conner thought he would pass out from the smell of strong perfume. He was glad he didn't have that issue with his wife. Regrettably, they still had this other issue.

Pam slowly wrapped her arms around her husband's waist. He'd removed his T-shirt and tossed it onto the chair beside the bed. She stood on her toes and planted a kiss on his lips. It was the best way she could think of to initiate what she now had in mind.

"I was just going to say I think we need to have this talk." She waited for Conner to put his arms around her waist but they remained at his side. "You, obviously, were going to say the same thing. That we need to talk." Pam looked into her husband's eyes and continued. "Conner, I got together with Jeff twice, and the only thing we did was talk."

"If that's the case then why didn't you just say that?" Conner removed Pam's arms from around his waist. "And it doesn't matter if all you did was talk, Pam. There are just some things I won't tolerate."

"Conner, when I tried to tell you that nothing happened, you just blew me off. You were so upset that it didn't matter what I was trying to say."

"You're right. I was going to say we need to talk." Conner walked over to his dresser and pulled out a white, short-sleeved, pullover shirt. "You know, as I was preaching that sermon earlier, I felt the Holy Spirit telling me to let it go." He stood with his shirt in his hand. "But as much as I want to get past this, I just can't let it go right now."

"I know." Pam smiled. "I made a huge mistake and I'll do whatever I can to make things right between us."

Pam grabbed the shirt from her husband's hand and tossed it onto the bed. A few kisses later, she lay beside him, both of them still partially dressed. As difficult as it had been to resist his wife's advances, Conner couldn't bring himself to move past a few kisses. He was dealing with a lot, including Renita's ongoing issues.

He hadn't yet told Pam about Renita's turbulent past. Although she was no longer his wife, she was still the mother of his children and he still cared a great deal about her. He wanted and needed for his life to resume some normalcy. There was enough going on. And he needed for Pam to understand that his kindness was not to be mistaken for weakness. He removed himself from Pam's embrace and stood up.

"You know, life has enough problems on its own. We do ourselves harm bringing on anything extra." He watched his wife put on the blouse she'd just taken off.

"I know, and I realize that," Pam said as she got up from the bed and went to stand next to her husband. She reached out to him and was rejected once again. He moved her arm and stepped backward.

"Pam, you really need to be a little more considerate in your dealings with others. And you can start with your own husband."

"I know. I'm human, Conner. Allow—"

"Allow you to make a few mistakes, right?" he responded accusingly, cutting her off.

"I would allow you to be human," she snapped back, wondering what Conner would say next. She was hoping he wasn't about to ask her to pack a bag and leave again. From the expression on his face, it was hard to tell.

"Let me start off by first explaining this to you." He paused. "Renita has dealt with some pretty rough things in her life. So before you continue to treat her with contempt, you should understand that."

"Conner, what are you talking about?" Pam's voice got louder. "You act as if I treat *that* woman like she's some sort of demon. Shoot, I rarely even see *the woman*."

Pam walked angrily to the closest and snatched a pair of white, linen slacks from a hanger. Conner watched his wife's overly dramatic behavior as she slid her left leg into the pants. He waited until she was dressed before he spoke again. Pam frowned as her husband imitated her voice as well as her demeanor.

"I rarely even see *that* woman. You act like I treat *the woman* like a demon."

Watching her husband wiggle his head while speaking in a feminine voice was almost comical. Pam had to struggle to keep from breaking out into a grin, remembering that she was upset.

"See? That's exactly what I'm talking about," Conner said in his own voice. "You're so quick to get an attitude. I can't even talk to you because you get so defensive. Learn to relax."

"I'm not on the defense." Pam rolled her neck. "I don't have a problem discussing anything with you, Conner."

"Must you roll your head and your neck like that?" Conner asked. "Your neck looks like it's about to fall off!"

After a few moments of silence they both laughed. Conner's was more like a light chuckle, though. His wife calling him by another man's name hadn't been easily forgotten. They were definitely going to need counseling. He even considered individual counseling for himself, just to be safe.

What Pam didn't know was that her mother-in-law, Viola, was the reason she hadn't been put out and wasn't on her way to divorce court. She'd told Conner to pray and "try hard" to work things out, and he'd decided to take her advice. He'd contacted an attorney but eventually informed the gentleman that he "wasn't going to pursue it right now." Pam had one more chance and, if she blew it, he still had the attorney's business card.

Four hours later, after spending some time with his daughters, Conner and Pam sat across from each other at one of their favorite places to dine. The restaurant in Hyde Park was a casual place with a hint of elegance. There was a large chandelier hanging from the middle of the main dining room ceiling and four pieces of African American art lined the walls. There was also a piece by Dali that captured your attention when you walked in.

White tablecloths adorned each of the 15 tables in the main dining room. The smaller dining area toward the back seated up to 20 patrons. Though not considered a big restaurant, it was sizable enough to draw a decent crowd. For a Sunday evening, both Conner and Pam were relieved the place wasn't packed.

"We should bring the girls here sometime," Conner said as he glanced around the restaurant. "I don't believe they've ever been here."

"Maybe Renita has brought them before," Pam responded with a shrug.

She wanted their dinner conversation to be about their marriage and how to move forward, not his twin daughters. There were still years left to discuss them. Right now, her focus was on keeping the man who sat before her happy. When she glanced at the chandelier, a wicked smile formed on her face.

"What are you smiling like that for?" Conner asked as he turned and looked over his shoulder in the direction of Pam's gaze. He wondered if she might have seen someone she knew.

"I was just thinking about what my sister Terri said to me." Pam smiled. "I'll tell you—no, I'll show you—later."

"Okay."

Conner was about to say something else when their server approached the table. Conner ordered the grilled chicken with mashed potatoes and asparagus, and Pam ordered the grilled salmon salad. Before proceeding to share some very personal details about his ex-wife, Conner decided to make small talk.

"So your co-worker—Darcy, is it? She seemed to really enjoy the sermon this morning." He took a sip of his lemonade. "But her husband? I don't think he'll be returning any time soon." Conner chuckled as he recalled the look on the man's face.

"Darcy enjoyed the sermon and meeting Aunt Polly. As for Sedric," Pam said and slowly began to nod her head, "I'd like to think he got something out of your message."

"Trust me. If Darcy returns next Sunday, she'll be returning minus her husband."

Conner mentioning Darcy caused Pam to think about Friday, when she'd confirmed that Janae was Jeff's cousin. That wasn't the part that had ruffled her feathers, though. It had been the part about Jeff having a wife. While she'd thought about it all Friday evening and, pretty much, the whole day on Saturday, a few tense moments between she and Conner as they got ready for church this morning managed to push it to the back of her mind.

As Pam was driving home from work on Friday, she had a strong urge to phone Jeff and ask him some questions. But then she remembered the issues she was already dealing with at home. A phone call to Jeff would have to wait. But if things went Pam's way, that call would be the one call Jeff would regret answering. Pam had already thought of a few unkind words she was more than willing to use, right before telling him to lose her number for good.

Their food arrived and they bowed their heads. Conner blessed the food. "Lord, we thank you for this meal and we ask that you bless the hands that prepared it. In His name, Amen." Pam followed with a soft *Amen*.

After a few forkfuls of grilled chicken, mashed potatoes and a couple of asparagus spears, Conner cleared his throat. It was time to explain some things to Pam about his ex-wife. He left out the part about Renita's therapist's recommendation that she attend a four-week retreat this summer, no family members allowed, including children.

Pam listened intently with a wide-eyed expression upon hearing about Renita's misfortunes for the first time.

"Wow, she dealt with incest from two different family members and was raped by someone who was supposed to be like an uncle? Gee, some family friend."

A restaurant hadn't exactly been Conner's first choice for sharing news of this sort, but the timing of it all just seemed to work out. He could see the genuine compassion in Pam's eyes as he talked. They'd been married for six months and now seemed as good a time as any to share what he and his ex had kept secret. When he mentioned to Renita earlier in the day that he'd shared with Pam the fact that she'd been through some pretty rough things, Renita had said nothing and asked no questions. But Conner realized that the day would arrive when Renita would want to know just how much he'd shared with Pam.

The fact of the matter was that he hadn't shared anything with Pam until now. Before he left Renita's home after his visit with the girls this afternoon, she divulged that the therapy sessions were helping and that she hadn't realized that so many other women had been through similar experiences. Renita also realized that Conner wasn't the kind of ex-husband she couldn't trust. Even though they didn't make it as husband and wife, she carried no ill feelings toward the father of her children.

"Yes, things have been difficult for her. So what you see is not so much an evil ex. It is a woman dealing with some deep-rooted issues."

Conner paused but Pam remained silent, allowing her husband to say whatever he felt he needed to say.

"You know, if I'm honest about it, I felt for a long time that Renita was the wrong woman for me, and that she was, indeed, evil on wheels."

That comment caused Pam to chuckle. "Evil on wheels, huh? That's a new one." Pam reached for her glass of water.

"Now don't get me wrong. Her issues weren't the only reasons we couldn't make it. In actuality, we really just weren't right for each other. We both realized that."

"After laying up and having babies." Pam sat back in her chair.

"Well, you know, Pam. It happens."

Conner pushed his plate away from him. His wife sure could be the formidable one. And she was so opinionated! He only hoped she would bend a little, as his mother would say. This was crucial to his and Pam's marriage. To Viola, bending a little simply meant not being so self-absorbed that you forget someone else is involved. "One person is usually not the sole reason for the deterioration of a marriage," she'd said.

Conner believed he was being led to stay and work things out this time. And he believed his wife when she said that nothing happened between her and Jeff. Even if that wasn't true, it was Pam who would have to suffer the consequences. It was her guilty conscience she would have to live with.

They discussed how to move forward in their relationship and agreed on counseling, though whether they'd seek it from their pastor or another source hadn't been decided. Conner admitted to Pam that he'd been ready to give up on their marriage because of the hurt he'd felt. And it wasn't just ego. He said he was more than willing to go at it as an unmarried man who assisted in raising two very beautiful daughters. He didn't need any added stress. And being an assistant pastor didn't change how he felt.

"I know what the Bible says about divorce, but I also believe the Lord wants us to live in peace, married or single," Conner said to Pam on the drive home. Then he quoted the verse from 1 Corinthians 14, verse 33 for good measure. And a few moments later, he decided to also quote verse 34 and 35, which got a rise out of Pam.

"What made you share all this now?" Dressed in a short, white, lacy negligee, Pam was ready to go to bed but not to sleep.

The look in her husband's eyes had her convinced he felt the same way. "Why are you just now sharing this with me? About Renita?"

"I heard you the first time. I just felt that, with the issues between us, I needed for you to know that I can only take so much. That's the only way I can describe it. She's still the mother of my children and I do care for her well-being. Then there's Raneen having that concussion. I'm just thankful she's okay. It just seems like quite a bit is happening all at once. I do trust that you'll keep what I've shared to yourself."

"Oh, now you should know me better than that," Pam replied, pulling the blanket and top sheet to the foot of the bed.

"I thought I did," Conner responded as he climbed into their bed. He propped himself up on one elbow and watched Pam use her fingers to smooth the short hairstyle he'd come to love so much on her.

"Okay, I guess I deserved that one." Pam climbed in beside her husband. "But you have to believe me when I say I promise to do better. I need to do this for me and for my peace as much as I need to do it for you."

"And just so you know," Conner began, placing his other arm around his wife's waist, "I am, by no means, a wimp, Pam, just because I'm willing to move past this. You let it happen again and I—"

"I know. I know." Pam cut him off. "But can we just agree that our matrimony has been redeemed?"

Conner reached over and turned off the light on the nightstand. "You're going to have to learn to bend a little, you know." He turned to face his wife.

"Hmm. That's what your mom said. I wonder what she meant—"

"Shhh—I don't want to talk anymore. Let's discuss that later on in the week. Better yet, call her and ask her yourself. What I want to know is what you were going to show me when I asked you why you were smiling earlier."

"Oh, yeah—that." Pam laughed. "It had something to do with me swinging from a chandelier. But since I can't do that, literally, we'll have to improvise."

She could see the huge smile on her husband's face as they lay in the darkness of their bedroom. Forty minutes later—but who's counting?—Conner walked into the kitchen and poured himself a big glass of water.

Whew! Wow! Incredible! I just hope she's still willing to have that kind of fun with me when she finds out I'll need to take my daughters for practically the rest of the summer, Conner thought. *I know Pam's not ready for that.*

28

"I can't believe my cousin's gone. I feel like I'm having a really bad dream." Hunter shook his head as Tricee reached over and gently patted his knee.

She'd picked him up from O'Hare airport and was driving them back home to their north side condominium. The expressway was crowded with vehicles, many of the drivers headed home after spending a Monday at work, no doubt. But Tricee imagined that quite a few of them had done exactly what she'd done—picked up a loved one from the airport. Out of the window to the left was a crowded train platform. The Blue Line train that ran from downtown Chicago straight to the airport was always filled to capacity with commuters on weekdays. For a lot of people, this July evening marked the end of just another day. That wasn't the case for Tricee and Hunter.

The late night phone call they'd received two weeks ago had been one of the worst moments in Hunter's life. When his aunt told him that his 30-year-old cousin had passed away in his sleep, it had been like reliving the time he lost his one and only brother a few years prior. Now, as Tricee glanced over at her husband, noting the look of despair on his face, she thought about the tension that had filled their home upon Hunter's admission that he wasn't ready to adopt. His revelation had been a shocker because, a year ago, they'd been on the same page regarding kids. They'd even met with Ms. Rous from the adoption agency on two occasions. So when Hunter dropped the bomb that he didn't want to adopt yet, a disheartened Tricee had to phone Ms. Rous and inform the kind, middle-aged woman that, unfortunately, there'd been a change of plans.

"Oh, hello, Mrs. Hatchett! Thank you for getting back to me. I have some additional paperwork for you and your husband to look—"

"Ms. Rous, I'm sorry." Tricee breathed a heavy sigh into the phone. "I wish I were calling to discuss my husband and me proceeding with additional paperwork. Unfortunately, there's been a change of plans."

"Oh?" The happiness in Ms. Rous' voice quickly disappeared.

Tricee could sense how her unpleasant news had also been unpleasant news for the woman assigned to assist them in the adoption process. Ms. Rous informed Tricee that while she was very sorry that Hunter had changed his mind, it wasn't the first time she had this to happen.

"If anything changes, you be sure to contact me, Mrs. Hatchett. Even if you just need to chat, I'm here. Give it some time. I've seen this sort of thing between couples turn around and work out in the end." Tricee appreciated Ms. Rous' encouraging words and realized that she was correct to a certain degree. Just not correct in the way Tricee had imagined.

Hunter had flown into Seattle to attend his cousin's services. Tricee tried to insist on going with him, but with her classes, a final exam to study for and a 30-plus-page research paper due—not to mention her professional responsibilities as Director of Partnerships and Programs at H&P University—Hunter convinced his wife that it would be best if she stayed home. She'd met his cousin once, at their reception. She remembered him being a pleasant young man with a wicked sense of humor. To Tricee, it had felt like she'd known him forever.

When Hunter introduced his favorite cousin to his new bride, the young man's mouth fell open and he rubbed his eyes.

"Aw, man! Hunter, you didn't tell me you married Janet Jackson's twin sister!"

Tricee blushed and laughed and Hunter shook his head and laughed. He was used to his cousin's creative remarks.

"I'm for real," the young man had stated with a serious expression. "She looks just like Janet. The only difference is the hairstyle."

So, whenever he called the Hatchett household to speak to Hunter, "How's Janet doing?" usually made its way into the conversation. Tricee and Hunter had even made plans to visit Seattle in the near future. Of course, now it would be a different visit.

"I know this is very difficult for you, Sweetie. I wish I knew the right words to say."

Tricee veered into her left lane to exit at Foster Avenue. This was a more convenient way to the north side from O'Hare, no need to drive into downtown. There was still at least another 40 minutes before they reached home, ample time for the discussion neither of them thought would ever happen.

"Babe, just being here for me is enough."

Hunter looked over at his wife, noticing the steady gaze she kept on the road. He placed his hand on her leg and rubbed it a few times. He thought his wife was so strong yet so tender. She was definitely not the kind of woman he could imagine any man wanting to hurt on purpose. His mother and two sisters adored her, and his sisters made it their business to inform her that she was "the best thing that could have ever happened to their bother."

"Tricee, when Hunter brought you to my home to meet me, I knew that you were the one for my son." Hunter's mother had shared her feelings with Tricee right after she and Hunter got married.

Tricee could recall a time before she and Hunter got married when they'd visited his mother one evening. Hunter had excused himself to make a run to the store. Upon his return, he noticed that Tricee and his mother would giggle like two teenage girls and steal quick glances at each other.

"What did you and my mom talk about while I was gone?" he asked Tricee later on that evening.

Tricee laughed. "Mind ya business, Hunter. Just mind ya business."

A smiling Hunter knew he was with the woman he wanted to spend the rest of his life with.

Admitting that he wasn't ready to proceed with the adoption process had caused his wife some pain, no doubt. But he knew in his heart that he hadn't done it intentionally. He felt better knowing that Tricee realized this as well. Now they were faced with another decision that was sure to affect their lives.

"You know I'm here for you. Always. I have to say, though, that I feel really badly for Samuel. It's hard when a child loses a parent. And in his case, he never really got to know his mom, did he?"

Tricee stopped at the red light. This warm July evening had many people sitting out on their front porches, riding bicycles or enjoying an evening run. The hustle and bustle of the big city never ceased to amaze Tricee, a St. Louis native who'd relocated to Chicago some 10 years prior. She'd stopped counting after a while.

People went to work, to school, and did whatever other things that were required of them. Many people were unemployed due to the weak economy, which—if you were optimistic like Tricee was—was on its way to becoming stronger. One thing was certain, though, in Tricee's estimation. Chicago certainly qualified as a city that barely went to sleep. Even in the colder months, it wasn't uncommon to see Chicagoans standing in line to get into a nightclub or a favorite restaurant. She'd come to love the Windy City and—having met her husband here and the fact that he was a Chicago native—she acquired a special love for the place.

When the light turned green, Tricee noticed that Hunter had failed to respond to her question about his second cousin, 7-year-old Samuel. She looked over at him, then heard the horn from the vehicle behind her.

"Oh, okay, Jimmy Mack. I'm going," Tricee mumbled as she pressed the gas pedal.

"Jimmy Mack? Where'd you get that from?" Hunter asked with a slight grin.

"I don't know. Just something I made up." Tricee shrugged.

After a few moments of silence, she offered an apology for the question she'd asked about Samuel.

"You don't have to apologize for asking about Samuel, Babe. You're just being concerned, that's all."

"Yeah, well, when you got quiet on me, I thought maybe you just didn't want to discuss it any further."

"I was just lost in thought, Babe. You're right. Samuel never really had a relationship with his mom. My cousin had him from the day he was born. His mother, unfortunately, chose to ignore the fact that she had a child. Guess she realized after the fact that motherhood wasn't for her. But thank God Samuel had a father and a grandmother who loved him enough to make sure he was well cared for. I know it wasn't easy being a single dad. And my aunt, Samuel's grandmother, has been a great help. I admire my cousin for being the dad he was to his son."

"If you don't mind my asking, was Samuel's mom at the service?" Tricee didn't want to ask too many questions but Hunter was right. She was asking because she cared.

"I don't mind you asking. No, she wasn't. I don't even think her whereabouts are known. Sad isn't it?"

Tricee drew in a deep breath. "Sad is an understatement."

"I know she wasn't there because I asked my aunt. I don't even know what she looks like."

Tricee shook her head. She'd taken off work at noon, and even though Hunter's flight wasn't scheduled to arrive until 7:10

PM, she'd wanted a few extra hours to get some things done and to "get her mind right."

She'd spent the past two weeks solo. Hunter had decided to spend a couple of weeks in Seattle to be there for his aunt who had the misfortune of burying her only child. During his visit, he and his aunt had a long conversation about what would be best for Samuel. While Hunter's aunt was his primary caretaker for the moment, there was no way she could care for him permanently. She was dealing with health issues and just didn't feel like she could give him all that he needed. When Hunter called Tricee to ask if she would mind Samuel staying with them temporarily, Tricee swallowed before answering. "Oh, my goodness! Of course, I don't mind!" She had a hard time holding back the tears.

After that call from Hunter, Tricee remembered what Val said to her the day she, Jackie and Pam had come over for their first Bible talk session. It was the day Hunter had walked in on them having a Holy Ghost-fest in their home: "Tricee, there's a reason you and Hunter aren't supposed to adopt right now." Val had shared what had been in her spirit. Tricee hadn't been able to receive it wholeheartedly then, but she was ready to receive it now.

Later on that evening as they prepared for bed, Hunter and Tricee held hands and prayed. They prayed for Samuel, themselves, and for all the other family members who had been affected by the untimely death of his cousin.

"I spoke to my mother and sisters," Hunter removed the colorful quilt from their bed. Even though night had fallen, it was close to 90 degrees. He had yet to comprehend why Tricee still needed a quilt on the bed. All he needed was a sheet. "They're very happy that Samuel will be staying with us for a while."

They climbed into bed and Hunter noticed the faraway look in his wife's eyes. During his flight home, he thought about Samuel and the changes that were about to take effect in the young boy's life. Both Hunter's sisters had mentioned something about taking Samuel in but Hunter's mind was already made up.

"I know you were interested in adopting a toddler," he began, wrapping his arms around his wife's waist, "but what—"

Before he could finish, Tricee turned to face him. "I think we should consider adopting Samuel."

Hunter shifted and propped himself up on his elbow. "Okay, you read my thoughts. But, Babe, let's pray on it to be sure this is what God wants."

"I can do that."

"He's a special-needs child, Babe. That can be a challenge you—"

Tricee cut him off again. "Let's just continue to seek God on this. He knows all about challenges."

Hunter nodded. "Okay, you're right. You're right." He glanced at the pink silk gown Tricee had on. "But for now, before we do all *that*, how about you let the kitty come out to play?"

Tricee laughed. "Okay, I guess I can let her out for a little while."

An hour and a half later, Hunter was fast asleep—and sleeping very well, thank you.

Tricee got out of bed and quietly walked into the living room where she stood silently next to the sofa. This was where her girlfriends had jumped around and shouted a few weeks prior. She slowly knelt beside the sofa.

"Lord, I don't know if I'm 100 percent sure that I'm up for a challenge such as this. But I do know that Romans 8:28 makes it plain. All things work together ..."

29

"Jeff, lose my number! And under no circumstances are you to contact me again!"

"Would you calm down and let me give you an explanation? You don't even know all of the details!"

Jeff was shout-whispering into his cell phone when his administrative assistant appeared in the doorway of his office. She put a hand on the knob of his office door and began to close it. He tilted his head and placed his cell phone against his chest. "Thanks," he said softly before putting the phone back to his ear.

The older woman smirked as she left his office. She was closing his door out of consideration. He must not have realized how pitiful he looked. She couldn't hear all of what he was saying—even though his tone was slightly louder than usual—but she could tell that whoever was on the other end was really letting him have it. She was surprised he hadn't closed his office door himself.

Back in Houston, sitting in his office, Jeff had received a call from Pam. She was blasting him about *this wife* that she hadn't known existed. Not that it made a huge difference. After all, she'd already decided that nothing and no one was worth losing her marriage over. It was simply the principle of it all.

It had obviously been a mistake to agree to have lunch with Jeff when they'd run into each other two months ago. Back then it had seemed harmless, until Pam realized she still had unresolved feelings. Her emotions had overruled her ability to make what would have been the better decision—to say no to both lunch and dinner.

Pam had still been processing all she'd learned from Darcy at work on Friday. On Monday and Tuesday, she avoided Janae Mays-Morrison as best she could. Thanks to the very busy start of a new week, that had been fairly easy to do. Besides, Janae was Darcy's client. And unless Pam spent a great deal of time in the residents' area of the shelter, she wouldn't run into any of the women.

Darcy had already arranged for Janae to sit in on one of the Monday classes: Knowing the Signs of an Abuser. Darcy spent Tuesday morning reviewing treatment plans for two other clients and part of Tuesday afternoon at a workshop that all of the social workers were required to attend. By 4:00 PM, she was on the phone, gathering all the necessary resources for her newest client. So other than a *Good morning!* And a *So glad you made it to our church yesterday!* on Monday morning, Pam and Darcy hadn't really had a chance to talk.

Wednesday would, no doubt, turn out to be one of the most memorable Wednesdays in recent memory. Not just for Pam but for Jeff, too. Pam had purposely ignored his call on Monday and was relieved when he hadn't tried to contact her on Tuesday. But she was determined to have the last word, hence, her call to him on Wednesday.

"Jeff, you know what? I thought meeting you for lunch was going to be two adults, who once dated, discussing things like two adults. Okay, I admit I was curious to see if there were still feelings for you, but I—"

"So be honest with yourself," he interrupted Pam as he loosened his dark blue tie. "Were there still feelings?"

Pam pulled her cell phone away from her ear and looked at it with her mouth wide open. *What?! You old arrogant ...* she called him a few colorful adjectives in her mind. She put the phone back to her ear.

"You know what? You're unbelievable! Still arrogant and truly unbelievable! How long did you think you would be able to keep up this charade of yours? And as for this cousin of yours, this Janae May—"

Pam suddenly stopped talking. Discussing a client was against the rules unless it was absolutely necessary, and then only with a colleague. Jeff might have been related to the woman but he wasn't employed by the agency. And Janae wasn't her client.

"It doesn't matter, Jeff. You were dishonest when we went out and you're dishonest now. Nothing has changed."

"Pam. Listen, please. I'm legally—"

Click. She hung up before he could finish his sentence. He immediately redialed her number. She picked up on the second ring.

"Don't call my number again! You hear me?!" Pam shouted one last time into the phone before she hung up again.

She drew in a deep breath, exhaled slowly and took a mental assessment of herself: *Okay. Okay. I'm calm.* A few minutes later, she had to leave her office and quickly make her way to the ladies room. She went into a stall, leaned over the toilet and barfed up the bagel and cream cheese she'd eaten for breakfast.

"Ugh. I guess that bagel didn't agree with me," she mumbled softly as she left the stall. She rinsed her mouth and washed her hands, glad that she was the only one in the restroom. The last she thing she needed was an *Are you okay, Pam?* from one of her colleagues.

After Pam's outburst, Jeff sat back angrily in his black, swivel desk chair. He looked up when he heard a light tap on his office door.

"Come in," he said, the annoyance in his tone hard to miss.

"Mr. Mays, Mr. Hung Sung is here to meet with you," his assistant announced politely.

At 65, she had the energy of a woman 20 years younger. Jeff was grateful to have her as his assistant, but given his demeanor today, you would have thought otherwise.

"Mr. Hung Sung?" He repeated the name as if he'd never heard it before.

He looked at his Seiko stainless steel dress watch before reaching into his back pocket for his handkerchief. For the beginning of July, Houston was unbearably hot. Wearing a long-sleeved white shirt, a dark blue tie, and navy pants, Jeff wished he'd opted for more casual clothes. But it was Wednesday, not causal Friday, and he was meeting with a very important client. One he'd obviously forgotten about thanks to Pam and her let-me-tell-you-where-to-go phone call.

"Yes, Mr. Hung Sung from Hung Sung's Pharmaceuticals. You're meeting with him this morning to discuss a potential co-marketing strategy using our blood pressure pills and their diabetes control pills." *Duh!* She thought silently.

Jeff's assistant observed the beads of sweat on her boss' forehead. She watched him wipe it with his handkerchief, then fold it back up and return it to his back pocket. She loved her job and

Jeff was a great boss, but he was obviously having a bad morning and was off his game today.

"Mr. Mays, you're scheduled to meet with Mr. Hung Sung at 10:00, another 15 min—"

He nodded and waved his hand, stopping her from going into further details. "Yeah, of course, of course. Let him know I'll be right out."

"Will do." She turned to leave.

Dressed in a tan, below-the-knee sheath dress with a thin white shawl draped around her shoulders, she reminded Jeff of his own mother. When she hesitated before leaving his office and turned back to face him, her concern *almost* made him feel better.

"Are you alright, Mr. Mays?"

She was holding a name tag for Mr. Hung Sung in one hand and a manila folder in the other. Jeff didn't know what he'd do without her.

"I'm fine, thanks. Uh, please hold any other calls for me until 1:00." He gave a half-smile and promised himself he'd apologize for his abruptness later.

"Sure." His assistant smiled and left his office.

After she left, Jeff typed a quick email and re-read it once before hitting the "send" button. After shutting down his laptop, he reached into his desk drawer and removed a folder with the name

Hung Sung written across the top. Then he picked up the receiver to his desk phone and dialed his assistant's extension.

"Yes, Mr. Mays," came the warm reply on the other end.

"Uh, could you book me a flight to Chicago for three weeks? Sometime around the 15th of this month, please?"

****

"See? Now you know God had a purpose for you here at this agency, and it wasn't just to serve the clients." Darcy's face was aglow as she stood in Pam's office. "He knew I needed to meet someone like you to show me the way to Him."

"Well, good. I'm glad to hear." Pam fanned her face with her hand. "Is it me or is my air conditioning not working properly? Good grief, I'm just having a bad morning. First I puke and now I'm too hot."

"You okay?" Darcy asked. When Pam gave a convincing nod, she resumed her conversation. "Well, I don't know, girlfriend, if it's you or that air conditioning. All I know is, thanks to you, there's a great chance I'll never know how hot it is down below. Glory!" Darcy began to shake her head. "Hmmm, Gracious One!" she praised.

Pam couldn't help but laugh, even though she could tell her co-worker was obviously still feeling His presence. After calling Jeff and telling him not to call her again, Pam had allowed herself to feel His presence, even if only for a few minutes. She was sure Jeff had gotten the message loud and clear and would not phone her again. Cousin at the shelter or not, there would be no more dealings with the man. She figured she'd tell Darcy about her phone call but not today. And unless Darcy mentioned Janae first, Pam decided that she knew all she wanted to know about her.

"You know, I've been at such peace since hearing your husband's sermon. I was able to get through these past two very busy days without complaining," Darcy remarked, fiddling with the silver broach that was pinned to her short, white, linen blazer.

It was hot outside and Pam's office was too hot—as far as Pam was concerned—but the air conditioning in Darcy's office was working just fine, hence, she was wearing a short blazer.

"I was also able to grin at all the white faces I had to pass on my way to work this morning. So, again, thanks to you, the white folks can exhale when they see Darcy coming."

Pam laughed. "Girl, you are crazy! Conner might not preach again until sometime next month. But I can assure you, you'll enjoy our pastor's sermons just as much. In fact, he gets way more into it than Conner." Pam chuckled.

"Oh, trust me. I *will* be coming back to hear your pastor preach. I sense that church is where I need to be on Sundays. We were thinking of coming this Sunday but Sedric and I decided to get out of town for the Fourth of July. I'm using a few vacation days so I won't be back to work until the 8th." Darcy glanced at the clock on Pam's wall. "Ten thirty. I have to be in court this afternoon at 1:00. Let me run. I'm glad our lovely boss allowed me to come in at 10:15. I ended up staying here until 7:00 last night." She turned to leave. "Talk to you later. Maybe we can do lunch next week. I'm taking off early tomorrow and I know you're looking forward to the holiday just as much as I am."

"Indeed!" Pam replied. She suddenly recalled Conner's comment about Sedric. "Darcy, so you and your husband will be coming back to church? Maybe next Sunday?"

"Yes, we're both coming back. Why?"

"Hmm. Well, Conner is convinced that *you* will be back but not your husband."

Pam scribbled a few notes on the front of a red folder and put it to the side. What Darcy said next had Pam giggling to herself even after her co-worker exited her office.

"Pam, allow me to let you in on a little secret. Darcy knows exactly how to get what she wants. It might take a little time, but I strategize very well." She winked at Pam and left.

Pam chuckled and thought about the issue Darcy had a couple of months prior, when her husband's ex-girlfriend would show up unannounced. "Obviously, she *does* have some sort of strategy," she mumbled under her breath.

Pam looked at her "to do" list and checked off the few items she'd taken care of for the morning. Unlike Darcy, Pam wasn't taking a half day tomorrow, so there was some relief in knowing she still had the rest of the day and all of Thursday to get things accomplished. Due to the Fourth of July holiday, however, the clients would have to wait until next Friday to go through any donated items. The staff members who were scheduled to work this Friday had arranged for the clients to enjoy a special Fourth of July lunch. Things were usually quiet around the shelter and the agency around the holidays, so the staff who was scheduled to work didn't mind coming in.

Next on Pam's list was to read and reply to any pertinent emails. She checked an email from her boss and quickly typed a reply:

I will ensure that all of the direct services reports, as well as the progress notes, are in your office before the end of the workday on Monday, July 6th. I will place them in your inbox and also send you electronic copies. Enjoy your vacation. See you next Tuesday.

"It's about time you took some time off. Even if only for a few days," Pam mumbled as she scanned through her other emails. She paused when she saw one from Jeff and frowned as she read the words *your phone call* in the subject line.

Oh, no he did not send me an email! she thought. She shook her head and drew in a deep breath. She contemplated hitting the "delete" key but her curiosity won over her indignation:

Pam, you know you can be quite the stubborn woman when you want to be. Instead of calling to give me an earful of what I did wrong (something you are obviously still good at), you could have kept your mouth closed for a second or two (is that even possible?) and given me an opportunity to explain my position.

As for my cousin Janae—yes, she is, for now, staying at the shelter where you are employed. She's going through a tough time right now, but I won't discuss all of that. I was going to mention to you that my cousin would be staying temporarily at the shelter when I felt the time was right. Either way, there is still so much you don't know.

I will be returning to Chicago in a couple weeks as I will be assisting Janae in getting back on her feet. Maybe, by then, you will have calmed down.

Jeff

"Arrrggh!" Pam pounded her desk one good time with her fist. A few seconds later, she hurried out of her office and back into the restroom. This was the first time she could remember puking twice in one morning.

30

"Wait, wait. Hold up, hold up." Jackie set the gift bag she'd just received on the floor.

She'd turned 38 the day after the fourth and her three closest friends were treating her to a belated birthday dinner. Since the beginning of the month, all four women had been kept busy with family, work, and everything else. This warm Friday evening of July 17th was the date that worked best for each of them.

"Let me get this straight." Jackie placed her hand on her hip. "You have a client at your agency—well, at the shelter ..."

"No, not *my* client," Pam corrected. "She's actually a client the other counselor will work with. But she's been assigned to work with Darcy, the only social worker I talk to outside of work."

"Okay. So then you find out she's Jeff's cousin. And on top of all that, you learn that he has *a wife.*" Jackie stared at Pam in disbelief. "Man! Can the plot get any thicker?"

Outside of planning this evening, the women hadn't spoken much. They did know that Hunter had lost a cousin and that he'd spent some time out of town, but Tricee had yet to share any other details.

Val noticed how different Tricee sounded when she'd called her last week, but when she asked whether everything was okay, Tricee had only replied, "Yes, everything's fine. Just really busy with work." Tricee had shared with them already that Hunter's cousin had passed, so Val decided not to probe. But she sensed that something else was definitely up. Whatever it was, she knew it would come out sooner or later.

Pam's behavior seemed normal, even though they knew there was still discord between her and Conner. "We're going for counseling, *maybe*," was all she'd told Val, even though Val hadn't asked. Val had to give it to her girl Pam. She just seemed to have a way of going with the flow, even when the going seemed tough.

Val had returned to work full time and, with her father in town to spend time with Sean, his 17-year-old step grandson, and Ashlyn, his 1-year-old granddaughter, both Val and Cory were looking forward to having some alone time. Val's father had even said that Sean's 7-year-old sister was welcome to join them for a summer outing.

"Oh, Dad, I'm sure Desiree and her hubby would love that," Val had replied. But as for him being successful in spending time with a 17-year-old, she and Cory just laughed and said, "Good luck with that."

Now, as the four women sat across from each other in a booth at the Thai food restaurant on Sheridan Road, the night was still young. They were taking Jackie to one of the blues clubs downtown after dinner. They could've gone to listen to jazz, reggae or blues—Chicago had quite a few places to choose from. But since it was Jackie's birthday, she got to choose. "Let's go listen to some blues," she'd said when Val asked what she would like to do. But she immediately said she had to get off the phone when Jackie began singing her rendition of B.B. King's "The Thrill is Gone."

"It does get thicker. The plot, I mean," Pam said before taking a sip of her iced green tea. "She showed up at my church a couple of months ago and tried to get Conner's attention."

Val shot Pam a look that said *Are you serious*? But Pam was prepared with a quick follow-up before anyone had a chance to comment. "Don't look at me like that, Val. I know when a woman is giving my husband the 'come hither' look."

"I don't doubt that," said Val. "It just all seems so … so …"

"Bizarre would be an appropriate adjective," Jackie said with a quick nod of the head for emphasis.

Val and Tricee snickered—though Tricee's was more of a forced snicker. She was choosing to remain silent for now. Besides, she was enjoying her Pad See Ew too much to stop eating. Her girlfriends had ordered the spicy shrimp fried rice. And while it was tasty, Jackie thought Pam's news was better.

Pam went on to explain exactly what happened at church that particular Sunday and how Conner admitted that he had noticed the woman. Not knowing too much about Janae—other than her address and the few things Darcy had shared—Pam had to wonder if, perhaps, flirting with other men was part of the reason there were issues in her marriage. But even if it was, Pam didn't believe any woman deserved to be abused. Any man either, for that matter.

Interestingly, just as Pam was thinking to herself that Janae looked older than her 26 years, Val asked, "How old is she? I'm just curious." She drank the rest of her Sierra Mist and smiled as the server quickly poured a refill.

"Actually, without sharing too many personal details with you ladies, she's 26. I was curious so I looked at her personal file the same day I got Jeff's email. I had decided to just push her completely out of my mind—remain professional when I see her at the shelter but just let things be. And then Jeff sends me an email and it made me curious all over again. I will say this, though," Pam pointed her chopsticks across the booth toward Val and Tricee before she continued, "she looks a little older than 26."

"What did he say in the email?" Jackie scooped up a forkful of shrimp fried rice.

Pam decided to give her friend a reminder before answering her question.

"And this conversation stays between us, because you ladies know I'm not supposed to and cannot share—"

Jackie cut Pam off. "Yeah, we know, Pam. You're not supposed to discuss the clients and their personal business. By the by, you know you can trust us. So, again, I ask, what did he say in the email?" Tricee couldn't help but laugh this time at Jackie's amusing behavior.

"Oh," Pam waved her hand, "it doesn't matter. I read it, deleted it, and that was it. I haven't heard from him since."

Jackie shrugged. "Suit yourself," she said with disappointment before finishing the rest of her meal. Just as she was about to ask Tricee how things were going, Pam spoke again.

"I take that back." She wiped her mouth and placed her napkin on her plate. "He did send me another email but I deleted it without reading it. If I happen to see him at the agency, I'll just remain professional. So I need you ladies to pray that Janae gets back on her feet quick!"

There was no need to ask why she'd made that last comment. It was obvious. Once Janae was gone—poof!—no more Jeff.

"Good for you, Pam, for moving on," Jackie said as she reached into her purse. "But you could have made my birthday even better by sharing what he said in that email."

They all laughed. It was Val who reminded her friend that, technically, it wasn't her birthday.

"Your birthday was 12 days ago!" she said with a smile. Then she excused herself and headed for the ladies room.

"Yes, and we apologize for having to treat you to such a late birthday meal," Tricee added.

"Better late than never," said Jackie as their server approached the table.

Tricee thought how much the petite Asian woman resembled the server who'd waited on her and Paul two years ago. They were in the same Thai food restaurant that she and Paul had dined in the evening they ran into one of Paul's exes. The two Asian women were probably related as the restaurant was a family-owned business. Tricee also remembered coming to this restaurant after she'd learned that her dear Aunt Jancie had passed. She'd just wanted to get out of the house and clear her head. That particular evening, however, her food had gone untouched.

"So how are you, Tricee? How's Hunter, and how's his family doing?"

Jackie's question interrupted her thoughts. Tricee planned to share her news with her girlfriends sometime this evening when the time was right. It was all about Jackie tonight and she wanted to respect that this was a birthday celebration. But she knew her friends well enough to know that her news wouldn't be considered an infringement on Jackie's party at all. She and Hunter had been holding their own prayer and Bible study sessions at home. And they'd met with their pastor to discuss and pray about their plans to adopt Samuel.

Other than Hunter's aunt/Samuel's grandmother; Tricee's parents; Tricee's half-sister, Annette and Annette's husband, there weren't too many others they'd shared the news with. They even made Pastor Downey promise he'd keep the news to himself until they were ready to share. Their pastor had laughed heartily and agreed to the couple's request.

"Oh, I'm fine. And Hunter's fine. Everyone's doing better, considering the circumstances."

"Well, I'm glad you guys are okay. You looked sort of down for a minute. But I understand. His cousin was so young, and to just go in his sleep …" Jackie paused and shook her head. "We've been praying for you guys …" Her eyes suddenly focused on something toward the back of the restaurant. " … of course," she finished absently.

Tricee turned in her chair to see what had captured Jackie's attention so completely. Val had just emerged from the ladies room. Pam was scrolling through her Blackberry, but she looked up when Val returned to the booth. Val was wearing a different hairstyle from the one she wore into the ladies room. Her three friends stared in awe at the mid-length, curly, red wig that sat neatly on top of her head.

"You have different hairstyle now," the petite server said as she nodded toward Val. "Very nice."

"Thank you." Val patted the ends of the wig. "We're done. May we have the check please?" She ignored the stares of her friends as they all gathered their purses and left the restaurant.

The four women stepped into the warm July evening. The 85-degree weather with a nice breeze off the lakefront felt perfect as they walked the three blocks to Tricee's Ford Taurus.

"I would've driven, ladies," Val said to no one in particular, "but Tricee insisted on driving since this is her neck of the woods."

"Cool," Pam said. "It's a good thing, though, that she and Hunter have two parking spaces. Otherwise, you'd have been parked on the street and who knows where you would've found a space."

"Yes, I figured she could just park her vehicle in my space for the evening. No big deal," Tricee said. "As long as the doorman knows."

"Girlfriend, I did bring an overnight bag in the event I decide to take you up on your offer to sleep over if I'm too tired to drive back to Forest Park after we take these two home," she said, pointing to Jackie and Pam. "I might have to move my car and find a spot on the street."

"That's not a problem if you want to stay over. And you'll find a space," Tricee said as she unlocked her car door with her key fob.

"Well, I'm just glad you ladies planned such a good birthday treat and kept me from having to drive," Jackie said. "Even though I'm only teaching twice a week, the drive from Beverly all the way to Northeastern can wear on you." She wiggled her head in a little celebratory dance. "And I'm only teaching this summer composition course for one more week. Once this class is over, it's vacation time for the Latham- Larsons!"

They climbed into Tricee's car, Pam and Jackie in the back and Val in the front. For whatever reason, Val felt that since she'd pretty much made all the plans for the evening, it was her right to ride up front. She'd made that perfectly clear when they'd all arrived at Tricee's house at the beginning of the night.

Val thought it was senseless for each of them to drive their own vehicles, with the lack of parking on the north side and for their venture downtown. So she'd driven over to Pam's house where Jackie's husband, Lem, had dropped her off. That worked out perfectly as the husbands ended up watching a baseball game together.

The breezy, 85-degree weather made for a perfect summer night in Chicago. While Tricee and Val had opted for dressy capris and short-sleeved tops, Jackie was wearing a tan, mid-length summer dress, and Pam had chosen some tan, linen, flared-leg pants and a white blouse with three small gold buttons.

"How do you like teaching a freshman summer class at the university, Jackie?" Tricee asked after they were all strapped in.

"It's interesting. Some of the students behave like they're still in high school, but there are a few who are quite mature. I do have a couple of middle-aged students. I like it, though. It's a great experience." Jackie rummaged around in her gift bag.

"You might decide to leave your position as a principal—"

"Not going to happen, Tricee. I told you that already." Jackie laughed.

Tricee came to the stoplight on Broadway and Granville and Jackie immediately spotted the McDonalds.

"Mmm hmm. A sister could really use a cup of coffee. Tricee, would you mind turning here if it's not too much trouble please?"

Val snapped her neck around to face Jackie and Pam. "Girl, we're trying to get downtown! And it's too late for coffee, anyway!"

Pam laughed as soon as the words left Val's mouth. The very red wig she was wearing and the way she'd just whipped her head around were comical. Not to mention the look on her face.

"Tricee, you didn't tell me Val was making your car payments," Jackie blurted out and swiped Val lightly on the neck. "Calm down, Little Orphan Annie."

"She kind of looks like that Raggedy Ann doll." Tricee couldn't resist. She knew one thing for certain. She knew that even when she had things weighing on her mind, she could always count on her three best friends for a joyful good time.

After pulling into the drive-through where Jackie ordered a small cup of coffee—black, no cream, no sugar—Tricee headed south on Sheridan Road toward the Lakeshore Drive expressway. Now felt like as good a time as any to share the news about Samuel.

But before she could speak, Jackie happily began to give a description of each of the gifts in her bag. Pam rolled her eyes as she announced each item.

" … a light blue, silk scarf; a pair of dangling silver earrings; some Autumn Mist body spray and lotion; a book, *Prayer for All Seasons*—hmm, sounds interesting—some vanilla-scented hand cream. Thanks again, ladies, for my gift bag! I like all my gifts." Jackie reached into the very bottom of the bag. "Oh, and a pack of Trident gum."

"That's mine." Without turning around, Val threw her hand backward over her head toward the backseat. "Give me that."

"Oh, yeah. By the way, Raggedy Ann—I mean Val," Jackie smiled as she nudged Pam in the arm, "You and Tricee don't have to give us a ride back to the south side. Lem told me to just text him when we were close to leaving. He'll pick us up and we'll give Pam a ride home. It's Friday, he doesn't have anything else to do."

"Okay, that works. And Cory likes my different hairstyles." Val giggled as she patted her red wig.

"Good for Cory," Jackie said before taking a sip of her coffee. "I'm not mad at you girlfriend. Do your thing."

As they passed the Lawrence exit, Tricee cleared her throat. It would only take another 20 minutes to reach the blues club and, once inside, she knew conversation would be limited. Besides, she couldn't hold it in any longer.

"Ladies, I have some news." She kept her eyes straight ahead.

"What?" Val snapped her neck again, this time toward Tricee.

"Okay, Val. I need you to stop snapping that neck of yours, because the red hair and the snapping is making me dizzy," Pam said and burst into laughter.

"Right!" Jackie said. "Girl, you'd better hope that thing doesn't fall off your head tonight while we're out." They all shared in the laughter. When it quieted down, Val asked Tricee to continue.

"Sorry, Tricee. What were you saying?" Val was looking at the side of Tricee's face and Pam and Jackie were looking at the back of her head.

Tricee glanced at Val briefly. "Hunter and I have decided, after much prayer and fasting, to adopt his cousin's 7-year-old son, Samuel."

Silence. Her three friends said nothing as they processed what they'd just heard. *So that's why she's been sort of distant,* they realized.

Val reached over and patted Tricee's right arm. "Oh, bless Jesus! Tricee, that's wonderful!"

"Wow, Tricee! You kept this from us? When did you guys decide? I can't believe you didn't tell us sooner!" Jackie scooted up from the back seat.

"I had a feeling something was up," Pam commented. "But I just couldn't put my finger on it." She mumbled *Thank you, Jesus* a few times under her breath.

"Well, we need to meet for another Bible session! This is just too much!" Jackie said excitedly.

"He's a special-needs child," Tricee said softly. "But I know he's supposed to be with us. I just know it."

"So you're up for the challenge?" asked Jackie as Tricee turned down the street where the Blue Light club was located. "Let me rephrase that. I know you're equipped to move forward as long as God is in it."

"Amen," Val and Pam said in unison.

Tricee explained the things she felt were important regarding Samuel, and hers and Hunter's decision. Samuel was obviously very bright. He recognized words that contained many letters and could count beyond 100, Hunter had said. He needed help with his speech, however, and continuing his speech therapy was crucial. There were also times, Hunter had explained, when he would talk louder than necessary. But according to his teacher and his speech therapist, these things were manageable with the right assistance.

Hunter had spent the Fourth of July holiday with Samuel, his grandmother, and a couple of other relatives from Samuel's mother's side. They seemed like nice folks, he'd told Tricee over the phone later that evening, but not one of them had seemed even remotely interested in taking Samuel in. She and Hunter hadn't yet discussed adopting Samuel when they'd had that conversation, but just knowing that her husband had experienced a loss—and that his little cousin had been left without a father—made for a sad holiday.

Later that same evening, Ruby called her daughter to make sure she was still okay. She'd wanted to visit being that it was a holiday and that Tricee had been home alone for two whole weeks. It seemed to her to be a perfect time to reschedule her canceled trip. But Tricee convinced her mother that sometime in August would be better. As it turns out, now that Tricee and Hunter have agreed to move forward with the adoption, Samuel would be with them in Chicago by then.

They were making arrangements to fly to Seattle to get Samuel within the next two weeks. Both Hunter and Tricee agreed that it would be best for him to get acquainted with them first, before allowing him to meet anyone else. Ruby understood and was elated that she would now have a grandson. Well, that's what she called him, anyway. August couldn't come fast enough.

Tricee went on to explain how she'd spoken with Samuel twice over the phone in the past week. His favorite foods were pizza, spaghetti with round meatballs—that got a chuckle from Tricee—and chicken nuggets. Chocolate was his favorite ice cream and his favorite toy was anything with Spiderman on it. When she asked him if he liked any vegetables, he made a sort of grunting sound. His grandmother told Tricee, after Samuel handed her the phone, "You should have seen the look on his face." Tricee responded with, "We'll work on the veggies."

Their chatter was briefly interrupted by Pam's ringing cell phone. She had the volume set as high as it could go.

"Hello?" Pam spoke loudly into the phone.

"She talking all loud," Val remarked from the front seat.

"Oh, hey, Sondra. What's going on?" Pam had only spoken to her cousin a few times since their lunch a couple of months ago. It was the day Jeff reintroduced himself into her life. Her mouth flew open when she heard what Sondra said next.

"Pam, I think I might be pregnant," her cousin announced in an exasperated tone.

"What! Sondra, you have six kids already! I mean, I know you and Spencer are married but what is he doing to you over there?"

After a little hesitation Sondra responded, "Well, Cousin Pam, uh, first he put his dingaling in my—"

"Girl, stop! You know what I mean!" Pam shouted.

Jackie stared at her excited friend and Val turned to look at Pam. Tricee glanced at her in her rearview mirror.

"Sondra, look. Let's get together tomorrow. It's Saturday. We can chat then, okay?"

"Pam, I know what day of the week it is. I said I might be pregnant, not suffering from amnesia."

Moments later, the women were walking into the club as the valet parked Tricee's vehicle. They found a table near the back of the club and ordered drinks—a ginger ale with a couple of cherries for Tricee and Val, a Diet Coke for Jackie, and sparkling water for Pam. The place wasn't packed yet, but by 11:00 PM they expected it would be. Filling up with people from various ethnic backgrounds, the blues club was evidence of the culturally diverse city. The patrons were black, white, Spanish, Asian, African, and Middle Eastern. Tonight, everyone seemed to have one common denominator—to have a good time.

It was definitely an over-30 crowd of singles as well as couples. Val was approached just as they sat down.

"Hello, Pretty Lady." A handsome man with smooth, dark skin smiled at her.

"Hello," she replied politely and smiled back.

His offer to buy her a drink was met with another polite response.

"Thank you, but no. I'm okay for now."

The man simply nodded and smiled. Even when he went to sit with who the ladies assumed were his friends, he would glance over at Val and smile.

"He smelled good, though," Val told her friends.

"Val, you're blushing!" Jackie teased. "Your cheeks are as red as that wig you're wearing!"

The blues singer sounded great as she belted out lyrics to many familiar blues standards. The band backing her consisted of one white guy on the horn, and two black guys—one on saxophone and the other on bass. A couple of times, the singer just stood back and allowed her band to play. Each musician was a master at his craft.

By 11:45 PM, Jackie was texting her husband who said he was on his way. The women decided to have another drink while they waited, white wine spritzers. They were pretty sure that listening to the blues while indulging in a little bit of wine wouldn't keep them from entering heaven. But Pam declined the wine. Her reason was met with three mouths open wide.

"I'm pregnant."

The ladies spent the next several minutes gushing over, carrying on about and hugging on Pam, genuinely happy for her and for themselves as they would become honorary aunts.

"So first you get a call from your cousin telling you that she's pregnant, and then you announce that you're pregnant!" Jackie raised her glass. "I'll toast to that!"

"Correction," Pam raised her glass. "Sondra *thinks* she's pregnant. I know *for sure* I'm pregnant."

"I bet Conner is so excited," Tricee added.

"He is," Pam smiled. *Even though he had the nerve to ask me if I was sure the baby was his,* she recalled indignantly.

Everyone was having a nice evening until they were leaving the club and ran into Jeff.

Epilogue

"Pam, are you okay?" Conner's daughter, Connis, was loading the dishwasher. She looked up when Pam came into the kitchen. "You look tired."

"Oh, Sweetie, yes. I'm fine. I just have a little pain in my side, that's all. Go and tell your sister to get ready so we can go to the grocery store." Pam gently stroked the top of her stepdaughter's head.

"Raneen doesn't want to go to the store with us. She says she wants to go visit Gransi. She misses our mom, too."

Okay, here we go, Pam thought. She exhaled as she sat back in the tall kitchen chair. It was a hot and muggy August morning, four days before the month came to an end and five days before Renita returned home from her "summer retreat." Pam hoped and prayed that the retreat had done her husband's ex some good. She meant that from the very bottom of her heart. But it would have been nice if Conner had told her before the last day of July that the twins were staying with them for the month of August. Well, practically a month. They'd stayed with their Gransi, Conner's mother, Viola, for one week.

Pam hadn't told her friends any of the personal information her husband had shared with her about his ex-wife. All she'd told

Jackie, Tricee and Val was that Renita was dealing with some personal things and that they would be keeping the girls for a while. No questions had been asked, bless their hearts. This was all the more reason Pam loved her girlfriends so much. But sometimes, loving her friends wasn't so easy.

Jackie phoned Pam the day after they'd taken her to Blue Light blues club for a belated birthday celebration.

"Pam, you have a moment? I have a question to ask you. Now you know I love you like a sister—a real sister—so please don't get mad at me." Jackie was whispering into the phone, talking as if she was afraid of getting caught. By whom, Pam had no clue.

"What is it, Jackie?" Pam asked.

"Well, I know you had dinner with Jeff back in May, I think it was. And I just wanted to make sure you hadn't slipped up and … you know?"

"What are you trying to ask me, Jackie?"

"You know. I mean, you're not pregnant by …"

Jackie didn't have a chance to complete her question. Pam caught a major attitude and allowed some words to come out of her mouth that she'd forgotten she even knew. It was bad enough to have her own husband ask the question. Even if he *had* chuckled when he asked.

It was a whole three days before Pam called Jackie back and apologized. Jackie apologized, too. She'd asked the question out of genuine concern and, deep down, Pam knew that. But it was still a painful question to be asked.

"I'll go talk to your sister. You go and change into something else. It's too hot for that long-sleeved shirt," Pam told Connis.

Pam walked into the bedroom where Raneen was making the bed. The child had been through enough in the past couple of months. First, she'd had that concussion, which, thankfully, only lasted a few days. That had been a scary time, indeed. Now she had to deal with not seeing her mother for a whole month. Both girls were close to their mom, but Pam could tell that Raneen was more of a mama's girl.

"Raneen, wow! You made the bed and put all of yours and your sister's clothes away! You are quick."

Pam learned that it was best to start off with a compliment and then ease into the real matter at hand.

"My mom used to get upset with me when I was little." She smiled warmly at her husband's daughter. "I used to take all day just to do my house chores. One day, you know what I did?"

Pam folded her arms and a sly grin formed on her face. Raneen shook her head. Pam could tell by the child's expression that she was hooked.

"One day, I promised my two sisters that I'd bake them their favorite cake if they cleaned my room for me. You know I have three sisters?"

"Yes," Raneen said softly.

"Well, at the time, I only had two. But anyway—they cleaned my room for me, so I had to keep my promise, right?"

Raneen nodded.

"I waited until my parents went to bed that night, then I went into the kitchen and started gathering all the ingredients I thought I needed to bake a cake: eggs, milk, water, butter, sugar, salt, orange juice …"

"Orange juice?" Raneen's eyes lit up. "You don't need orange juice to bake a cake."

"Oh, you don't? Are you sure?" Pam gave the child a once-over. *How do you know?* she thought.

"I'm very sure, Pam." Raneen giggled.

"Okay, well, anyway—my sisters never did get their favorite cake and I ended up having to clean up a messy kitchen all by myself."

Conner stood in the doorway listening to Raneen giggle. He was surprised that she and Pam were even having a conversation.

"Raneen, I know you miss your mother. She'll be home in five days, okay? You can wait five more days?" It was more of a statement than a question. "Besides, I enjoy having you here. " *Wow, did I really just say that?* Pam was genuinely surprised at herself. *Well, I do. Sort of.*

Conner raised an eyebrow, wondering if he was in the wrong house.

"I can wait five days," Raneen said, picking up her sister's pajamas and hanging them on the lowest hook on the door.

"Good. Now we need to hurry to get to the store before they run out of all the things I need for dinner."

Raneen looked past Pam at her father who had slowly entered the bedroom. "Daddy, Pam tried to bake a cake with orange juice." She giggled and turned to Pam. "Can we bake a cake for dessert?"

"Not if you girls plan on using any orange juice," Conner said.

He and Pam laughed when they overheard Raneen telling her sister about the orange juice cake.

"Glad to see you and Raneen getting along." Conner kissed his wife on the cheek. "Funny how you waited until they only had a few more days with us."

Pam gave her husband a punch in the arm. "I didn't plan it this way," she said. Then she put her hand to her forehead.

"You okay? Why don't you go lie down. I can do the grocery shopping." Conner placed his arms around Pam's waist. Even though she wasn't showing yet, he could feel a slight bulge in her belly.

"Oh no, I'm fine. Really. I had a slight pain in my side a little while ago, but I'm okay. I just need to stop trying to do everything at one time. Did you deposit the check?"

"Yep, I sure did. We'll open a separate account or maybe even think about a CD."

"Hmm, a CD. I don't know. Let's definitely look into a few other options."

The father of Raneen's friend had written a $15,000 check for both of Conner's daughters. He'd told Conner and Pam, Conner passed the information on to Renita, that he wanted them to use it to start an education fund. Although Conner and Pam had tried to tell the doctor and his wife that the money wasn't necessary, they were very grateful for their generosity.

After a trip to the grocery store and a quick stop by the cleaners, Pam and the girls arrived home with several bags. Conner talked Pam into waiting until Sunday to cook the dinner she was originally going to prepare that evening: baked Tilapia, mashed potatoes and gravy from scratch and steamed vegetables with shrimp.

"Let's just order a pizza instead. It's Saturday," Conner said. "Besides, you need a break."

Pam relented but the girls still wanted to bake a cake. There was plenty of time for that, though. She promised the twins they'd bake one later, after she returned home.

Pam grabbed her cell phone and purse and headed out the door. While she and the twins had been out shopping, Tricee had called and asked if she could meet the rest of the crew for a late lunch. It was only 2:00 in the afternoon and all three women had a couple of hours to spare. Jackie and Val were already at the café when Pam arrived.

"Pam, I'm so proud of the way you handled seeing Jeff last month at the club. You just put your head up and walked right on past him," Val said.

"Oh, I so agree," Jackie added. "He had the nerve to ask if he could talk to you for a moment. Ugh!"

Val imitated Pam's reaction to seeing Jeff that evening by sticking her nose in the air. "Jeff," she tried to imitate Pam's voice, "I'm out with friends. Take care." Val giggled as she picked up the glass of water the server had just placed in front of her. "He really just needs to leave you alone. It's funny that he would show up at the same club, though."

"That was purely coincidental. He'd mentioned in his email that he was coming to Chicago around then, but I didn't pay it any mind." Pam gave a wave of the hand.

"*Now* you share what that email said," Jackie complained. "You could have shared that back then." She playfully nudged Pam in the arm. "If I'd known he was coming to town, I would have suggested that we stay in and order take out."

Just then, a smiling Tricee entered the café. "What's so funny?" she asked, hanging her purse across the chair.

"Nothing. Just Jeff," Val offered. "Why the big smile?"

Tricee was no more interested in hearing about Jeff than she was in finding out who would be signing with the Chicago Cubs next year. "Ladies, I'm so glad you could meet me this afternoon. I wanted us to see each other before things got too hectic—even though they already are. "

"I can imagine. So when can we meet Samuel?" Val asked. "How long is it going to take before everything is final? Do you guys have a court date set up? How is he doing?"

There were a ton of questions and rightly so. So much had changed in just the past month. Tricee had finished her classes for the semester and was planning to enroll again for the fall. She had a lot on her plate, but she knew, with God's help, that she could handle it.

Samuel was attending a summer school program for special-needs children and they'd found a wonderful speech therapist. Once school started in September, he would start seeing a child care specialist one-on-one.

Tricee and Hunter had looked into several schools—on the north side as well as the south and west sides—but they decided on the one closest to where they lived. Not only was it the most convenient as far as location but it just seemed a better fit for Samuel's needs. Fortunately, this particular school had been the only one with two summer school sessions. Samuel had been able to begin the first week of August, a few days after he arrived in Chicago. The other schools' sessions ended in mid-July.

There had been a lot going on but Hunter and Tricee were receiving the support they needed. Between Hunter's sisters, his mom and a few church members, things weren't as hectic as they might have been. Samuel's first Sunday in church hadn't gone so smoothly, however. During the service, he became fidgety and, ultimately, Hunter had to take him out to the lobby. And bless Pastor Downey's precious heart. He made the announcement about the new addition to the Hatchett household—after Tricee and

Hunter gave the green light, of course—and had the new family come to the altar for prayer.

The adoption process was a whole other ball game. Ms. Rous from the adoption agency put them in contact with someone from another agency who handled cases similar to theirs. She was an angel, just as pleasant as Ms. Rous. There were court dates that had to be set up; a ton of forms that needed to be read, signed and submitted; and other red tape that came with adoption. Tricee and Hunter realized it wasn't going to be easy, but they were willing to take the journey.

"Oh, my! Where do I start? Well, I was thinking that the weekend after Labor Day would be a good time for you guys to meet him—that is, if you're available. I'd like for it to be sooner but I just don't see how to make that happen." She tossed her head back and giggled.

"We don't have any plans," Pam said and smiled as she noticed the twinkle in Tricee's eyes. "I'll mark it on my calendar."

"We've had our vacation already so we should be good for that weekend," Jackie said and picked up her cup of black coffee.

They each ordered turkey and Swiss on a whole wheat Kaiser roll and iced tea. Pam ordered extra pickles and mushrooms on the side. Her friends said nothing as she removed the turkey from the roll, sliced the pickles into small slivers and placed them—along with the mushrooms—on top of her turkey. "It tastes better like this," she explained.

"Oops, we forgot to bless our meal," Tricee said. After saying grace, she picked up where she'd left off. "It could take a year or maybe longer before it's final, but we were also told that things could move along rather smoothly."

"Is your mother coming to visit soon?" Jackie asked.

"My mom's been here since last week. She's a big help, but I had to take her aside and tell her, 'Ruby, you can't spoil him too quick. Give him some space. He's still adjusting, for goodness sake. You might scare the child.'" That got a chuckle from her friends.

"Is she staying with you guys?" Pam inquired. Hunter's and Tricee's three-bedroom condo was spacious and Pam was curious to know whether they'd made room for Tricee's overbearing mother.

"No. She and Boyce are staying downtown. But I do believe they'll spend a few nights with Bev, Boyce's sister. That'll work out much better. You ladies know, Ruby—well, my mom— can be a bit overbearing at times."

"I was just thinking it myself, girlfriend." Pam laughed. She quickly moved her body to one side when Tricee threw a mock punch at her.

"I fell in love with him as soon as I saw him." Tricee's friends could see her eyes misting up as she spoke. "He wanted to sit next to me on the plane so we could read a story together." She took out her phone and scrolled until she found Samuel's picture. "Look at my baby! Isn't he so adorable? I don't know how I ever lived without this kid in my life." She gave up trying to fight back the tears.

Tricee was heaving and sobbing, though she was trying to do it quietly. An older couple looked in their direction.

"They're happy tears," Val explained to them. "God is so good!" The couple smiled and nodded.

A few seconds later, Jackie and Val were crying. Pam looked over at the older couple and noticed tears in the woman's eyes.

"I'll be back, ladies, while you cry. I need to use the bathroom." Pam reached into her purse for a tissue and handed it to the older lady.

In the bathroom, Pam took her cell phone out of her purse. She quickly dialed a number and spoke aggressively into the phone.

"Darcy, this is Pam. I've decided to put in a transfer to go to another agency. I was hoping that Janae, your client, would've been able to leave by now since her cousin, Jeff, has been helping her out. I don't feel like I should have to play dodge ball every time he comes to the shelter. He's doing this on purpose, trying to make things difficult for me."

"Pam, let me see what I can do. Don't let this fool … " Darcy paused. "Please don't let this man make you transfer and leave your job. We need you at the agency. On Monday, I'll contact a few of the other agencies and see if there's any space in their shelters. In the meantime, just ignore him. And if he really wants to act a nut, we'll take whatever action is necessary."

Pam thanked Darcy and hung up. She hoped that by early next week, Darcy would waltz into her office with some good news: Janae is at another shelter. But for now, she had another prayer request that only God needed to hear.

Lord, only you know the reason I feel so uptight over what my husband and Jackie asked me about this life I'm carrying. I'm dealing with too many different emotions right now and it's causing me to not be able to think clearly. But this, too, shall pass. You know all things and you know my heart. Please remove this unpleasant feeling and give me peace about the situation. Amen.

"Pam, you okay?"

She hadn't heard anybody enter the restroom but when she looked up, Tricee was staring at her with a concerned look on her face. She walked over and stood next to Pam.

"I'm okay." Pam wiped a tear from her eye. "There might be a long road ahead of me, Tricee. But I'm okay."

Proverbs 3:7

Be not wise in thine own eyes: fear the Lord, and depart from evil.

Resources:

Autism Speaks.org (website)

Autism Society of America

(Not a complete listing)

www.ingramcontent.com/pod-product-compliance
Lightning Source LLC
Chambersburg PA
CBHW062001170626
46813CB00001B/3